FIRST EDITION

SORIN BANU

Cover: Rodica Tița
Translation: Mirela Adăscăliței, Horia Cocoș
Edit: Metamorphosis Editing Service
Print: ENv0.23 17.05.2020

www.tentoria.org
www.facebook.com/tentoriathebook

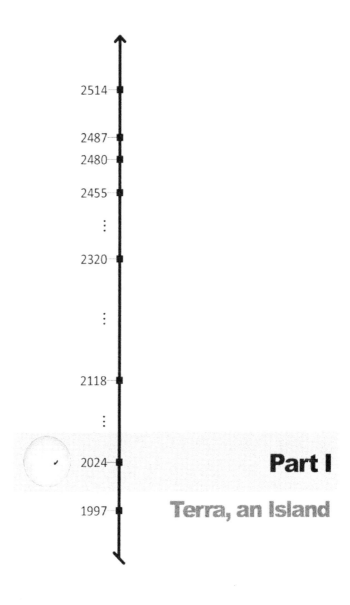

2514

2487
2480

2455

⋮

2320

⋮

2118

⋮

2024

Part I

1997

Terra, an Island

Chapter 1

"Mankind has made great strides in goods manufacturing," the Governor of the Island pontificated.

Acclamations lifted the roof of the congress hall. Cameras were busy rendering his likeness and millions had their eyes glued to him in their homes.

"We are enjoying them to the fullest and lead a happy life in the company of our families and our loved ones on the only spot of land in the middle of a vast ocean surrounding the Earth—this blessed land hemmed in by such a wealth of water. We are blessed!"

Again, applause heaved while the fine upholstery of the boxes and birch wood exquisitely covering the walls did nothing to dampen them.

The Governor lowered the excitement in his voice. "But then again, everything is grounded in strict rules. Humankind must be conscious of the limits it cannot surpass and must firmly abide by the Constitutional Governance Code."

There was a mystical ring to his words as they fell upon a completely silenced hall. The spotlights yielded him a unique aura and, although his stature was hardly imposing, he was perceived as towering higher than the uppermost row of the massive amphitheater. From the top row, he appeared a mere nebulous blot on the cream background of the stage. Yet, one was able to perceive the authority of his lips as he spoke, the prominent cheekbones that had never been slapped by human hands, and the commanding spark in his aging, honorable eyes. All were riveted to him, unable to move.

"Failure to comply is not an option." He scrutinized the gathering. "By upholding the limits we are showing respect for ourselves, our families, our friends; respect for humankind... but, most of all, we are showing respect for this Island. We become part of it, part of the cycle of life that was given to us. We are showing respect for the planet!"

There was another thundering peal of applause. The Governor raised his hand and a deep silence fell almost at once, as if the people present knew they were being followed or that someone up there might look favorably upon their show of compliance to the supreme authority.

"I thank you for your vote, for your vested trust, and for this new mandate. I promise that as long as I continue to be your Governor, I will keep things the way you have always known them!"

With that, the smartly dressed gentleman with a grizzled bushy beard and a shock of white hair concluded his speech. Cheers flooded the hall, lingering even after the man left the stage. That was only natural; after all, he was the most important man on the planet.

Chapter 2

The sun was about to set. It had been floating there, right above the horizon, for hours on end as if it were in no mood to hide behind the ocean. The man savored the smell of algae brought by the ocean breeze and the sound of the waves crashing against the rocks strewn across the sand. It was that summery time of the year that was dearest to him precisely because the days were so very long. Mr. Jefferson, a clerk at the local post office, knew nobody to thank for the Island lying so far up on the Northern Hemisphere. He enjoyed going out around midnight to admire the sun's late procrastination and forget all the worries alongside his dog, just the two of them walking the waterfront.

His pupils suddenly grew dim. A dazzling light coming from the sky, high above the sea, flooded the beach. The man took a step back, then another. The source of that light was barreling down to Earth. With every second ticking away, an object like a strange aircraft came into sight. *Where's that coming from?* he asked himself, aghast. The display went on at a bewildering speed: a failed landing attempt followed by a muffled blast; the impact was violent.

A few seconds later, all that could be made out was a shattered wreck on the sea's surface several hundred meters off the shore. A large wave made the man push his dog back before he tripped and fell into the sand. It looked like nothing he had ever seen. He tried to get up, but curiosity and fear kept him fastened to the soggy beach. Only the dog tried to leave but was held back by the leash, which remained in the clenched fist of his petrified master.

An incandescent light emerged from the upper part of the ship, rolled down along its frame, and on the pieces severed on impact, pulverized everything behind it like a cigarette burning to the filter. The clerk's lungs were suddenly unable to accommodate the air he needed to breathe while his heart struggled inside his chest. He was still numb with astonishment, unable to budge an inch.

The ship and the remains were destroyed to the last grain of matter and the incandescent line vanished. It looked like everything had dissolved into the sea.

All Mr. Jefferson could hear now was his heart beating and the waves slowly returning to normal.

He wanted to flee to safety, but he was running short on time. The seawater in front of him stood up as if some transparent creature was emerging from the deep and made its way towards him. Marks formed on the sand as if the creature was now stepping on the beach, water dripping off of it. *A force, a life form.* His mind faltered. The clerk waited no longer trying to make it out; it was moving too fast. He wanted to run away but only managed a few steps before a light struck him in the back. He fell onto his knees, paralyzed, hitting his head hard against the sand.

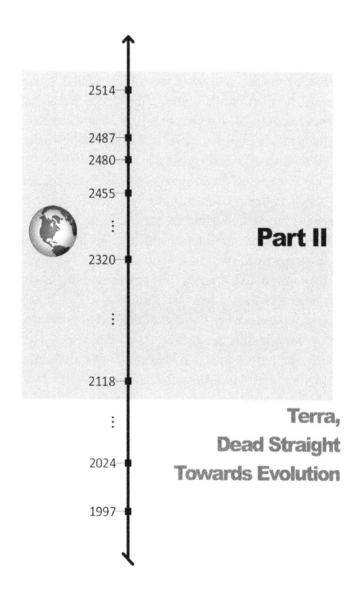

2514

2487
2480

2455

2320

2118

2024

1997

Part II

Terra,
Dead Straight
Towards Evolution

Chapter 3

"Wonderful cities are about to be wiped out, blameless people will die, and thousands of years' old heritages that have defined the culture and history of our planet will disappear! What a shame. All that for the rotten lust of power - much too rotten not to afflict nations all over the world."

The Commander spoke in a low voice, seemingly only to himself. He glanced briefly at the paper-thin screen which showed several faces twisted with emotion. "I am listening, gentlemen."

"I confirm!" came from one of the teleconference speakers.

"I confirm!" joined in another voice.

"I, too, confirm!"

While the voices of many presidents, ministers, and high ranking generals were heard one after another, the coordinating commander reviewed the plan that had just been devised. It had been debated for many days, and he was not even sure if they'd reached the best conclusion. Too straightforward and risky, he told to himself. *We should have thought harder...and not use bionic people.* Wrinkles formed between his eyebrows. Though these beings were the first real success in achieving both a physical and intelligence augmentation, he was still afraid at the thought of creating so many and letting them loose to control the outcome of a war. "The special troops", as they'd all agreed to call them, were in fact the first army of bionic people ever created. There were ten thousand robot-people packed full with flesh concealed chips, behind their human appearance, with brains set on precise targeting programs meant to smother the hotbeds fueling conflicts all over the world.

The commander thought only a sick mind could have produced such a thing; a mind that took advantage of the desperate wish of nations all over the globe. The individuals in the "special troops" had different specializations in respect to their assigned objectives, ranging from genuine killing machines to diplomats of the highest level. They were trained, educated, and equipped to fight physically as well as withstand inclement weather; they could be good spies, but also influence large masses of people or bring leaders to power where needed. Economical, political, and religious control were the most important fields at which they took aim.

Upon the last "confirm", the commander ceased paying attention to his own thoughts. He didn't need to listen to everyone. They did nothing, after all, but repeat the same word, which rang gloomier each time it was uttered.

"The last confirmation duly given," he ended the sequence curtly. "I declare the whole approval process complete. As a commander-coordinator of the operation, I order the initiation of phase one, whose main objectives are as follows: destroying the enemy command centers and work points, attacking and disabling information and communication systems, and sending special troops to previously designated areas."

Thus the spark of what was to become a new world war was lit—the war that spawned the first generation of

Tentorians, the so called "special troops" sent to "previously designated areas" in the first phase of the operation.

The commander-coordinator as well as all the others present there on that historical day didn't live to see the outcome he feared most. However, they did get to witness the good part of the plan. With the help of that ten thousand-being army, the world war came quickly to a conclusion, and several years later, the Tentorians completed their tasks. The more unfortunate ones perished while many of those who had survived bore scars of war.

The commander's fears were realized later, after his generation faded away. For reasons their creators would never grasp, the Tentorians who were still alive began to gather and form a nation. Several centuries later, what a worldwide alliance had created to back it in establishing peace proved to be its number-one enemy.

Chapter 4

"We are a race superior to the common man," Kaligor said to the throng gathered before him as well as the other Tentorians watching him all over the world.

He stood up on a podium of rotten wood within a roomy concert hall that had been left in disrepair. In the weak light projected on him, he looked altogether grey—a stale, metallic grey mass. Once, he had been fonder of color, but now he relished the glints of technology. The cold blood of an old fashioned soldier of fortune still ran through his veins while his bald skull shone eerily in the dim light. Some of his people allegedly said that he'd had an intervention done and had completely discarded the roots of his hair in order to obtain that perfectly taut skin which made him appear even more inhuman.

"Our forebears," he carried on excitedly after a brief break, "...WE were created to serve people, but our mission was over a long time ago." He straightened his broad shoulders, ideally matching the width of the nasal septum. "Now we are a nation!"

The several thousand Tentorians stamping their feet made the walls vibrate as their frozen gazes bore through the heated atmosphere.

"...A nation that has continued to procreate, to grow on an evolutionary scale!"

The stamping muffled his voice once more. Stark contrasts were everywhere in sight: between the cobwebs in the corners and the sophisticated state-of-the-art devices worn by some of the Tentorians; between the mold formed on the dilapidated podium and some of the spectators' perfectly white teeth; between the pale hue of the few still-functioning neon lights and the sparkle of the powerful LEDs glittering in the crowd.

Those assembled were in contrast as well, according to the specialization they still carried in their genes. Some were time-worn and aged yet bulging with muscles and shiny weapons; others wore formal suits and held themselves in seemingly flawless genial postures. Still, there was one uncanny similarity amongst them all: their smiles were mere perfidious grins and hell was reflected in their eyes.

Kaligor took a deep breath and continued in a voice that sounded like rusted metal. "My dear brothers, the time has come at last to stand up for ourselves, to enjoy the qualities we were endowed with, the genetic superiority which we can still develop, and, more importantly, to pass them on to our heirs!"

The clatter in the hall cracking under the audience's feet interrupted him again. He stopped them by lifting a hand.

"I am here, in front of you, because I want to give you good news. The petition we have all signed requesting to be recognized as a nation here in Iceland has finally been answered." Taking his time, he arranged the collar of his black shirt, covering his whitish, vampire-like, wrinkleless neck. "From now on," he said louder, "we are officially a nation!"

The stamping and cheers became deafening. He sized them up and thought proudly that the handful of mercenaries of yesteryear had bred so fast in the last two centuries to become a force to be reckoned with.

He bellowed, this time allowing the flood of enthusiasm to show in his voice. "From now on, when we say Iceland we say Home!"

The clamor of the wound up crowd completely drowned out his voice. The landless nation that had migrated to Iceland from all corners of the world was now officially recognized and embraced with open arms.

ONE WEEK LATER. SWITZERLAND, THE LABORATORIES OF "FUTURE CRYONICS INC"

"Today we have a patient for de-icing-revitalization." The nurse straightened the collars of her fitted white dress.

"Nemilo. What kind of a name is that?" the doctor attempted a joke.

The woman tittered and continued to analyze the patient's data in the file scrolling down against her contact lenses.

"As I see," the doctor pondered, "Mr. Nemilo needs a fair bit of work. We need stem cells type AD34 for most of the tissues afflicted. We need to get some for the entire range of functions."

The woman frowned. "Are we to prepare the Glasgow lab?"

"Hmm...yes, we are going to need the best we have to get this fellow in top shape. Here it's written that he was hacked to shreds in an accident—no description. The classified ones again! By the way he looks, I'm surprised they were able to keep him alive until freezing time." He continued scrolling through the file on his contact lenses. "Have we informed the next of kin?"

"A rather distant relative will be here today to assist."

"Very well. He'll have some story to tell. One less history lesson for us." He rolled his eyes.

Shades of grey danced in front of the black eyes. He chased the shadows away, but hundreds of little star lights filled his vision. Then the white equipment surrounding his bed came into focus in the form of different rounded shapes he couldn't recognize.

"You are in good hands. Do not worry," the doctor reassured the man.

The distraught patient searched the doctor's face for anything familiar. His mind was hazy while thousands of painful tingles ran through his otherwise numb body.

"Welcome to 2320, sir...and to our laboratories," added the man dressed in white from head to toe.

"What...who are you? Where am I?" mumbled Nemilo as he fearfully climbed out of bed.

He found the style of tight-fitting clothes worn by those in front of him altogether bizarre. He could find nothing in his memory with which to associate them.

"All I need is for you to be calm now. You'll get answers to all your questions. In a few minutes, your memories will also come back."

Nemilo ceased examining the serene face of the man in white. It conveyed warmth and confidence.

"You've just traveled through time, Mr. Nemilo, through our cryogenic laboratories. Someone took great care of you and brought you here right when you were about to die from multiple serious wounds."

"Humphhh." The patient exhaled loudly and shut his eyes, striving to mentally return to the past.

"You have defied death by way of cryonics," the man in white went on. "The medical technology of your time would not have saved you. Now, 200 years later, we had all that was necessary to deice you in life-supporting conditions and fully cure you."

Nemilo smiled subtly.

"What really matters is not to get scared. With the help of cutting-edge medical technology, we were able to bring you back into very good shape, thoroughly cured. Mr. Eliot here is one of the best living psychologists." He pointed to the man next to him. "He is going to help you quickly overcome this moment and explain to you how you came to be here, the fortunate beneficiary of a completely recovered body, after staying in a frozen state for two centuries."

"I don't...remember all that much. My head hurts."

"You will recover; don't worry. The pain will die down. One thing I can tell you for sure: you were full of metals and electronic devices. I don't even want to know if they came with the accident or had been placed in before that." Silence supplied the answer the doctor already knew. "That's about all I wanted to say. We'll catch up later. For the time being, all I can do is wish you luck with your new life. Perhaps this time you'll manage to stay out of trouble for longer." He flashed him a shining smile, shook his hand, and started to leave. "Oh, it slipped my mind. You have a visitor!"

An hour later, he had been shown an entire history book. Kaligor, a young descendent of the Tentorian family that Nemilo remembered vaguely, stood next to him providing data.

"...You will be able to live forever," the hoarse voice strongly echoed, further raising Nemilo's interest.

"Huh. Right now I feel feeble, like a...normal, powerless man." The visitor followed him, grinning and letting his ragged eyebrows relax. "No visualizing lenses, no enhanced audio information, nothing. Not even my arms are as strong as they used to be."

"Don't worry," Kaligor cut in. "You will forget the antiques you were wearing inside you and fall in love with the new technology. It makes us stronger without having to wear almost anything. It's amazing how far we've come in the last two hundred years! Practically, this technological progress could be the one to keep you alive forever!"

"Big words, big words," Nemilo mumbled.

"Technology has gone so far that we can recreate or rejuvenate any tissue, any organ, including the brain. Soon enough, we'll be able to make perfect human clones, from physiology to memory. Pure madness!"

"That is our field: pure madness." Nemilo laughed.

Kaligor shut his eyes for a second and a smile dawned on his face. He was satisfied to see that the man who had once been the fiercest Tentorian leader, a soulless chief apt to crush anything with his bare hands to achieve his objective, was coming round nicely. It had taken dozens of enemy troops to remove him from the game; many had been sacrificed to take him down. The story of all his exploits had made a legend out of him, and a handful of Tentorians knew he was the ideal leader for what they were plotting.

Kaligor knew Nemilo was ready. "The Tentorians need a leader. Now you are a martyr, resurrected from the dead. Most of them will follow you."

Nemilo brightened. The thirst for power was imprinted in his genes. His angled face became more pronounced and his tired black eyes were no longer able to hide the monster returning to life.

"We have big plans," Kaligor continued, "and for that we need many Tentorians and someone to lead them. We'll go down in history."

"Why not?" Nemilo grinned inanely. "Oooh, I love this planet!"

Chapter 5

ANOTHER TWO CENTURIES LATER. APRIL
10, 2514. NORTH AMERICA, TENTORIA

Xilo's imposing figure outlined by beautifully crafted, top-quality clothes and wrapped in a black and gold mantle, was the only element that conveyed a noble note to the room. The rest was just a jumble of the latest technology meant to strictly serve the purposes of a command center overrun with all manner of devices more virtual than real and having nothing to do with aesthetics or humanity.

"It was a big success!" he boasted while relishing the image scrolling down his retina.

A cargo airplane and a few fighters were returning to the Tentorian city. He took it in and a dull thought sprang in his mind: *Well, it looks like a military base.* Military-style organization had been one of the staples of Tentorian culture for the last several decades. The greyish-white of the metallic buildings and the modular architecture made out of cubic structures dominated the landscape. Civil constructions, pyramids hundreds of meters wide also made out of cubic structures, had a filthy, degraded look about them.

The man let his eyes wander over the airbase. From up there, he could see its stately mass right in the middle of the city, inside a circle a few kilometers in diameter. On its edge, within each quadrant, four huge, cube-shaped identical structures rose. Above, hundreds of fighting aircrafts assembled nose to nose in star-like formations of five. There was something about their shapes that aroused his admiration: downward-folded wings, stingrays supporting the entire machine against the ground; a design both simple and scary, no windshield, engine, or other such elements jutting out from the fuselage. The planes were connected to the base by means of umbilical tubes running a few meters from their bellies down into the buildings themselves.

Between the four gigantic cubical constructions, several hundred meters away from the center of the base, four cargo airships had been stationed—one against each building. Xilo's eyes sparkled. He admired these most despite being conical and not as streamlined as the fighter airplanes. Instead, their size was staggering. Each had six huge propulsion engines standing dozens of meters long. They sat there like some soulless colossuses waiting to be flown towards new territories.

Xilo had watched one of them precisely when it landed. An ear-splitting roar rolled over the entirety of Tentoria, making its way through the most hardened walls while swirling dust clouds swept the ground like a hurricane. The debris then rose in the sky and blanketed the sun, which ceased to shine minutes on end over large acreages of land.

The fighter airplanes kept coming back from the mission, looking like flies beside the conical behemoth airships, while hundreds of troops returned through the military base underground. The black protective suits covered them completely. The matte material of the ruggedly-textured, graphite-hued helmets absorbed any ray of light that dared touch it. Behind them, the cold faces of the Tentorian warriors hid, dizzy with their latest conquest.

"Is this what you call a great success, capturing resources

that will last us for just a month? Let's be real here!" Nemilo snapped his last few words through his jagged lips.

Xilo went from the image projected on his retina to the reality in the room, then to Nemilo's face framed by shoulder-length black hair. He answered modestly: "Those resources did not belong to anybody. We fought for them with a few mobs and won them without raising the wrath of any nation. That's what's important."

"I am sick and tired of these scraps!"

"And what do you suggest we should do?" Xilo voiced his annoyance.

"We could be bolder. We are a force no one can stop. We are a nation superior to all the creatures on Earth, and yet we are always so careful. A hundred thousand Tentorians are sitting on a few dozen square miles and we're mostly concerned with our resources running low each month."

"I must remind you, Nemilo, that the last time we sought to expand our power, dozens of nations jumped at our throats. I do not think we're quite so strong."

Nemilo's upper lip twitched unintentionally while Xilo's mind flew to ages passed—the reputation Tentorians had built for themselves. They had once been a nation of superior beings, just as Nemilo had desired from the very beginning. 40 years earlier, they conquered everything they had set their minds to, like all-out performing machines; they almost ruled the world. The last generations were 90% created through technology; they were hardly humans anymore. Xilo knew the other nations were inferior to them because of laws or ethical norms. Of these, the most important was the Luxembourg Treaty, concluded in 2321, which placed a limit on the use of certain technologies in the medical field and banned a series of body-transforming practices on humans. Just by not adhering to this treaty, the Tentorians had achieved a fundamental lead. After all, they wanted to fully take advantage of technological progress.

Now Xilo feared the risk of repeating the same mistakes. This time, he had to set limits on the greedy Tentorians. Not a long time ago, in the 25th century, the thirst for power swept them too far while the murders, dirty routines, and terror spread all over proved to be concepts that went well with the name of Tentoria. They had come close to sparking another world conflict. The creatures engineered to be peace-enforcing special troops in the 2118 world war had turned against the word's system of governance three centuries later. Xilo recalled shuddering with horror at the fact that it did not take long for the world's great powers to realize the imminent peril. They saw the need to form an Alliance to fight back with the same illegal weapons...and that they did.

Xilo cracked his lips, still engrossed in the past. "I do not think we are so strong," he repeated.

"We are even stronger than that," Nemilo pressed on, clenching his jaw. "We survived the great genocide of last century!"

"But at what price?"

"It doesn't matter. What does not destroy you makes you stronger. We can be better than them with this technology!" He flung his arms open and his prominent veins, pumping hot blood, streaked his well-defined forearms. "I have a dream, a dream in which our great nation once again comes to rule the world. We are number-one in the food chain; the world should be ours by right. There's no way an inferior race could be stronger than us!"

A handful of officers present in the room avoided any

interaction, pretending to be busy with the coordination of the returning fleet.

"Nemilo, with all due respect, let's not bring up the same issue all over again." Xilo sounded commanding. He clenched his fists and leaned forward a few degrees, staring daggers at Nemilo to remind him who was the ruler.

31 years after the Alliance had fought back, silence prevailed. Tentorians had been driven out of Iceland, chased away from every corner of the world, and isolated somewhere on the eastern seaboard of North America. Those who were still around had been granted that piece of land to build a city of their own. The plot of land had been given to them to keep the thought of occupying any other territory far from their minds. What they called Tentoria was only a few dozen square miles. Here, just a handful of Tentorians—too few, thought Xilo—were still trying to shape a principle-based nation to erase the label that had been branded on their foreheads, but most found it hard to live a life free of crime or giving in to their cravings for power. Right after installing the new Tentoria, the new leader— Xilo—was appointed: a Tentorian accepted by the Alliance who had undertaken the task of integrating his people into the ranks of the world's nations.

"Brothers," an officer cut in, "an operation has just been successfully concluded. Let's enjoy this victory no matter how minor might it be."

Nemilo's features became contorted with hatred. "Kaligor, I need to talk to you," he growled to another officer and left the room in a rage.

Kaligor followed him to the corridor, looking over his shoulder to make sure nobody followed.

"We must do something, Nemilo. I'm telling you!" he

snapped. "You can't lurk in the shadows any longer; you've got to hit back! We are Tentorians. For us, space and time have no limits."

Nemilo blew his top. His hand jumped like a snake and pinched Kaligor's chin between his thumb and the rest of his fingers. "I am four hundred years old; don't you tell me what to do, you idiot."

The officer raised his palm to his face and swallowed his words.

"I have a plan," Nemilo hissed, and a contented grin spread on the officer's face while wriggling himself out of his superior's grasp.

"But what about Xilo?" Kaligor asked.

"We'll deal with Xilo, too."

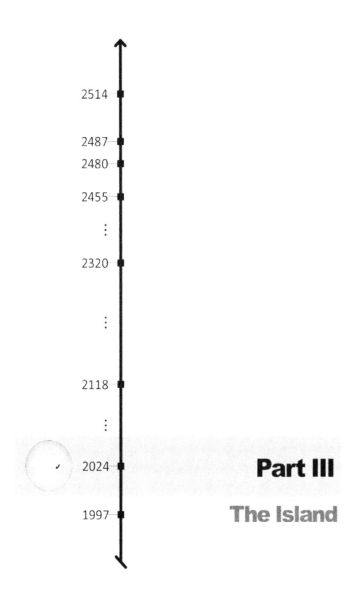

2514

2487
2480

2455

⋮

2320

⋮

2118

⋮

Part III

2024

1997

The Island

Chapter 6

The makeshift garage served as the pit stop of the kart circuit. Wearing jeans and a simple T-shirt, Cole was flat on his back next to a kart, tinkering with its engine. A kid of about ten stood next to him, anxious to get back into the race.

"All right, big champ," Cole said to him, "your super-kart is fixed."

"Okay!" the kid beamed.

"You have to really step on it; just touching the throttle won't protect it. This bad boy here tears through asphalt like butter, pal."

"Thanks, Cole!"

"C'mon, get in. It's almost closin' time."

As soon as the kid jumped into his kart, Cole started to push it to the track gate.

"Five more laps and the race's over, so, my friend, show me the best you've got...now!"

As the kid's kart joined the others spinning in earnest, the sun beams shone from the west, probing through the trees that surrounded the area, and the sky was still blue. It was a perfect karting day; *a perfect day to work!* Cole mused, taking a deep breath and relishing the smell of green foliage mixed with exhaust and the magnificent hum of the karts. He had been working on this job for a while, and though not one his parents would be proud of it, he simply loved this job. *"The sweet buzz of vibrating engines against the green backdrop of the forest at the edge of the track, under the deep blue sky,"* was how he enjoyed describing his workplace.

Two mothers were seated in the small arena, watching their children and cheering whenever they passed. Cole threw them a casual look and knew they were ogling him. They seemed to forget for a while it was for their kids' sake they were there.

The young man had turned 27 and looked more handsome than ever. His snug T-shirt gave away only a slight hint of how well-built he was; the rest was up to the two ladies' imaginations. He did not necessarily pose as a tough, macho guy, seemingly unaware of his own charm or knowing how to make good use of it. Nevertheless, he was the kind of man for whom a single glance sufficed to bowl a woman as she cast him wistful eyes. He threw another glance, just to make sure. No, he wasn't wrong; the two women were still looking at him. He turned away shyly and went on surveying the track.

The voice of another young man by the starting line drowned the sound of the engines. "Last lap, boys!"

It was Jimmy, his workmate and best friend since college. Had there been a line of work called "a lad who's all up to mischief", he would have been the perfect candidate.

The two began parking the karts, as they did every evening the moment each of them returned to the so-called pit stop. The last kid arrived and the last "Good bye, see you next time!" was heard.

"See you next time, boys!" one of the mothers said, each word caressing her lips. A last charming glance over her shoulder at Cole, and she turned back to her kid.

Jimmy patted his back. "You rotten schemer!"

A smile flickered in the corner of Cole's mouth while he shrugged. He remembered a similar scene back in college, when the girl in their history class couldn't settle on one of them. She liked them both, but she needed to make her pick. Back then Jimmy had been the victor, with an equally poised shrug. It was he who got to be her partner for prom night because he was the joker type. The type you could happily listen to for hours on end—something terribly appealing at that age. *He's the same guy he was back then,* Cole mused. *Actually, no. He's put on a few pounds,* he joked. *Being a little fuller becomes him...he is even funnier.*

"Would you like to see one more time who's better at karting? At least there's one thing I'm better at than you."

Jimmy's challenge brought him back to earth. "There may be one thing you're better at," the attractive young man smiled, "but not this!"

They turned their attention to their boss' booth, waiting for a sign of approval. That was what they loved most at the end of the workday, and their boss was far too kind a man to not let them chase each other on the track. He knew those laps made them love their job even more. He nodded his approval.

"Whoever comes second in five laps pays for the next beeeers!" Jimmy screamed after pushing his friend as they sprinted towards the karts. "The race has already started." He laughed.

"Screw you!" Cole retorted, running to the second kart.

The two sped on the track, laughing their heads off like some zippy kids bursting with life.

Thirty meters before the finish line, Cole was about two

karts ahead when a twitch violently jerked his temple.

He stepped on the brake suddenly, freezing the kart. He saw black for a second, as if the image of the steering wheel, which was still imprinted on his retina, was obscured behind a leaden blanket, but it was only for a split second. A moment later, he felt nothing anymore; everything was back to normal. However, he couldn't stop feeling bitter, about similar painful moments he went through every morning. *Now it was only a short spell!*

"Yeah!" Jimmy whooped, dashing past him, his wild laughter still heard after he crossed the finish line.

"High five!" Cole said while slipping on a clean shirt. "You're good, but there's still room for improvement. If I wasn't going through a moment of weakness right there..."

"Yeah, yeah, sure. You still have to pay for the drink!" Jimmy playfully slapped his back.

"Hey," Jimmy added, shaking his hand, "tomorrow I'll go to the car dealership. The five years for my jalopy are gone."

"Wow, at last!"

"Yes! I got a letter from the House of Environment that says as of today, I am allowed to buy myself a new car if I want to. And of course I do, dammit!" He raised his voice excitedly. "Will you come with me look at the new models, see if one ticks all my boxes?"

"No make is enough of a lemon to go well with you, buddy," Cole laughed, "but we can only hope. Why not?" He winked and slapped his friend on the back, then ducked to avoid being repaid in kind.

"You two should go home, lads. It's late!" the boss said.

Cole raised his head and watched the orange sun. He nodded briefly and lapsed into a smile as he turned back to Jimmy. "See you tomorrow, pal."

"See you...and don't cry all night long! We both know you lost to a karting god. One day I'll grant you a rematch." He smirked and saluted him military style.

He didn't notice the broad smile on Cole's face as he ignored him, throwing the rucksack into the trunk. He slipped behind the wheel and saluted him, raising two fingers to his temple.

The red sun painted long shadows on the highway. Although it wasn't very late, Cole's off-roader was the only one speeding by with the windows down and Bon Jovi playing at top volume on the local radio station.

"*It's my liiife!*" Cole sang enthusiastically. He shouted as loud as he could, as if trying to make himself heard by the entire planet, "*It's now or never, I ain't gonna live forever, I just wanna live while I'm aliiive. It's my life!*"

The aroma of warm pancakes filled the kitchen. Christine hummed some tune while the radio in the background broadcasted a crosstalk between two entertainers:

"*... Science House has designed a sunscreen that is going to protect us better against the sun overexposing burns,*" a female voice was saying.

"*We are so lucky!*" a male voice cut in by cracking a joke. "*There are only five years since they said they'd do this in*

2019." It was obvious how he felt about the news. "*Believe me, Carol, those guys are soooo fast…*"

"*Let's go easier on these jokes, John. Someone might hear us.*"

The entrance door slammed shut.

"Good evening, mother, father, Mathew!"

"At your age, you should be saying, 'Good evening, darling wife' and maybe live in your own house already." She raised her voice on the last word as if singing it.

Cole stopped short halfway up the staircase, took some steps back, and poked his head through the kitchen door. "If only I could find the right one! Mmm, it smells so good in here. What are you cooking?"

"What do you think? Your favorite: blackberry pancakes."

Christine knew she could never go wrong with that dessert. Cole's mother was a beautiful, well-groomed woman, always close to her two sons, and a good friend. Although well into middle-aged, no one would have said she looked past 40. Her hazelnut dyed hair was only slightly longer than Coles', not quite reaching her shoulders. If it wasn't dyed, it would have been but a grey mass stricken with many white hairs. When she was younger, her hair had been like Cole's: ebony black. It was so much like his that he once said, "Mum, you're going to have to stop cropping your hair short like that or maybe dye it another color. It's strange; it looks like watching myself in a mirror each time I see you."

Cole couldn't stand the temptation. He went into the kitchen and grabbed a hot pancake, chewing on it and staring blankly at the ceiling as if he were in heaven. "Mum, did I ever tell you that you're wonderful?"

"Well, yeah," she replied and kissed his forehead. "How was work?"

"The same old adrenaline-packed karts, but please don't say:"—he mimicked his mother—"'I'm still waiting to see you get a serious job.'"

After that, they both smiled broadly.

"Where's Father?"

"He had to drop by his office for a bit. Just texted me he's coming back."

"And Mathew?"

"Your brother's in his room, I think."

"Okay, Mum, the roll call's done for the evening! I'm going upstairs to my room."

And out of the kitchen he went, taking the stairs up.

"Cole," she stopped him on his way, "Doctor Tang called. He said you need to make an appointment to see him and discuss your test results."

Cole paused for a moment, took a deep breath, and continued climbing to his room. He would have felt no shivers running through his body if not for the memory of his strong morning headaches; he'd forgotten how long it had been since he'd woken without them. *Why did the doctor ask me to make an appointment? He could have sent me the results directly.* When he got to his room, he lifted a calling card off his nightstand, grabbed the handset of his landline phone, and dialed.

Chapter 7

The car dealership sprawled over less than three hundred square meters. It looked rather like a neighborhood store, with a large window and three car models on display. The car dealer had assumed a haughty attitude in front of Jimmy and Cole. He was a nerdy kid with heavily gelled hair and too small a tie to pass for a top-notch salesman. However, he proudly presented them with the new car.

"This car has had a facelift, a complete interior redesign, and..." his eyes bulged as if he was waiting for their excitement, "it now comes in black leather too!"

"C'mon, man," Jimmy moaned, "that's disappointing! All you could do in the last ten years is a redesign? These look like the cars our old men used to drive 20 years ago."

"And not even one measly horsepower more?" Cole whined too.

"You know the regulations!" The seller tried to take the company's side. "We could have boosted the power, but the Governor's rules are clear, people. That is the limit set in the Constitutional Governance Code to keep the roads safe."

The two friends listened to him silently, their hopes dashed.

"The good side is," the heated seller raised his voice, "that ten years ago only two models were sold on the entire Island; now we have three!"

"Okay, okay, all well and good, but why did you discontinue the Bluetooth, man? I read that on your website;

now we're back to square one."

The boy shrugged. "Once again, the same rules...everything for safety. It seems they found out Bluetooth might irradiate us."

The nerd lowered his voice in an attempt to become more convincing. "The House of Health wants to remove it from all devices. Haven't you heard?"

"Hell no!" Jimmy snapped in desperation, also keeping his voice down. "I like wireless connection; I want progress, man!"

"Instead," the seller went on after a brief silence, "it comes with a new set of headphones and guess what?"

The dopey excitement fully caught the two friends' eyes.

"We are giving it for free!"

Cole shot Jimmy a mildly dazed look. "Wow! You are sooo lucky, pal!"

He started laughing, then smiling and putting up a serious expression when realizing that the heavily gelled salesman didn't get the joke.

"Seriously now, I say you should take it. The make looks cool enough, bro, and it's brand new!" He patted his shoulder gently. "I wish I got the okay to change my own car."

They carried on turning round it, closely followed by the dealer keeping his head up high, pleased with yet another successful presentation of the new model.

"Let's take it for a spin." Jimmy was fed up with just looking.

Cole raised an eyebrow. "Okay, so I get to drive?"

"You wish, friend. You wish! You just stick to your old car."

With that, they both jumped into the car like two excited

children.

"Are you sure you don't want to come with us?" Jimmy taunted the guy after letting down the window.

The seller stared at them, flabbergasted. What he expected to hear was more in line with an invitation, not this question. He stammered ill at ease, "Unless you don't want me to come with you...?"

"Nooo," Jimmy assured him. "Don't take it personally! Of course we'd like to take you, but my manner of driving...you don't want to know! And with all those road security rules, bah. Believe me, you can never know. Better stay safe, man. I'm buying it anyway! I haven't got too many options on this planet, have I?"

He turned to Cole and pulled a face, about to burst out laughing. The curly thick mane framing his stout face emphasized his expression more, prompting Cole to raise both hands to his mouth in an attempt to muffle his laughter. Then he coughed in his palms to avoid a *wrong* interpretation of his gesture.

"Yes, indeed, no...don't you worry. It's okay," the resigned salesman managed to mumble. "Drive safe!"

"Vrroom, vrrooommm!" Cole burst out, driven more by the moments spent together with his chum than the car itself.

Chapter 8

Just by his smile, one would have been able to tell it was one lovely summer morning. Although it was rush hour, the city looked anything but overcrowded. Cole explored the low-rise buildings through his windshield, searching for the sun he liked watching on the horizon in all its crimson splendor. Perhaps he could have enjoyed himself more spotting new car models—his life's passion—except he knew them all by now.

He realized it was much too quiet and turned on the radio. The last tunes of a song spread through the air. "...*Forever young, I wanna be forever young. Do you really want to live forever...?*"

The DJ cut back in as the song ended, "*Who doesn't want to live forever? 'Forever Young' from Alphaville.*"

Shivers ran through the tips of Cole's fingers. *Why does my head hurt every morning? What could be so serious?*

The radio speakers brought the light back to his expression: "*This is a lovely morning! Wake up and enjoy life, my friends!*"

He negotiated one last turn to the right, smiled at two pedestrians taking the crosswalk to the other side of the street, drove another hundred meters, and pulled into a free parking spot. He appeared confident with his hair well-groomed and his face clean-shaven. The building next to which he had parked bore an inscription: *St. Charles Clinic.*

"*Let's move on to our next tune...*"

He turned off the radio, breathed deeply, and made for the entrance.

Half an hour later, the doctor was sitting in front of him with the results of a cerebral CT scan. Behind him, a series of scans, clipped onto backlit glass screens to be visualized, showed different perspectives of Cole's skull.

"How is that possible?" Cole's shaky voice asked for the umpteenth time; there was still no answer.

He sat in a chair with his head cupped in his hands and the expression of a man who'd lost everything in a matter of seconds. Tears welled in his eyes. They hung there, trying not to betray his manliness, or simply because it would have been too easy for them to run down his cheeks; they could not just form streaks as they did in any other fit of sobs. These were the tears of a broken man. The doctor's hand on his shoulder did nothing to help; on the contrary, it made him understand the gravity of the news he'd just received.

He did not have the strength to get to work. Cole sat on a bar stool at a pub not far from his workplace. The glass of whisky in front of him could have been the twentieth since that morning; it was evening now. Cole had gotten dead drunk in a joint where all anyone cared about was the drink in their hand or the sandwich on their plate.

An inebriated old woman babbled in earnest with a woman at a table close by when the young man cast his eyes at them by chance. They both raised their chins, disgusted, and turned their eyes to the Governor's photo sitting on the uppermost shelf of the bar; the Governor's portrait watched. Seemingly, the Governor meant a lot to the owner. If not for the booze, he could have taken the place for a drugstore. The white-blue walls, the wooden floor, the tables, and the chairs were flawlessly cleaned and taken care of while in the bar behind the counter everything was carefully lined up.

Cole's faint cry cause everyone in the joint to stare at him.

"Why...? Why?" he shouted. "A miserable disease! Why the devil can't they find a solution for this cancer?"

The bartender wanted to reproach him but changed his mind and solved the issue by himself. He took a napkin from a pile sitting nearby and began to wipe the whisky drops Cole had spat through his teeth. The young man managed to catch the eye of some clients at the tables, shooting curious, demure glances his way. Usually they dropped in only to have a drink, but today it was something else.

The bartender stopped polishing the glasses and filled one up with ice and a drop of whisky. "Take this glass on the house, boy! You'd better quit drinkin'...and most of all quit shouting like that. You know that's not allowed. The guards will come and take you to the police station."

Cole sized him up casually, grabbed the glass, and muttered, "I'm 27, man. It's unfair! You start having some headaches and then *bang!* the answer: cancer! Cancer? Son of a bitch!"

"You've got to stop drinking; it'll do you no good! You've been here since this morning."

A few minutes later, Cole left the bar, teetering on his feet. It was already late, and the street was deserted. He worked his way to the car, got behind the wheel, and sped off with a jolt.

Chapter 9

Morning settled over the forest, which was full of life. The green foliage merged with the moss-covered ground and the ruby hues of lupine flowers. The sound of dewdrops running down the leaves of trees blended with the hum of insects and the sung chit-chat of blackbirds. A dewdrop fell off an oak bud, breaking into dozens of beads against the rear-view mirror of Cole's car, now abandoned at the edge of the road. The door hung wide open and traces of his footsteps grew fainter and fainter in the moist soil as they distanced themselves from the car. A few more marks and the contour of a shoe sole pointed the way towards Cole, who lay sideways on the ground, mud and dead leaves caked into his clothes.

He hardly cracked open his eyes, feeling all the whiskey he'd thrown back the day before behind them. He wouldn't have minded the headache, which was there every morning anyway; now it throbbed much more violently in his temples and forehead. Everything from the night before seemed fuzzy now. He could barely focus and failed to budge an inch. Once he tried to move his body was sapped of strength as if he were hogtied. He would have rather liked falling asleep and lying there forever.

A rustle of leaves could suddenly be made out amid the chaos swarming in his temples. He opened his eyes wide. Something was moving there, but one meter away. *Strange,* his thoughts echoed. *It's neither an insect nor an animal, but I can't see anything!* A chill went through his entire body and stopped in his forehead; the pain sheared through his brain. He was not afraid—the hangover held too much sway over him to be afraid; this was the mere instinct of self-defense that had turned itself on from deep inside his subconscious. Out of nowhere, an invisible, shadow-like shape passed through the leaves. The chill now plunged deep into his chest. He felt it like an arrow with sharp iron heads at both ends now stuck between his heart and his brain. *I cannot be this delirious!* He rubbed his eyes.

Nothing seemed to be there, just the same green, waxy leaves. He hardly made heads or tails of it when that "something" started to inch away from him. He immediately sensed the sound of steps on the fresh soil. *There's no such thing!* He concentrated to the utmost when examining the carpet of leaves. *The leaves are...pressed...by something.* The shadow seemed as if it were running, disturbing the dead leaves as the steps grew farther and farther away. He followed it through heavy eyelids until it faded away altogether amongst the trees.

Cole was baffled only to be terrified a few moments later. Then curiosity started to push its way into his mind. He worked hard to raise his head off the ground and searched again. Nothing. He heaved a sigh of relief. *It must have been the alcohol.* He took advantage of a brief moment of lucidity and looked around, and Cole shuddered at the thought of having slept there. He gave up thinking. He laid his head back on the ground, shut his eyes, and covered his face with his hands. The hangover pulsed throughout his body and he found himself powerless and despondent. He felt soil all over his body, but also inside of him.

Chapter 10

The young man sat on a wooden doorstep with some nuts and bolts in front of him. He picked them up one by one and threw them from one small pile into another. He was far away when Jimmy's voice brought him back.

"Yo, man. What's up with you?"

Cole turned his head the other way and then to the ground.

"C'mon, Cole. You can't keep this up! You haven't punched in for two days, and today you're acting like this. It's obvious you're not yourself."

At long last he looked up from the ground and squinted at Jimmy. He stood still for an instant. He had to tell his best friend to relieve some of the burden weighing on his soul.

Ten minutes later, the friends were sitting side by side on that same doorstep of the storehouse, both at a loss for words.

"Life sucks, man!" Jimmy's voice was frayed with disgust. He held his head low, staring at the bolts Cole had stopped moving to and from. For a second, he dared throwing him a quick glance then returned to the pile of bolts.

"And this is a unique form of cancer," Cole added, seemingly coming to terms with the thought. "As if any form would not be quite enough. The doctor says it comes up in just 0.1% of all patients. How lucky must someone be to get this one-of-a kind type?" He forced a smile.

"Luckier, for sure, than whoever's got this disease

without a friend called Jimmy by his side." He made a feeble attempt at winding him down.

A smile dawned again on Cole's lips, this time a more natural-looking one, content to have even this simple respite. Their eyes bore through the ground and silence ruled for a few seconds. Eventually, Cole plucked up his courage and raised his head. He made a terse frown as if having recalled a small detail.

"And that weird moment yesterday morning, when I woke up in the forest with a hangover..."

His friend searched his face without a word for more of an explanation.

"Perhaps the disease has started to act on my brain."

Jimmy raised an eyebrow.

"There was something like a shadow back there, or like a force stalking me; and when I noticed it, it vanished. It ran away."

"My Gosh," Jimmy blurted out. He shut an eye, staring at him, and added joyfully, "C'mon, brother. You were dead drunk! I see leprechauns when I drink."

Cole arched his lips but went back to thoughtful quickly. "I'm telling you, man. It was something as if from...up there. My whole body shook."

Silence fell over them again.

"You believe in something way beyond the Governor?" Cole asked. "Something much greater, far away somewhere in the Universe?"

"It doesn't matter, bro'. It's worth nothing what I think. Something is up there for us though," Jimmy assured him, lifting his eyes to the heavens. "You'll be fine...you'll be fine!"

He clenched his hand for a fist bump. Cole responded with a brief touch. They both heaved and eyed the horizon.

Chapter 11

Saturday at lunchtime the entire Williams family was in. Today was special for Cole's family; they were scheduled to receive the Governmental Overseers' monthly visit. His mother, father, and brother were all elegantly dressed, waiting in the living room. Although the Overseers hadn't arrived yet, they sat respectfully on the couch. Christine's listless gaze stuck to the gauzy curtain-covered window. Today she had chosen to wear a cheerful dress, straw-colored with blue printed poppy flowers. She hadn't done so for the visit necessarily, but she had felt a need to infuse herself with some wellbeing—through clothes if nothing else.

The reality of the news she'd been given ate her up inside without mercy, a razor-toothed grinder. She shook off her bitter thoughts, straightened her back, drew a breath of air without trying to suppress the sound, and forced a beam of light to shine in her eyes in order to instill an iota of enthusiasm into the two wordless men framing her. She took George by the hand then smoothed Mathew's back with a soft pat.

Mathew, Cole's younger brother, was that thirteen year old kid whom anyone would have called brilliant and he'd always been attracted to architecture, engineering, technology, ships, and life's practicalities in general. He had matched his blue short-sleeved shirt with his favorite bowtie: white, decorated with one little boat on each side.

Not many months back, he had sneaked tiredly into

Cole's room while he was sketching.

"You're in here drawing instead of coming out to play," he interrupted. "You're not even tinkering on the car engine. That'd be more exciting."

"You're not so young anymore, Mathew. Now you can wile the time away without me too."

"With what? Instead of toys Mum started buying me clothes. Look for yourself; now she's got me a white bowtie—white as milk! She says it goes with all my shirts. There isn't the faintest strip of color on it."

He opened his palm and showed him the bowtie, despondently.

"Dressing elegantly is important, Mathew. Girls will like you more."

Paying no attention to Cole, the younger brother swept his eyes over the room and stopped short on the sheet in front of his brother.

"You're drawing cars again?"

"This time I'm making a kart. Here, d'you like it?"

Mathew shrugged indifferently. "Kinda."

"With such aerodynamics it can reach 80 kilometers an hour."

"It's okay," Mathew said, still untouched by his brother's passion. "I'd have liked it better if you'd drawn a boat."

Cole gave him a wry smile, but because he loved his little brother dearly he asked him to hand him the bowtie for a bit and to sit quietly next to him, asking no questions while he made it into "the prettiest bow tie in the world". When he finished drawing a design on it in pencil, he added, "Go and tell Mother to sew two colorful boats on these contours. She should make the flag at the top of the mast red, the sails blue, and the boat itself red."

After seeing him hurrying down the stairs straight from Cole's room, blushing with excitement and with his bowtie held as high as possible—and after much pleading and protests against the pencil washing off of it—Christine had given in and sewn it in colored thread, just as Cole recommended. Since then, Mathew always wore it at the meetings with the Overseers to remind them what he most wanted for his career. The visit on that Saturday was a special one for him: he was to be given the answer to his application to enroll in the college he deeply desired to attend.

"Father," he wanted to know, "why are the Overseers coming over every four weeks? Couldn't they drop in let's say...every ten weeks, or simply mail us a letter with the results and what they want from us for the next period?"

Their father, George Williams, was a respectful man when it came to the authorities and everything pertaining to laws and regulations. That was the way he had been brought up; that belief relied not on the fear of getting punished, but instead on his own view of discipline.

"Because those are the rules," George answered. He felt the line of buttons on his shirt and then his sleeves as if performing a final check-up. "They want to see us, they want to talk to us, they want to listen to our problems."

After the silence returned to the room, George realized he failed to convince the boy, who had lowered his head and stretched his arms on the couch in line with his legs. He got up from his seat next to Christine and sat on the other side, inserting Mathew between him and Christine. He ruffled his son's hair then ran his fingers through it, combing it like a treasure. The soft strands stretched for a moment then curled back. It never stayed straight. Although the color was the ebony of his mother's hair, the curls were definitely George's.

"Because we are people, Mathew," he carried on, "and do we remember the main communication rule?"

The boy answered on the spot, "'Never communicate with another person on the phone, by mail, or via the Internet when you can do it directly face to face'." The boy kept his voice low.

The same line, to the last word, could be read simultaneously on George's lips; it was a rule known by heart.

"That makes us human…and gives us true feelings," George added while Christine's hand went over Mathew's knees then gripped her husband's hand to show her support. "Face to face communication," he repeated, "not through computers or SMS. Just what you're doing now, Mathew."

"Yes, I know," the boy stopped him, still keeping his head bowed, "you told me that last week too."

The doorbell rang. Christine stood and opened the door for a gentleman and a lady.

"Please, do come in."

Both people were in their late forties, impeccably dressed in demure suits in nuances of white and grey. They each held a file labelled "*Williams Family*" with their address printed on the outside. They both behaved formally but tried to convey an air of offhandedness and it was hard to tell whether it was phony or coming from the heart. The lady Overseer also held a tiny box in her hand.

"How are you, dear Mathew?" she asked. "You're growing so fast; you get taller with every passing month, and it seems to me you're trying to turn into the handsomest boy in the neighborhood, too!"

"I'm fine. Thank you for the compliment," Mathew answered politely. "And how are you?"

"We are very well and happy to be seeing you again. We've brought you some cakes," she told him in an air of simple and formal kindness that was all by the book. She handed him the box.

"Thank you very much! Did you cook them?"

Christine shot him a smile and laid her hand on his shoulder, suggesting wordlessly that he cease asking such questions.

"No. I got them from a good tea room," the Overseer helped her, "but you've got to believe that they cooked them tastier than I would have."

Mathew smiled politely.

Christine pointed to the loveseat. "Please have a seat." She took the other one in front of them, as did George and Mathew. Now they were in the same positions as just before the guests arrived.

The two Overseers cast an eye around for the fourth member of the family. George felt obliged to offer explanations.

"As you can imagine, the news of this disease of Cole's...has devastated us all." His hand grasped Christine's hand; she was about to burst into tears. "And in such moments, Cole does not want to..." he hesitated, "talk to anyone. We chose to leave him alone in his room—"

"We're sorry," the male Overseer cut in.

"But if you want, I can try and call him again" George shouted his name, but there was hesitation in his voice as he stared at the staircase.

The male Overseer stopped him. "We're sorry. No, you shouldn't disturb him."

He looked for visual approval, which came from the lady Overseer. "We understand his state perfectly. We only hope he'll come 'round soon and that all will be fine."

A wave of silence rose and was then shattered by the calm words of the lady Overseer: "Let's have a look at last month's assessment and the novelties in the Code and the Catalogue of Rules."

The two opened their files to page one, watched attentively by their hosts.

"Food consumption," she began with the proper intonation for a chapter heading. "Here everything goes within the normal parameters for your family. The rules of the House of Health have relaxed somewhat on quantity and diversification but grew tighter as to quality. From now on there shall be a cap on some staples, especially those with high sugar contents." She looked at Mathew earnestly then smiled at the parents. "What do you think of these new rules?" she asked, trying to start a conversation.

Christine rushed to answer before her husband. "Well, unlike others, I think these rules are very beneficial." She patted George's stomach and smiled meaningfully.

The male Overseer dashed the joke. "Then...do you believe there are rules that aren't beneficial, Mrs. Williams?"

"No," George cut in, shooting a phony smile to Christine, "I only believe this wasn't such a brilliant joke."

"Yes, certainly..." she backed him drily.

Silence. George felt a heavy lump forming in this throat down to his sternum. The joke seemed inappropriate to him. The image of the Governor and the insignia of the Island abruptly sprung to his mind, an instinctual association he disliked.

The Overseer dropped the issue, moving on to a new

---

section. "Let's see now...'Computer and Internet use'. For the second consecutive month you have exceeded the allowed time limit per citizen. For that reason, I regret to inform you, the Government shall extract 120 points from your citizens' credit."

Christine almost stood from the couch.

"That's too much for meagre computer use! That is progress; that's the future!"

George calmed her down, gently patting her back. Every time he heard the word 'Government', a code of personal conduct activated itself within him. His mind would redraw with great clarity the whole leadership structure of the Island: Governmental Overseers, Houses specializing in different areas, and the Head of each House at the top; above all the Governor, in whom he placed his deepest beliefs and who loomed high above his humble existence.

The male Overseer tried to formally wind down the conversation. "It could be worse. Believe me, Mrs. Williams. This decision is endorsed by article 985 of the Constitutional Governance Code. We must obey these rules. The Government reached the conclusion that it isn't good otherwise, therefore what goes beyond a certain limit will be penalized. I need to remind you that if you exceed the limit of allowed hours again next month, the number of points you will be penalized shall double and your Internet access shall be immediately suspended for no less than one month."

"You may wish to look more carefully into the young men's Internet use," the lady suggested.

Mathew lowered his head, but in his mind he rushed forward to the chapter long-awaited by him, which was still not in sight. *Why didn't they start with that? They knew that's what interests me the most. Usually that's where they start.*

Nobody said another word more on computer usage. The lady Overseer flipped a page in the file and changed the tone of her voice so it was more cheerful. "Instead, you received 34 points as a reward for using the car under 60% of the average. The Government wishes to thank you for that. However, I would like to remind you that your oldest son is 30% above average. We shall talk to him next time, given his current condition. In conclusion, I'd say we can regard this section as a positive chapter for the Williams family."

In his room, Cole lay on the bed, hearing faint, jumbled fragments of the conversation with the Governmental Overseers. A subtle shade of puzzlement and nonchalance took over his expression. He kept staring vacantly at the ceiling, thinking of nothing at all. Nothing stirred the faintest trace of interest in him; everything rushing through his head concerned the news he had been given. He no longer saw the meaning behind any of the things around him, or the meaning of his own life.

The LED of his landline phone started blinking. A few seconds later, the answering machine took the call.

"Cole, what are you doing, man? Yesterday you skipped work again...the boss's worried. You must get over this; there might be a way—"

He picked up the phone.

"Hey, man...you must get over this!" Jimmy repeated. "Shirking work and not answering your phone will not make you feel better. I promise I'll let you win the next race," he joked, seeking to change the tone of his monologue. But he got no answer. "Cole?"

"There is no solution, Jimmy." Silence broke at the other

end of the line. "I checked a hundred times on the Internet."

"In that case, all you need to do is think positively. They may find something soon enough."

He said that rather awkwardly, trying to sound upbeat, but Cole didn't buy it. Jimmy changed the subject before getting back to Cole's answer.

"How's Mathew? How are your folks?"

"They're...it's that stupid monthly Government visit again."

"And you're off the hook, you loafer! You see, being sick means some perks, too," he tried to make the best of it then became serious. "We had ours too, last week. I have the feeling they want to limit us more and more; shut us off from all the cool stuff. On the one hand, we can't complain since we're leading a good life. On the other hand, I don't know what to say, man...we have to obey rules blindly and not question the decisions made by the Governor. Sometimes, I don't know, I find them too—"

"Well, what should I say? I don't care anymore. I don't give a crap about anything now."

He said it blankly, as if he hadn't even been listening to what Jimmy was saying.

"Okay, man, I can see it's not your best day. So...see you tomorrow at the sermon and after that let's have a beer in the name of the Spirit." Jimmy tried to jazz up his conclusion.

"All right," Cole agreed, "let's meet tomorrow."

He did not give Jimmy time to add anything else. He hung up the phone and turned to the computer screen, where a page on his type of cancer lay open. It was an article he had already read dozens of times. He did not hesitate to cast another glance over one paragraph: *"Once diagnosed,*

---

this type of cancer is impossible to cure except by surgical removal of the tissue involved. If located in the brain, the patient's chances of survival or remission are minimal."

Another link, another article; this time with photos of patients in an advanced stage of the disease. *"In the second stage, the patient manifests emetic states and possibly the paralysis of the lower limbs. In the final stage total paralysis sets in."*

"Why, why, why?" Cole's words bounced desperately off the walls.

He grabbed his head in his hands and fell on the floor. Shutting his eyes, he tried to forget everything.

Half an hour later, he was lying in that same spot on the cold hardwood floor. After opening his eyes, he realized that nothing had changed. He had not forgotten anything, the bad dream wasn't over, and the same annoying voices of the Governmental Overseers came from downstairs, droning on: *"The applications we've had of late..."*

"...for the Maritime College," the lady Overseer carried on spewing information, "have been plenty."

Mathew was following her very carefully.

"That means Mathew will not be able to attend."

The boy felt like he had been squashed under a boulder.

"Madam," Christine replied, "that is the only maritime college on the Island, which is to say...on the planet."

"I understand too well, but on a careful analysis of the applications in this field it follows that the places are taken for the next ten years. With the deepest regret, we inform you that the young boy will not be able to embrace this profession."

"But I want to become a navigator!" Mathew reacted with

conviction, like a child whose favorite toy was taken away.

"Dear Mathew, a specialized crew is already in place. This isn't just about ships and sailing. Many a danger can be lurking on the high seas. I wouldn't have recommended you the remaining places anyway. There are so many beautiful trades you can still choose from."

"But it's not fair! I want to build boats! I want to sail!"

He went to the library and took a globe with the little island marked on it in the northern hemisphere; it was white at the poles and the blue of the boundless ocean spread all over the rest of it. George had kept it from the first part of his life, when he had been a real long-haul seafarer. Back then when sailing the Earth far and wide, he used to withdraw into his cabin in the evening, give it a spin, and set his finger on a point, saying: *We are now here.* Since Cole had come into the world, however, he had decided it was too risky to continue as a sailor and changed his work to remain home near his family.

"All this expanse of water," Mathew said gloomily, pointing his finger randomly on the globe, "I want to sail it. I want to travel around the globe like Father did!"

"Mathew, you know it's dangerous and can be done only by attending the Maritime College. Unfortunately, as we have pointed out, the places have been occupied."

"But not—"

"Quiet, Mathew!" George intervened. "You heard the lady Overseer. We'll find something more interesting for you together."

He then shifted his eyes to the Overseers, pretending he had the situation under control, but his heart was with his child. Mathew fell silent, but still George heard him sobbing and out of the corner of his eye, he saw his child looking sadly at the globe.

"We're sorry for that," the lady added.

"I reckon that was all for this month," the gentleman Overseer concluded. "We should let the Williams family relax on such a beautiful Saturday."

She agreed. "Yes, of course." She stood along with him. "I hope we were not much of a nuisance for you."

"It was a pleasure to have you visit us," Christine assured them.

A leisurely smile cracked both of their lips.

"We wish you a wonderful month! Send Cole our best wishes and let's hope all will be well," the gentleman Overseer said; then, standing in the doorway, to Mathew: "And don't spend too much time on the computer!"

Chapter 12

Rows of people dressed completely in white flowed into the enormous building. They were grouped by families and ambled demurely in silence. The white, commanding building was shaped by rectangular sides, and its entrance was spread across a wide platform that people got to after climbing a few stairs.

There they were greeted by a gigantic double door, also painted white; the humongous size was meant to signal the importance of stepping through the entrance. It was a Sunday and the place where the city's residents gathered was a house of worship. Above the door, a symbol was carved in stone—a star delineating a heart-shaped corolla flower in the center.

Some minutes later, the place was packed. It looked rather like a large conference room, each chair taken by a person wearing impeccable white.

"...by worshipping the purity of this Land, we worship ourselves, we worship our body and mind, we worship our family, the people close to us...we worship our Governor, the Heads and the rules that have been given to us."

Thus went on the sermon given by the gentleman on the stage, dressed in a white tunic and a simple grey ribbon going round his body from his right shoulder to his left hip. He did not need a microphone; the silence was unbroken.

George proudly wore his perfectly ironed shirt strewn with patterns handcrafted by his wife. He was in his early

60s and for as long as he could remember, he had loved to come immaculately dressed to this house, to be together with the other citizens, with his friends and neighbors, to listen to the sermon and contemplate. Next to him sat Christine, holding his hand, and although she did not share his blind convictions, she, too, listened attentively. All in the same line sat Mathew, Cole, and farther away Jimmy and his own family.

Cole was dejected. His face was gloomy and his mind was in another place, where nothing had meaning, where his life might as well have already been over. *Why live a couple of months more? It will all be over sooner than I would have liked anyway. I want to die...now!*

He looked at one of the white walls, at the grey painted words: "*We trust our Law and Governor*". Detached, he shifted his sight to another one: "*The purity of our soul is not for granted, it must be built in our lifetime*". Somewhat to the right, in larger letters than all the others, was inscribed, "*The Code is Holy*", and more inscriptions surrounded the great hall from floor to ceiling. For the first time, Cole read them all together.

Christine threw him a brief look and understood that he, too, was far and away, thinking that soon he would no longer be with them. Her baby—*her soul*, as she used to call him when he was but knee-high—would never again sit in that line and listen to the sermons with them. She wasn't a strong woman, or maybe it wasn't even possible for her to be one in the face of such a prospect, so she could no longer conceal her tears.

"...we must love one another," the pastor's discourse droned on in the background, "but also respect the Island; this wonderful gift we have been given. We must thank the heavens that we have been born and that we are living in these times; this very moment with all it has to offer, be it little or more than that. And we must also be at peace with the idea that, at some point, we shall cease to be. A restful and grateful thought should prevail in each of our minds; namely that a force larger than our powers of comprehension has given us the chance to be one of the 12 million inhabitants of the Earth. In the Code and the Governor we trust!" the pastor uttered poignantly and at the top of his voice.

The entire crowd followed suit, causing the hall to vibrate harmoniously: "In the Code and the Governor we trust!"

Cole couldn't stand the pressure building inside his head anymore and shouted, "That's stupid!"

Dumbfounded, the crowd all turned to him.

"Can the Governor or this stupid law help me live my life whole? No, I do not want to be at peace with the thought of dying in less than a year!"

His emotions and the realization of the mad rashness of his outburst stifled his outcry, still eerily reverberating through the farthest nooks and crannies of the large building. It seemed as if the full outpouring of his heart had stopped in his throat and sapped the strength from his voice. In just a few seconds, he felt completely drained. He had to free his mind. He looked around, waiting for an answer to his unanswerable question while desperation and hopelessness filled his eyes.

The people stared at him in alarm, as if something bad was surely about to happen to him at any moment. They looked at him with compassion equally for his condition and for what might be in store for him in exchange for such an outburst.

Jimmy placed a hand on his shoulder, attempting to calm him down, and so did Christine, but to no avail. Cole stood and began pushing his way out of the row of seats. A rustle of whispers went through the entire hall when two people wearing white-tinted grey tunics sprang up. His father quietly waved at them to make them understand he would deal with this and followed Cole. They seemed to embrace George's proposal and desisted.

"Stupid!" Cole shouted one last time from the aisle, followed by his father at some distance.

George stepped out of the building and quickly down the stairs. "Please wait!" he said, panting two meters behind Cole's car, which was parked on the street next to the site. The engine started and the door slammed shut. He could only watch as the car sped away.

Chapter 13

A sharp rumble cut through the suburban slumber; Cole's SUV was running flat out. A rumble also ran through his gloomy thoughts: Wha*t sense does it make to go through the little time I've got left? It's time I say goodbye to this world.*

A few kilometers later, Cole turned on to a forest road. The speedometer needle pointed 120 km/h and he kept accelerating. A hard rock tune made the speakers vibrate as he took his hands off the wheel and looked up at the sky—a white cloud floated high above—and looked back at him. *I'm sorry, Mother...Father...Mathew...* Silence enveloped his thoughts. He felt at peace. He smiled. *I am ready to merge with nature.* Sun rays pierced the curtain of tree leaves. He smiled again. *This is wonderful.* He closed his eyes. *Now I can go.*

The front of the car slammed against a wooden barrier set in the middle of the road that read *"STOP! DANGER! ROAD CLOSED"*. In a careless, slumberous gesture, Cole turned his head to the right and half opened his eyes to watch shards of the sign flying past him.

A shadowy outline formed in the distance, seemingly running parallel to him, rushing through undergrowth and offshoots. *No, that can't be!* He gripped the wheel and stepped hard on the brakes. A cloud of dust cloaked the car. He turned off the radio and for one or two seconds caught his breath. Cole's heart thumped as if about to leap out of his chest. He opened the door and broke into a jog towards the place he'd seen the shadow.

It felt like running through a void or an insulated tube. He heard only his steps in the tall grass and his hard, wheezing breath. A terrible curiosity urged him to run faster. He was hot on the trail left by the bizarre shape: unsettled leaves, torn twigs, the trampled grass; he was getting closer.

Suddenly, any trace the shadow had been there vanished. He stopped, too. Cole looked to the right then to the left, then at his scratched arm blistered in reddish stripes. A branch had done this. *I don't care. I'm ready to die anyway.* He checked his wild breath, concentrated for a moment, and listened.

A rustling right above him in the tree. As Cole raised his head, he saw the same translucent shape jumping down to stand in front of him. The ground trembled, the leaves blew away. He felt lightning travel through his body from head to toe, warming each drop of blood in his veins. *An invisible monster, an energetic vibration, a magnetic field, a spiritual apparition?* Through the filter of his logical mind, the shape was beyond depiction. He strained to the utmost, waiting for something terrible to happen. Cole felt a human faltering, he felt himself seen, looked over. Then the shape began to recede. *Is it running away?* A devilish inquisitiveness took hold of him again; the mad chasing resumed.

The sound of rushed steps crushing twigs, saplings, and leaves combined with Cole's racing pulse and mind as if he were hunting. He jumped millimeters away from an animal trap, avoided a fallen bough, and continued his pursuit, but it was getting farther and farther away. He was losing it.

A howl of pain broke from the trees up ahead. *It's*

a...woman's scream! He caught up with it and was petrified. The same transparent shape, barely visible, was next to a huge animal trap.

His heart froze, and the air stopped filling his lungs; he went numb. The transparent shape transmuted, inch by inch, into a human body.

"What are you? I'm not afraid!" he screamed, panting and kneeling on the ground.

By and by, a red haired young woman wearing body tight, black and grey gear appeared before his eyes. The metal trap was sunk entirely into her torn right foot. She gazed at him with shivers of dread and clenched her teeth as hard as she could, struggling not to show her pain. She grabbed the massive iron teeth and pulled them enough apart to get her profusely bleeding leg out.

Cole watched her, petrified. He forgot to even breathe. She looked him in the eyes for a second and, without hesitation, pressed her finger against a large rectangular watch she wore on her left wrist. It seemed like a flash of pain ran through her body as she clenched her teeth even harder, but soon the bleeding stopped as if by miracle and the flesh on her leg started moving, tightening up little by little. The wound was visibly healing under Cole's shocked gaze.

From the way she acted, it seemed her pain was never-ending. Neither of them moved. The only proof of what had transpired was the blood trickling down the leg of her torn trousers; the wound was completely healed.

Cole involuntarily broke both their numbness when drawing a full breath of air. She followed suit. Adrenaline still ran through their bodies when their eyes met for a second; the terror seemed to vanish. The wonderful creature scrutinized him without making any other gesture. She first analyzed his black unkempt hair, perfectly framing his oval face, then the brown eyes, beautifully contoured under the thick, slightly elongated eyebrows.

For a moment, he was under the impression he saw her trembling slightly, as if a strange unknown feeling had invaded her whole body. The light of her green eyes was enough to make him tremble all over too. The angelic features of her face and the beautifully curved contour of her lips made no sense in all the things going on around him.

The green-eyed redhead stood up in just two moves, took another look at him, and started running without looking back. She got lost among twigs and bushes while Cole was still down, shocked, staring ahead in rapture and taking deep breaths.

Chapter 14

The same lost gaze stared straight ahead as Cole waited on the checkout line while a television set droned on in the background:

"...the laws of the Code are made to be upheld. Only united and at peace with these rules can we hope for a better future together. Society cannot evolve out of its own inertia; it must be guided and modelled. Together we can sustain this path, which must be smooth, restrained—"

"Hellooo!" the harsh voice of the saleswoman broke him out of his stupor. "Are you going to buy those, or you just want to take them for a walk to the cash register?"

The stout lady sized him up, obviously annoyed, pointing out the products in the cart which had been waiting for a long time to be placed on the belt. Cole woke up as if from a deep slumber in the middle of a supermarket. Too much had been going through his mind these last few days. In the end, he reacted.

"Yes...I'm going to buy them, of course."

He moved the products onto the belt then into his bag after she scanned them in robotic-like movements. After he paid, he left the store and dialed a number on his mobile phone. The wide, badly finished buttons looked so slippery to him. The phone stuck to his ear was the only object his body still felt. A state of shock smothered his still-blank sight, drowned in the recollection of the images in the forest.

"The person you have dialed is not available right now.

Please leave a message after the beep."

He felt relieved at the simple fact that he was about to leave a message. Even before uttering the words he knew his voice would be unsteady:

"Jimmy, I have to talk to you. I saw something...extremely weird. It has nothing to do with my illness, believe me! I saw something unusual out there in the forest. A...creature, an alien—something which...I don't know, man. Something not from the Earth."

He fell silent for a few seconds.

"Call me as soon as you get this message."

In another part of the Island, a man twitched; it happened at the exact moment Cole had pronounced the word "alien". He sat comfortably in his regal chair, in a room packed with surveillance monitors, when—on the screens in front of him—all information connected to that call was rapidly displayed. Among them, the map with Cole's coordinates and the image of his ID card were shown. Other screens also presented the young man's profile and data clustered over diverse fields. The man looked meaningfully to his left, to two other people sitting in similar chairs. They were watching, frowning at the same screens. Then they turned to him, aware of the importance of the news they received and its effects.

Chapter 15

"Hi, Cole, I heard your message. Tell me what's going on, man. You're scaring me."

"I can't talk on the phone. I feel like I'm being followed. This is totally mad! Can we please meet at Dino's in half an hour?"

"Okay...let's do that. Take care!"

Half-light ruled the little street lined with buildings no more than three stories high. The two car models, parked on both sides, made the street look even bleaker. Cole quickly found a parking spot, killed the lights, and carefully glanced around; he was in no hurry anymore. He took his time searching all three mirrors. It looked like nobody had tailed him. He climbed out of the car and rushed to the bar with the large luminous sign: Dino's. At that time, just a few customers milled about. When Cole entered the pub, he had the feeling they all knew why he was there. Even if he had seen the interior dozens of times, the wooden furniture with rustic accents, the yellow and green lampshades, and the high ceiling all looked mysterious to him.

The two young men each had a half-empty mug of beer in front of them.

"Wow!" Jimmy exclaimed cautiously.

"I'm telling you," Cole continued, "I searched the forest after that for more signs and nothing at all."

Jimmy stared, completely absorbed.

"Believe me, she was not from this planet!" Cole went on. "I don't know how she appeared, how she healed herself, or how she vanished."

His chubby friend went numb, shocked. He mustered the strength to take another sip of beer from the mug that seemed heavier now than when full.

"I had better report this to the Government," Cole added.

"No," Jimmy said firmly, "I bet the Government already knows. Or maybe they are all in it..."

Cole wanted to say something but was cut off: his mouth remained half-opened.

"Or not, I don't know...it makes no sense! You may... have met an alien from somewhere far away."

"Bah!" Cole was still searching for a better explanation. "Fine, it's an alien...let's assume as much, but you see, it's done me no harm. So they want to study us? Protect us? Save us? From whom and why? Or maybe they want to send us a message—"

Jimmy broke in, whispering, "Or maybe the Government is hiding even more fishy things. They could run a special space program which we have no clue about!"

Cole took two gulps of beer in a single breath. "For the time being, I'd say to keep it secret. I am afraid of nothing— aliens or the Government. I'm dying anyway!"

"Shut up, man! Don't think about dying no more." He

threw the pint back. "Very well, a secret it shall be, if that's what you want."

Ten minutes later, the two friends left the bar. Outside, they first threw a suspicious glance to the pole-mounted camera and then a thorough look around. Fear had dissolved into the blood that fed their bodies. Jimmy also cast his eyes into the sky, trying to spot anything abnormal. A passer-by looked at them in a strange way. They felt as if in a bubble or in the middle of a play on stage. For a moment, they put their suspicions aside, shook hands, and gave each other a brief hug.

"Good luck, man. Take care!" Jimmy cheered him up. "Call me if there's something wrong."

"You bet I will." Cole quickly turned away and started towards his car, shrugging on his hood and hiding his hands in his pockets.

A patrol vehicle passed with two guards inside, its emergency lights off. He threw a quick glance at them, who also kept their eyes on him while driving slowly by. He couldn't make out whether they were looking at him as they would have looked at any other citizen out on the streets so late at night or if they were interested in something in particular. He did not care to know. He pretended to ignore them and went on his way to his car in the same rhythm, not a step faster or slower. Cole could have sworn he had seen the camera change its position to face him but did not dare to look up and make sure. On he went, minding his steps and pretending to ignore that as well. He slipped behind the wheel and started the drive home.

For about a minute, a car followed him. He started keeping his eyes on the rear-view mirror, whole body ablaze and a few drops of sweat forming on his forehead. He took a fast right turn and the car behind him rolled ahead. It wasn't following him, but Cole kept his eyes on it until it was out of sight.

A tire screech jolted him forward as the driver in front of him slammed on the brakes at the very last moment. Instinctively, Cole also stepped hard on his brakes.

The yelling coming from behind the slightly open driver's door completely broke him out of his thoughts this time.

"Are you a moron or what?" the angry driver shouted. "Can't you see you've got a yield sign? Are you trying to kill us both?"

Cole raised his hands and lowered his head.

"Unbelievable!" the other driver snapped, climbing back in the car shaking his head. He then left the crossroads mumbling something about Cole's relatives.

The young man heaved a sigh of relief. He just sat there, frozen in the middle of the crossroads, unable to touch the pedals any longer. The shiver in his legs kept irking him. *Calm,* he told himself. He took a deep breath. *I must come back to earth.*

He started the engine and continued on his way home.

Chapter 16

The dog-eared posters pinned up side by side displayed an entire hall of fame of vintage cars and motorcycles; the room was a teenage haven. Any empty spaces on the walls had long since vanished, covered with prototypes drawn by hand and newspaper clippings; everything was connected to motorcycles, cars, or karts.

The smell of a heated computer permeated the air as Cole sat at his desk. He had been navigating the Internet for several hours now, searching for that redeeming answer that would allow him to sleep better at night. He typed: "eyewitnesses confirmed alien sightings". The search engine returned several pages of results. He clicked the first link and an article with theories about the Universe loaded on his cathode ray tube monitor. He explored the screen carefully until his eyes rested on a segment of text: "...there isn't any clear evidence regarding the existence of other beings in the Universe, only speculations..." He navigated to the second link, where another title caught more of his interest: "Is there any form of extraterrestrial life out there?" The paragraphs succeeded one after the other in front of a pair of eyes greedily seeking an answer. Why do I expect to find something else than I already know? He went through different sections which talked about stars, galaxies, and supernovas. The vastness of the Universe could warrant the conclusion that there should have been extraterrestrial life, yet nothing was conclusive. Nothing! Another section and the map of the Earth sprung into view, marked with dots where alleged eyewitnesses sighted "strange phenomena" or were in situations where they thought they'd seen "something"—only flying saucers, abnormal marks on the soil, and nothing of what Cole had hoped he would find. Most of the places reported were on the Island; the rest were in various parts of the ocean.

Page after page, the space between his eyelids grew ever dimmer and Cole had to blink harder to manage. It was late and he was rundown. He rubbed his eyes, frustrated at finding nothing meaningful. He would have gone to bed but was in no mood. Cole wanted answers, to have a plan. He took a few turns round the room. *What should I do? Can I do anything? Should I do anything...or merely let time go by? Should I say something to anyone else?* He was so utterly alone in front of such a large mystery. He checked his wall calendar briefly: Sunday, July 14, 2024. It was a day behind; he turned the leaf to day 15. The corner of a poster came off the door; he glued it back. Overpowering pressure crushed his temples. He pulled the drapes apart and looked outside with one eye only, trying to go unnoticed. Nothing. He looked again more carefully, this time showing himself in front of the window, standing up straight and fearless. *I am afraid of nothing. I don't care!* He pulled the drapes back and returned to his bed. He lay on his back, *only for a moment*, staring at the whiteness of the ceiling. His lids closed slowly and sweeter thoughts began to invade his mind. He fell asleep.

The harsh material tight on his wrists made him uncomfortable. It had nothing to do with his dream. Suddenly, a terrible headache seized him. Cole could hardly open his eyelids and tried to focus on something in the room. *Two shapes...Two people? What's that?* His heart froze. He jolted once but realized he couldn't budge an inch. *My hands and feet are tied up!*

Two brawny men dressed in black seized him. Cole struggled hard and found out that he didn't stand a chance. The strings twisted around his wrists and the four strong arms had riveted him to the spot as effectively as a straightjacket.

"You...!"

A palm covered his mouth and he went silent. The sound of tape peeling off the roll pierced through his stomach. The heavy hand opened his mouth for a split second.

"Hel—" Cole managed to blurt out before a handkerchief was forced into his mouth and the tape was immediately stuck to his face.

He felt a strange chemical taste on his tongue while another roll surrounded his head and covered his mouth in yet another layer. His bloodshot eyes, bulging out to the utmost and swimming in tears, stared at the two men. A grey sack went over his head, turning redder and redder, ready to go off. It was the umpteenth time during the last few days when he had to listen to his own moans and his jerky breath thundering in his ears along with the murderous rhythm of his heart. His attempt to spit proved to be no use; if anything, it made his state worse.

He felt himself lifted up through the window and then taken down by way of something...*like a pulley*. He wished he saw something else besides the black of the sack on his face. A few steps and another pair of hands dug their fingers into his flesh and dropped him off somewhere. Adrenaline had long since replaced the terror, but Cole could still do nothing. He realized that the substance in the handkerchief had begun to take effect. He heard the sound of a sliding door—*I'm in a car...a minivan*. Slumber seized him without his consent.

A black minivan drove away from the Williams' home in the dead of night. All lights were off in houses and the whole neighborhood slept quietly; the only sound that could be heard was crickets.

In another part of the Island, three men carefully followed the monitor scrolling the entire scene. They sat in their enormous chairs and looked at the van. A few centimeters above each of their heads was a small cap-like device held by a bent arm starting from the back of the chair. In front of them, dozens of monitors showed a bizarre range of information: on one of them there was a 3-D map of the entire Island, which was covered by a translucent cupola similar to a magnetic field or protection shield. Above, tracking images provided by radar filled the screens, and to the left images sent by surveillance cameras popped up; all accompanied by the cold background of radio communications.

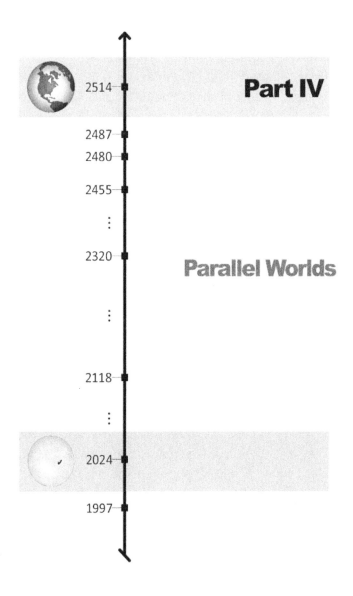

Part IV

2514
2487
2480
2455
⋮
2320

Parallel Worlds

⋮
2118
⋮
2024
1997

Chapter 17

His aching head told him he had slept a long while.

Cole suddenly remembered everything, but no longer felt a string wrapped around his wrists or a tape covering his mouth. He opened his eyes in terror. The room, which looked more like a prison cell, proved he wasn't dreaming. Cole lay on a bed covered by a rather foul mattress and wearing exactly what he'd been wearing in his bed at home. He hardly had time to look around the room when he heard a plod of heavy steps. *They're coming this way!* He scanned the cell again in a desperate attempt to break through. The immaculate white, windowless walls did nothing to help him. The metallic clank of the old lock resonated all over the room. Cole was out of time; all he could do was huddle by headboard and stare at the door.

Through the doorway came a man wearing a green military uniform, a plate of food in hand. "Eat, you must be hungry."

The plate was dumped on a chair as Cole watched without blinking. The uniform, made up of trousers and jacket, was flawless, as if it had been ironed right before he entered. Polished black leather boots were strapped tight over his tucked-in trousers. The buttoned-up jacket was girded on at the waist with a weathered gold buckle attached to a wide brown leather belt. A holster made of the same leather hung on his right side. It most definitely wasn't empty; it hung too heavy. Cole noted the safety catch was on and appreciated it would take the man some time before he could use his pistol. He immediately felt his chest tremble and didn't want to think of it. Then he looked up at the man's epaulettes; there were no marks, but pinned on each collar tip was a slip of black fabric shaped in an all-too-familiar symbol: a flower inside a star. Suddenly, Cole felt both more secure and bewildered.

When the man moved to leave, Cole asked with self-assurance, "Who are you? What do you want from me?"

"You'll learn soon."

Then the door slammed behind him.

Cole leaned against the edge of the bed, anxiously waiting for something to happen. The food tray had been long empty and by the hunger gnawing at him he would have bet hours passed since he'd been kidnapped.

The same metallic clank and the door opened again. Instinctively, Cole withdrew to the head of the bed.

"You must know that we are civilized here," the military man reassured him as he stood in the doorway. "Please, come with me."

He jumped out of the bed and followed silently. Another man, wearing the same garb and waiting for him outside the cell, came along as well.

The military man stopped in front of another door, opened it, and said in a blank voice, "Wait here a few minutes please."

Cole stepped in warily. The room was much like the ones police used for interviews in action movies: a table, two chairs, a lamp, and a wall with a mirror. He hardly had enough time to have a look at it, for a black man of average height showed up. He looked as if worked up by countless thoughts, a state perfectly befitting a man on the shady side of his prime.

"Hello, Cole," he said.

The young man took a step forward. "Why am I here, and what do you want from me?"

"Hello, my name is Chris McCain," the man said, ignoring his question. "You can call me by name. Nice to meet you too."

He stretched his hand to shake Cole's, who responded in kind, slightly faltering.

"I shall cut to the chase. We have been notified about your last third-degree encounter," Chris explained without wasting time. "Also, we've noticed that you've started to spread this information and I can tell you in all sincerity, that's not good for our community."

I knew I was being followed. He turned his head sideways to avoid visual contact.

"You are now in a building on the northern part of the Island. You must have many questions and you are probably confused and afraid." He broke off to wait for his reaction; Cole had none. "I'm going to tell you a real story, and yet it is so different from what you know that you'll have a hard time digesting it. Let's hope that knowing the truth will make you feel better."

Still lost for words, Cole turned his face towards Mr. *Smart Guy*. He was baffled by him; a trusting, deep, calm voice. He wore an impeccable tunic, looking much like a preacher in the house of worship, except it was completely grey.

"Take a seat, please."

Cole sat down without losing sight of him. He felt a huge void in his stomach.

Without further delay, Chris spoke in the same even voice. "What you saw there, in the woods, is not from outside of Earth. It is a so-called bionic person, the result of mankind's evolution up to the present moment."

Cole squinted. "I thought I knew how far we evolved or what we have here on Earth. We aren't that advanced, are we?"

The tunic-wearing man said nothing, so the young man found himself forced to add, "A...bionic person? First invisibility, then she cured her wound in a matter of seconds...but then she also felt pretty human to me."

Chris closed his eyes and, after a small break, said, "The year we are in is, in fact, 2514, 490 years later than you think—than the *Island* thinks."

The room began to spin along with young Cole Williams. All strength drained from his body, evaporating. He went suddenly pale and managed with difficulty to stay present.

"Another important aspect is that when I tell you this person is from Earth, that does not mean he comes from our Island."

"You are lying!" Cole bellowed. "You're lying to me! This can't be true! There is nothing else on Earth except this Island."

Chris lowered his eyes and shook his head.

"No, no, no..." Cole whispered to himself.

Chris took a remote control out of his pocket and pressed

a button. A projection started from behind the mirror and landed on the opposite wall. Planet Earth, with its Island and vast ocean, just as Cole knew it, revolved around its axis.

"This is the Earth as you know it now," he explained.

The young man's eyes widened as he waited for the next image. Chris did not keep him in suspense too long and pressed the button again.

"This is the Earth...as it really is. As you can see, it is different from what you learned in school. There is a lot more dry land above the ocean, which form the so-called continents, and there are a lot more small islands out there."

Cole gawked at the screen in amazement. He felt like he was floating somewhere in the air and could not feel his legs anymore.

"Perhaps you're asking yourself why all these things have been kept hidden from you, from your friends, from mankind as you know it?"

"You bet!" Chris noticed how tense his jaw had become.

"We hid them because we are afraid of ourselves—of the human race." Cole was only more baffled, so Chris thought a moment. "Let's go back to the past," he changed his approach, "to the real 2000s, when mankind kept making discoveries and applying all that technological advancement to everyday life at an exponential rate. In the field of medicine, we started by replacing human organs and constructing artificial arms and legs. They continued with artificial heart implants and inched forward towards substitutes for every organ. Everything was still rudimentary in that century and was done only in the name of medicine, all with the best of intentions, based on compassion for suffering people."

Cole followed the flashes projected on the screen;

---

snippets from the real 21st century. Images and pieces of news showing all kinds of accomplishments scrolled on even after Chris had stopped talking.

"All that was initially fine, but against the backdrop of the mad commercial race for more and more technologies and products, bigger and bigger sales, and an increased diversity," he raised his voice, "people's demands developed. Their appetite for entertainment through these advanced technologies also grew exponentially: touch-screens, smart-phones, an intelligent, and then even more intelligent, Internet, voice and visual recognition, digital projection glasses and lenses, 3-D images that looked more and more real, intelligent video analytics, drones, self-driving cars, robots..." Chris drew a breath. "Augmented reality, invisibility, atom teleporting, stronger and stronger artificial intelligence, more and more intelligent robots...a virtual world on constant development...and I could go on for a long time."

"Wow," Cole whispered. His face was numb.

"Unfortunately, bad things were not long forthcoming. First there was the negative impact on social behavior; then came the nanotechnology progress which, in time, was beyond control. That gave rise to nanobots, those minuscule robots that cannot be seen but can work for us on such small scales you cannot even believe. Everything that was previously known underwent a revolution. By such small forms of artificial intelligence, we can control and change anything, starting from atoms, molecules, and cells, up to objects or human body parts." He lowered his head. "It's just a matter of the human imagination...and this should sometimes be confined."

Cole half-opened his mouth but gave up on trying to

speak. Chris carried on, more restrained this time, clearly ashamed of the race he was part of.

"The medical field merged in time with the commercial one. More and more sophisticated procedures were being performed to reconstruct various body parts. Eventually, almost perfect replacement techniques were developed. Sick or disabled people became well again in a matter of days. By the 23rd century, the average life span had reached three hundred years. No one wished to die anymore."

The young man sensed all this data spinning madly inside his head, his sight blurred, and his throat felt as scorched as desert dunes under the relentless blaze of the sun.

"Water…" he murmured.

Chris raised two fingers to the mirror.

An Asian man stepped into the lobby of a Governmental building situated somewhere in the south of the Island. Three notches on his chin enshrouded the mystery tale of older scars. He approached the security officer sitting behind a small desk; the man was a head taller than him, sturdy, armed, and sporting a flawless military posture.

"How can I be of help, sir?" the officer greeted without taking his eyes off him.

"Good day. I am here for meeting with Mr. Smith." the Asian man spoke in broken English, missing a few syllables.

The officer cleared his throat. "I don't believe we have any Mr. Smith working here. What's the first name?"

"Alan."

"Still no," the officer articulated cautiously. "Just a moment. I will double-check" He searched through a small register.

The Asian man returned a barely sketched smile and lightly rested his hand on the desk without indicating any devious intentions. The black costume he wore was a size too large and strived to seem somehow diplomatic despite the rumpled white shirt underneath.

When the officer was almost done, a thread-like black stream trickled down his guest's index finger towards his hand. He felt sudden tingles running through his hand, and raised it off the desk. Then it reached his arm and shoulder. Instinctively, he put his hand to his throat and, a moment later, collapsed as if he'd had a seizure.

The guest stared as if nothing had happened. His right iris went red and a series of data scrolled across his pupil as if on a virtual screen: attack indicators, plans and details of the building, possible targets. Written more distinctly than any other information, however, was: *Eliminate the entire personnel in the building. Do NOT destroy any computers.*

One second later, another man wearing the same type of clothes entered the lobby; a massive man with blond hair and with a tousled beard that looked as if it had been trimmed with a shard of glass. He walked like he knew where to go and what to do.

The two assessed the room with lifeless gazes when a mini-drone flew from the Asian man's hand. It had sprung from a device somewhat like a large rectangular watch and now it went into the corridor of the building, searching thoroughly like a trailblazing scout.

They scanned the surroundings, then unbuttoned their suits and exposed their weapon harnesses accommodating two submachine guns each and multiple magazines. They released the catches, and their eyes met for a quick confirmation before they started down the corridor, following the mini-drone. A second mini-drone flew above them, disappearing into the building.

"The hunger for resources and power changed the entire world," Chris went on explaining on the other side of the Island. "I admit such facts are hard to buy because there has been so much progress. Five hundred years is a very long time when you have exponential advancements. If we only look at the years 1900 to 2000, an entire technological history—which you must be by and large aware of—unfolded in a mere century."

Chris broke off, haunted by a host of gloomy thoughts.

"I have...a million questions exploding in my...head," Cole said clumsily. "How did you manage to keep the Island isolated from the rest of the world? How did you hide it all?"

The man shut his eyes for a second. He knew he had to tell him more than he wished.

"In order not to evolve towards what is outside the Island, first we had to keep technology under control. Our Island is a pseudo-dogmatic land controlled by strict rules.

From the outside, we are seen as a so-called communist and religious nation. In fact, it may be even worse; we are seen by many as a sect. We are also called 'old-fashioned Earth people'."

A small hesitation, but Chris let it pass. "Only by means of this organization, by means of these authoritarian laws and regulations, can we keep things under control; keep them to where they were at the beginning of the 21st century."

"Marvelous," came Cole's taunting remark.

"We must then protect ourselves from the people outside. There is a very...complex mechanism in place to keep the Island under protection, isolated from adventurers, from people who may have all kinds of intentions, even if they are only driven by curiosity."

"Complex...?" He raised his eyebrows, waiting for Chris to explain more, but he didn't. Cole risked a bluff. "You told me far too much for a mere Islander. I don't think you want to brainwash or murder me though."

"Fortunately for you, we have no such intentions." Chris cut him short just as caustically.

"You need me for something. Otherwise you wouldn't have told me all that."

"So it seems."

The remarks were spewed in quick succession.

"Then I want to know the truth to the end."

"I see you came to your senses. I didn't expect you to digest all this information so quickly."

"If only you knew..."

"I can see it'd be hard to keep you in the dark about much."

"As I was saying," Cole regained his confidence, "I wish to

know everything. I won't cooperate otherwise."

Chris turned inconspicuously to face the mirror, then closed his eyes and resumed just as calmly as he had begun.

"There are twelve 'Erudites' that control all behind a sophisticated mechanism, behind the Houses and the Governor. I..." He hesitated again even more visibly, "I am one of them."

His image was projected differently in Cole's eyes. He once again took stock of every detail of his flawless tunic: the embroidered collar with the emblem of the Island at the two corners encircling the curve of the neck; the dark buttons covered in grey leather forming a line meant to command respect; the dark grey silk-embroidered sleeves.

"We are, in a way...just like the bionic people," he added. A shadow of sadness showed itself fleetingly on his face. "We are the only ones on the Island using state-of-the-art technology implanted in the brain; we are exactly what people are not supposed to become. We are the only interface to the control, monitoring, and defense system of this patch of land. We have taken an oath to use this technology solely for the protection of the Island and nothing else."

"I surely hope you keep your oath," Cole muttered.

The look Chris threw him made him understand his comment had gone a bit too far.

"Let's return to the purpose of having you here."

The young man leaned towards him, giving him his undivided attention.

"Starting from the description you gave, our opinion is nothing can be worse: we are having a Tentorian visit."

Cole measured him from head to toe, nonplussed.

"In Latin, an ancient tongue outside the Island

'Tentorian' means 'extended one'." An unpleasant thought beset Chris and made him lower his chin. "That's the name they were given when created, with reference to their artificially extended, overdeveloped capacities. It also means 'those with no soul' in the Maori dialect. That's where their leaders had understood the Tentorians' name to be derived from and that's how they liked to be called from then on."

Cole opened his mouth only to hear himself speak. "They seem rather...defiant."

The Erudite agreed thoughtfully. "The girl you have seen in the woods must be a Tentorian. It surprises us that she let you live after seeing her."

"That's what you need me for, isn't it?"

"We are interested in working with you, Cole, and indeed, that's why. If she did not kill you on the spot, we may take into account two hypotheses: either they want something in particular from you—and we are curious as to what that is—or the girl behaves differently, at least with you, and that might be an advantage for us. Therefore, one of the very few options we have is to try to find out the answer together."

Cole shook his head. "Wait a minute. How can I be sure you've told me the truth?" He lowered his head thoughtfully. "So much new information about my life and just about all there is." He stared Chris in the eye. "How can I know you're to be trusted, that you don't have other interests? You've kidnapped me from home the way they do in gangster movies."

"The matter at hand is extremely sensitive. No one must find out about it. We couldn't have simply come to your home and explain all those things nicely. And yes, you have no choice, you must trust us—in particular, me."

Cole angrily stood and paced around the room. "Just splendid!"

Chris seemed unwilling to learn more from his reaction. His palms met in front of him and he crossed his fingers, opening his eyes wide as if ready to let out an even more painful truth.

"From all that is out there, Tentorians are the greatest threat to mankind." He glanced at the mirror without a particular reason. His reflection stared back at him, but in a darker hue. "Most of them are the remains of a mercenary army used in the 22nd century World War."

Cole groaned.

"What is it?"

"Nothing, except I still can't believe it: the 22nd century, World Wars...that means they were waged on the entire...globe?"

The Erudite nodded.

"Please go on," the young man said.

"Tentorians couldn't care less about the law. They use technology without restriction, without restraint, ignoring the laws of ethics and many others. What's even worse is that they like to appropriate new territories and new resources and they are eager for power."

"And now they're on our Island," Cole pondered, worried.

"I think you know that better than me since you saw one yourself."

Cole's lips tightened to a thin line as he smirked. "From what I understood, you—the Erudites—have perfect control over all that enters and leaves the Island."

Chris' phony smile looked on the same par with that open irony.

"Normally nothing from outside can penetrate our

shield."

"What...shield?" Cole stammered.

The Erudite looked like he had no intention of telling him that either. But otherwise, it was difficult to convince Cole of the entire truth. He hesitated for a moment then pressed the remote control a few times. The Island was projected on the wall, surrounded by a hemisphere-like semitransparent shield.

"That one!"

The young man stood agape, waiting for more explanations.

"Two months ago, we lost contact with one of our reconnaissance aircrafts." Chris deliberately paused to emphasize *our*. "It was an unmanned ship, remotely steered. It then remerged on the radar one month ago and it all seemed fine; the ship appeared to be empty. The system let it pass through the shield, but as we later realized when we asked it to return to base, it wasn't us who were in control anymore. It attempted to land somewhere at sea, and at that exact moment we sent the command for it to self-destruct, hoping that nothing from outside would actually reach the Island."

"Apparently you were wrong," Cole helped.

"It seems that was indeed a mistake. Now we think the Tentorians managed to stow at least one person into the ship: the girl you have encountered."

"And what danger could such a cute redhead pose?" Cole threw the question through a grin.

"We don't know at the moment, but do not underestimate them. Besides, our aircraft could have accommodated between five and eight people without extra cumbersome equipment." For a brief moment, the Erudite looked lost in reckonings. "As we know them, that's more than enough to make up an army."

A mini-drone sneaked through the half-open door of a room in the Governmental building. Two men were working, each at his desk.

"What's...that?" One of them cowered, pushing his chair half a meter back. *A...flying object.*

The massive blond-bearded Tentorian burst through the door, hands hidden behind his back.

"That's my pet," he answered while pulling his hands into sight, each holding an automatic.

In a split second, bullets rained on the two men while family photos on the desk were splattered with blood.

The hulking beast opened two drawers and scanned them quickly; he then touched one of the computers and images flew past both on the screen and on his lenses.

"Nothing in room 1.02, Chan," he said as if the other Tentorian were beside him.

"Okay," the latter confirmed from somewhere along the corridor.

Another burst, this time smack through an office door, made the building shake. The bullets hit their targets precisely; the thud of the fallen confirmed it.

"I am going into 1.04," Chan announced.

On the other side of the door, an officer was down,

pierced by bullets. The weapon he held failed to fire a single slug.

"Nothing in 1.04," came some seconds later. "I am going into 1.05."

The two Tentorians went loose on their killing spree, taking out anything in the building that moved. Their augmented vision, advanced information processing, mini-drones, and sharp shooting gave the government employees no chance whatsoever.

Armed officers barged into the corridors in an attempt to stop them but were no match against two killing machines running about like bloodthirsty lions tearing through a corralled gazelle's offspring. The Tentorians made no distinction between civilians and armed people, killing them all indiscriminately.

One floor after another, the two went through all the rooms, searching with haste, opening closets and drawers, checking each box and scanning each document. The drones also scouted, flying in all directions.

"I go up to top floor," Chan uttered curtly from the staircase.

An officer jumped from a banister straight onto his back. Before the intruder realized what was going on, his neck was throttled by a sturdy arm and made him drop his weapon.

The Tentorian managed to size the officer up briefly. He was one of the biggest Islanders he had seen. When falling on him, Chan might have even broken a rib. He cussed, and though clearly worked up, succeeded fastening a smile on his face. He tried to struggle out of the grip, cursing again. It was harder than he thought. He had to resort to what he knew best; stretching his hand to the officer's head, a stream of nanobots trickled towards it. One second, two seconds...the officer fell flat as if struck by thunder.

The man brushed off his clothing leisurely then retrieved his weapons and continued upstairs.

"Problems?" the blond Tentorian's voice resounded in Chan's head.

"Nah. A mouse."

Ten minutes later, at the entrance of one of the rooms on the last floor, a body of an employee lay lifeless. The huge Tentorian was busy scanning information from a computer when Chan entered the room. He went straight to the cabinet against the wall, opened it, thrust his hand into a pile of documents, and said to the bearded blond in a bored voice: "Todor, check these too."

He threw them into the air. Todor looked up from the computer for exactly four seconds and pointed his eyes at them, unblinking until the last piece of paper had landed on the floor. That was all the time he needed to scan them. The two mini-drones hovered in the corners of the room, sending the last captured images of the documents as well. The fragments of text now came together. "*No useful information*", their lenses displayed.

"We're done in this room." The bearded Tentorian didn't wait for Chan to confirm and headed out to the last row of offices.

Minutes later, several employees shook with terror as they lay on the floor with their hands at the back of their necks. They peeked at the sturdy bearded man when he turned his back on them and didn't dare to even think they might be able to fight back. A door on one wall had caught the hulking beast's undivided attention. It was different from what he had seen in this building. It was large and made of massive metal. The edges were swollen with rust and there was no handle as if it was not used too often. Instead it had a combination lock. Todor laid a finger next to it and allowed a nanobot stream to trickle out.

He didn't have to wait long before the door opened. The light revealed a room no larger than three office rooms filled with hundreds of weapons carefully arranged in six rows of racks and cabinets.

He paced half of the storage room nervously and returned to the door. "This is a 20th century weapons storage!" He pushed his forehead through the air and hissed a profanity through his teeth. As that didn't calm him down, he banged his fists hard against the door and seized one of the men lying on the floor by the collar, pressing his face against a desk.

"Where are you hiding your last generation weapons? Where's all that new technology shit?"

"I...what? I have no idea what you're talking about!" The terrified man hardly stammered out each word.

Todor spit another shower of cusses.

"Where are those filthy Erudites? Where the hell is the Island's monitoring room? Where, man? Where?"

"What Erudites? What room? Please, I know nothing, I swear!"

The bearded man burst with rage and took his hand off the man who had died of fear. "What the hell is this, the House of Morons?"

He took another pile of papers and threw them in the air. Another quick scan and the pages arranged themselves on the man's lens. He zoomed in on a note at the bottom of one page: "*Level II classified information*".

He shouted another profanity.

"*Calm down,*" Chan transmitted to him. "*I think I found*

something here, in a database. It's in 5.10. Just check this out."

The dispatched information showed up on Todor's lens.

"Hmm," he mumbled, "secret locations accessed by security patrols on a daily basis. The same routes, a large number of high-level big shots, a security classification far beyond what these sorry asses in the building have access to. Bingo! I think it's time to get the hell out of here."

He headed for the door, all eyes fixed on him. In a curt gesture, he lowered his weapon to his shoulder and fired into the man still leaning his head on the desk. Then he riddled the others with bullets too.

„Bad news and good news, boss," Chan transmitted to another side of the Island.

"Bad?" a whisper-like, low hoarse voice asked.

"We found no last-generation weapons around here. We have none, but apparently they haven't geared up either. This could be a good thing for us."

"How stupid and indoctrinated they are. And the good news?"

"We might know where the Control Center and those darned Erudites are."

"You'd better be sure!" the hoarse voice threatened.

The young officer knocked twice on the door and without waiting for an invitation, hastily entered the room.

The Erudite stared at him eagerly. "Yes, Martin. Is it urgent?"

He drew close to his ear and whispered, "We had an incident at the House of Security, sir."

"What is going on?" Cole butted in. The two men went to the door without answering. "I still have questions to ask!" he protested, standing from his chair.

His gesture paid off in the end, for the Erudite came back. "Make it quick, please."

"For instance," the young man said, "how was it possible to hush this enormous secret? How was it possible for people to remain clueless? We have so many history and geography books that make it all credible. How did we get on the Island? History was passed down through generations, wasn't it? When did it all start, if you say we've isolated ourselves on account of the technology that would have affected us later in the future? How can it be that 12 million people believe we are alone on planet Earth, on this measly Island? My father sailed around the Earth and all he saw was water—at least that's what he told me. How come he doesn't know? Who built the shield and all that?"

Chris shook his head. "Cole, I can't answer all of your questions. All you had to know, you now know. Take care and keep this information as your deepest secret. From now on you shall observe the same rules and the same Code as yesterday." He took a break as if to draw one last conclusion. "We must find that girl and for that we need your help."

The door closed behind him.

Cole leaned against a wall and flowed down to the floor. He raised his eyes to the ceiling and grabbed his head. His mind still refused to fully take in the reality that had just been revealed.

Chapter 18

Several thousand kilometers off the Island, Xilo treaded the corridor of the Tentorian presidential building. The office door opened automatically to disappear into the wall while the Tentorian entered.

"What's happening on the Island?" he thundered from the doorstep, completely ignoring the Tentorian officer and the fact that he was sharing a drink with Nemilo.

"Xilo," Nemilo greeted, "I wanted to tell you, things took a turn for the worse and I considered it necessary to intervene."

"You're lying! I've been closely following what's been going on and I know very well that things did not 'take a turn for the worse'."

Nemilo rolled his eyes, and for a moment the white replaced the black onyx of his irises.

"You had no right to act without my approval!" Xilo insisted. "You know well enough we are not allowed to make any mistakes on this mission."

"Fine, fine...I sent them there to squeeze some information from a government building and things degenerated from there. They were attacked."

"Do not take me for a fool, Nemilo!" the Tentorian leader admonished, almost breaking into a roar. "That was an attack; a slaughter. We had a plan—an objective there; now you have started a war!"

Xilo's main promise to the nations had been shattered. All he had to do was make sure Tentoria refrained from aggressions towards other peoples and respect other laws and territories. He had tried many times to change the Tentorians' way of thinking without success. He had also tried to set an example to those who saw perfection as the ultimate goal: he had let his hair turn grey and several wrinkles were etched into his skin. Many people said he had failed; with his youthful appearance, he didn't seem to be in his 60s or 70s—at least this was the age he liked to think he projected to the world. However, physical appearance no longer carried any meaning in Tentoria. Anyone could have been the perfect model; the progress of technology in cosmetic medicine was within anyone's reach.

Nemilo changed to a seemingly cooperative tone. "Xilo, no matter how much we hoped we could easily talk our way into the Island, we found out they're being pretty well organized and pleased with the life they lead there...and it might not work. We can conquer the Island in hours with our technology; all we need is find a breach to go through—"

"Man," the firm voice of his leader interrupted him, "we have promised to improve our communication, collaborate with other nations, and better our relations with them. Where is all that in what you are doing?"

Nemilo grinned. "Nations have stopped following what goes on down there. This territory is not included in any treaty. No one sees what's happening down there—they are cut off from the world. They have practically ceased to exist!"

"But not like that! We said we were going to collaborate with them."

"I do not collaborate with inferior races. They reek of stupidity and enjoy those primitive, ancient feelings," Nemilo concluded.

A dark veil seemed to descend upon old Xilo's face. "I forbid such thinking in the presidential building and throughout the Tentorian territory!" he snapped. "The mere fact that we have no limit to our technology does not by itself mean we are superior!"

Nemilo poured himself a strong drink. He raised it and bowed his head to the officer in the room.

"Remember what happened last time?" Xilo carried on, goaded by the leisurely attitude of the shaggy-haired man. "Nations can decide at any moment to change the treaties or even break them...and they will start building weapons again to fight us. Again there shall be a massacre in the ranks of the Tentorians. We must use our brains; we must act intelligently. The end does not justify the means. Can't you see a fraction of our Tentorian brothers already desire peace? They've had enough. I hear some of them are inclined to accept limitations in technology use."

"Rubbish! Much too small a fraction, but some few and far between rebels. You are blinded by your ideals. The laws of the Earth are more important than what you're busy regulating here," Nemilo barked and placed a hand on Xilo's shoulder. "Evolutionism is a fundamental law you have forgotten, old man!"

"I forbid you to think that way or I'll release you from your duties immedia—"

He did not have enough time to finish his sentence. A light-beam-like dagger sprung from Nemilo's hand and penetrated deep into Xilo's stomach.

The shaggy-haired man stared into his eyes. "I, as

caretaker President, wish to take my land back!" he pronounced.

He then turned away and thrust the dagger even deeper. He couldn't look into his eyes anymore. The officer in the room slipped behind Xilo and thrust another dagger into the nape of his neck. The old leader fell down. No more thoughts went through his mind, no more sounds came from him. Nemilo's face remained frozen for only a moment.

"Get me Kaligor!" he ordered the officer while extracting his dagger from Xilo's abdomen.

"I'm getting a connection right now."

"*Yes,*" came the low hoarse voice from the other end.

"It's been taken care of," the shaggy-haired man put shortly.

"Gooood. Here...it's only half done. We found no newer weapons in the building, but we've located the Control Center."

"Ahem!" Nemilo droned.

"It's going to be much harder without weapons."

"I see no way of sending you weapons on the Island—at least not anytime soon. How are you on time?"

"They will probably send reinforcements to the Center soon. Time is running out." The deep voice of Kaligor flooded like acid through the shaggy-haired man's temples.

Nemilo swore. "We must stick to the plan."

"It's possible! We'll get help from our allies here; the Ragons."

"Yes...fine, keep it up then! Make the most of the technology you have. You are an elite team out there. They don't stand a chance in front of you, not even if you stormed them by yourselves without the Ragons."

"Understood!"

Chapter 19

The few infiltrated Tentorians had turned a decommissioned powerplant into their temporary base one month earlier. They did it along with their Island aids, a gang of mercenaries with military training easily identified by their Asian features and neck tattoos in the shape of a humanized dragon; the Shadow Ragons gang.

In one of the makeshift offices, some 15 persons were gathered around in a circle. Kaligor's hoarse voice sounded just as ruthless and commanding as it was low and poorly articulated.

"This is our new plan. For our first mission we were provided with scouting, reconnaissance, and survival gear. We're eight Tentorians with eight devices. That's all we have." He pointed at his hand device which looked like a large, rectangular watch.

Kaligor, the head of the Tentorian mission on the Island, had a frozen old-style mercenary appearance to his eyes; he was bold and had a distinct Russian accent when speaking English. Although there was no trace of Russian blood in him, he now felt it as his second identity, after that of Tentorian. Some of the Tentorians lost their specialization in time. Others, however, came from families who, despite having evolved with the new technological era, still liked to retain their sense of belonging. Kaligor was one of them—the offspring of a Tentorian elite specialized in "search, recognize, and destroy" activities, specially created to act on Russian territory.

His Tentorian team was with him along with the most important members of their hosts—the Shadow Ragons.

"So we'll work hand in hand," Kaligor went on, looking at Hoshito. "I hope you have put together the best possible team to make up for the primitive resources you have here."

"I told you, the best trained one hundred people." Hoshito was not mincing words. "They can't wait to wipe out this backward system and lay their hands on the fruit of progress."

"There's loads of crazy technology waiting for them out there." Kaligor grinned. "You cannot even begin to imagine the extent of the inventions! Let's first lay our hands on the Island and then you'll be able to see everything."

A barbaric roar of approval echoed throughout the room. Only Powalski, one of the Tentorians did not join them.

"Let's see what primitive metal you've got here," the bald commander said to Hoshito.

Hoshito, the boss of the Island "Shadow" hirelings and the host of the Tentorian mission, was a ruthless soul disfigured by the many scars on his face; one was from an older slash, standing out more clearly on his left cheek. The modern-day executioner was always ready to kill for money and power. So without making his guests wait, he made for a large metallic case and opened it.

"The primitive metal we have around here," he pronounced.

He stood there, hand held out to the crate full of weapons and ammunition and a smile in the corner of his mouth.

"Boom, bang, yeah!" shouted Kaligor. "I love antiques!"

He drew close to the crate and picked up a pistol. He loaded it, lodged the muzzle tightly against his left palm, and pulled the trigger. Some took a step back in shock.

"Bloody hell, that burns!"

He gnashed his teeth and gazed in morbid satisfaction at the hole in his hand which had already begun to shrink. His bleeding stopped in a matter of seconds; the hand was fully healed now. He told himself he had achieved the desired impact the second he looked upon the frozen faces of his Asian hosts.

"Do we happen to have any larger antique junk?" He wiped his palm on his trousers.

Hoshito nodded to his people and three more large crates sprung open. The setting sun shone red through the window and reflected upon the pile of weapons: rocket launchers, grenades, antitank machine guns.

"Bigger than this?" The host smiled.

Kaligor stood with his mouth proudly open. "No, this size suits me fine."

The Ragon guards watching over the perimeter of the temporary base greeted the passing car. Behind the wheel was Claire, a young, red-headed green-eyed Tentorian woman. Just several hundred meters behind her, she had spotted three other men setting up a device. *What gear are*

they installing over there? she asked herself. *A pipe, a turret, surface-to-air weapon? What shit is that?*

She went on to the building, where she stopped the engine, still puzzled at all that hustle and bustle. Metallic cases were being unloaded from a truck and caught her eye. *Military armament?* Two men sized her up indifferently while carefully carrying a case away. She climbed out of the car and pushed her way through, staring at them over her shoulder as she entered the building.

The door of the room those 15 men were in got slammed to the wall. Claire stormed in.

"What is going on here, are we razing governmental institutions as of late?"

"Ooops!" Kaligor reacted, clown-like.

"What...?" Claire let out in surprise.

She looked at all those in the room. Failing to make out why nobody said a word, she spoke again. "Boys...? We've been brought here to analyze resources, people's behavior, the state of things—"

"Yes," Kaligor interrupted, "and up until now everything has gone according to plan. It's time to move to the second part: the occupation."

"What occupation?" Claire raised her voice. "I was told the most serious thing that could conceivably happen here was a peaceful negotiation after convincing these people they are backward and have been lied to concerning the planet's evolution. Now we're occupying them? In this manner? Where did this idea come from?"

Kaligor smirked at the others, showing all his teeth. Then he turned his wry face to her. "Let's say there has been a small change of plans. Let's say we've been thinking we are running out of time and...how about we invade the Island this very evening?"

His last words hit Claire like a leaden shower.

"That's nonsense!" she fought back, which made his smile freeze. She wanted to have a seat in order to wind herself down. She fiercely hoped she could make him change his mind. They had certainly not seen things the way she had. She took a breath. "It's now been a month since we started observing this world. As for myself, I have rediscovered the miracle of being human; the miracle of being surrounded by all that beauty."

Kaligor raised his eyebrows while Claire pressed her hand device twice and pointed at the three monitors in the room. "Look at the screen."

The nature images filled the space with light and colors. They were recordings captured by the mini-drone during reconnaissance missions she liked to watch every night before falling asleep, but Claire wouldn't tell them that.

"Rivers are actually like that," she said. "*They* don't have to transmit false impulses to the brain in order for you to see such things. The grass is green and its smell makes you feel like you're being reborn. Animals frolic in the wild with no control and people do not keep them there just for the pleasure of seeing or hunting them."

Silence reigned and Claire hoped even more to make them understand.

"And the locals—these people making up 'the sect' we see from outside—are wonderful." Recordings of daily life of the Islanders were played on screens. "They laugh real laughs, they make mistakes, they are scatter-brained and clumsy the way normal people should be." She looked at a few of her people around the room, trying to read astonishment on their faces. All she encountered were pale, inert expressions.

"They work hard with real, palpable things and don't rely on technology alone. They have real dreams and love the way a person is supposed to love."

Images of parents with their children, running and laughing on playgrounds, caused all who watched the monitors to stare in bewilderment.

"Impressive!" Kaligor stopped her. "I am mad about this island. Let's grab it! But I don't need old-fashioned Earth people," he concluded sarcastically and then split his sides with laughter as he turned around for approval.

They all followed, letting out an inane laughter. All but Claire, who stared at him, no longer blinking, and Powalski, who looked at her equally concerned.

"Miss Claire," Kaligor said, assuming an outright haughty stance, "just in case you have failed to grasp my point, our cute reconnaissance mission is over. I've got instructions to do our best to deactivate the Island's protection shield and allow our fellow people to enjoy all that beauty."

Kaligor looked to the others with a blank expression as if once again conveying a clear message.

"Hell yeah!" Osman, a strapping Tentorian standing two meters high, backed him in a deafening shout.

"We've all been trained to fight," Kaligor added. "We are Tentorians and we can do it. It's in our blood."

"That doesn't mean we must be inhumane!" the redhead cut him short. "I don't want to go on with this mission any longer. I signed up for a reconnaissance and I believe I have the right to say no to anything else." The bright red of capillaries turned visible on Kaligor's face. "I choose not to bother them, and I'll convey my opinion to the people back home. Perhaps we should learn from them!"

Powalski braced himself and barged in: "All that was

planned beforehand. We've been lied to. I think we should have been consulted on this matter. With all due respect, dear comrades, after seeing how things are here on the Island, I share Claire's position."

"And exactly what are you going to do with that position, Mr. Powalski?" Kaligor growled.

"What am I going to do with it? I'm going to shove it up your ass and request this mission be aborted at once! I'm going back home."

An icicle-like shudder ran through Claire's heart.

"Max," Kaligor yelled in a thicker Russian accent, "connect me to Mr. Powalski's house."

"Ahem, yuuup!" another Tentorian who looked more like a failed rapper answered.

Not bothering to give any thought to it, he turned to a military laptop-like device, activated the Island's outside connection, and honed in directly on the house of Powalski's parents. Powalski's mother showed up on one of the monitors. She was in the guest room, setting a candle on the table, unaware anyone was watching.

"Filthy bastards," Powalski flew off the handle. "What business do you have with my mother? I shall report you!"

Kaligor raised his arm a few centimeters then let it drop. Powalski's mother collapsed instantaneously.

"No! You bastards! nooo!" The terrified scream of the young man froze the building. Then he fell to his knees as if mowed down himself.

"Shall we see what your father's doing, Mr. Powalski?" the mission leader asked.

Powalski stood powerlessly on his knees, tears welling in his eyes and gasping.

"You shall pay for that!" Claire burst out, stunned.

"Max, put me through to the young lady's father too!" Kaligor ordered.

"Wait!" Claire yelled.

"Unfortunately for you, you don't have a very large family, Miss Claire."

"Wait!" she shouted again, this time at Max.

She saw in his eyes a metallic indifference to the orders he executed. He could not tell the difference between a dead bug and a dead person. He was part of the new generation of the so-called "soulless children", descendants of Tentorians specialized in cyber-offensive actions. He bore no more sentiments. For such a specialization to even be conceivable, many functions of human genes had been abandoned in laboratories, making room for other software processing ones which were needed to penetrate any IT system and take control of it as quickly as possible.

Utterly lost, Claire looked around for any ray of hope. Her eyes were red with unshed tears. *Kaligor is a monster. I should have known that!* She squinted at her ghastly boss as he searched for a weapon. Powalski would lunge at him at any second.

Powalski noticed and went fast for his neck, bowling him over the weapons crate. Then he squeezed until his boss' face went bluish. Nobody tried to pull them apart. They helplessly watched the pain-stricken young man strangle Kaligor with his full strength.

Hardly breathing, Kaligor reached for a semiautomatic in the pile of weapons. One second later, the horrible sound of the bullets thundered in the silence of the room. No one breathed, no one blinked. Powalski, too, stood still. His hands loosened around Kaligor's neck while blood wet the back of his punctured coat.

Another burst was fired from the same weapon until the magazine was empty. Kaligor finished spewing the ammo into Powalski, who now struggled to delay his own demise. His ruthless boss turned a blank stare to him, face and body blood spattered, not feeling the faintest bit of pain. The deep wrinkles on his forehead and cheeks looked like seams hurriedly patched onto the face of an iron mannequin. He turned to the weapons crate, took out another magazine, and replaced the old one. He then rested the barrel of his pistol against Powalski's breast, next to his heart, and pulled the trigger again. The lifeless body vibrated with each bullet until it yielded and the last slugs flew straight through the freshly dug tunnel the weapon had created and into the ceiling.

Blood dripped down the bald man's eyebrow and onto his cheek. One second later, he pointed the weapon at Claire and hissed, "You still believe we must not carry on with our mission?"

He did not get an answer; the silence spoke for itself. Claire desperately tried to keep calm and lower her heart rate as the others waited for a reaction that failed to come. The girl just stared vacantly, pupils murky with hatred while the weapon directed at her did not budge.

Todor's flat, thick voice broke the silence. "Boss, you're not planning to leave us with only half the team, are you?" The Northern Tentorian gazed at the bald man's reddened face.

Kaligor knew if he squeezed the trigger again, the team would fear him. He had taught them a lesson, and that was enough. He now had Claire under his thumb along with her father. She wouldn't dare step out of line again.

"Good, that's what I thought!" he said to Claire, pushing

away Powalski's lifeless body.

Todor turned and pointed at the mangled corpse. "With that, my friends, there are only seven of us left. To my mind, things might stink worse for us now!" He sucked his teeth and raised his eyes to Kaligor. "That was not part of the plan, boss."

"Not necessarily," Kaligor retorted. "Hoshito, do you want to live forever?"

The crinkled man watched Kaligor in astonishment as he leaned over Powalski's body, drawing a knife from one boot and thrusting it into the back of his neck. A few seconds later, in the bald man's palm lay an oval, barrel-shaped little capsule a few centimeters long. Scores of wires hung from the bloody capsule like tree roots. He pressed a small mark on the barrel and the roots withdrew.

"Sit down and keep your chin low," he dictated to Hoshito.

Although frightened, the Ragon chief obeyed.

"This will hurt a bit, but you're a big boy."

The device self-activated upon making contact with Hoshito, and when setting it on the upper side of the man's nape, it began pulling out its roots once again until one by one, they pushed their way through his skin.

The other Ragons in the room could no more conceal their fear. One with bulging eyes dared to raise his hand to wipe the sweat off his forehead. Another could no longer keep his trembling chin under control and made up his mind to clench his jaw harder. In the meantime, the capsule was doing its job, penetrating Hoshito's head millimeter by millimeter.

He yelled through vice-like clenched teeth, turned up the whites of his eyes, and caught the arms of the chair with all his might, making it shake. Another outburst and he pulled them loose then slammed the mangled wood into the ground.

Little by little, he stilled. On the surface of his skin only a few traces of blood remained along with a tiny, red, T-shaped luminous mark. The capsule had been implanted, and the T glowed at the back of his neck, similarly to the other six Tentorians. The seventh—Claire—was the exception.

"You see?" Kaligor grinned towards Todor. "We are eight again."

After unclasping the rectangular device from Powalski's hand, he turned back proudly and put it on Hoshito's.

"You've just been implanted with one state-of-the-art system. It's rare enough even back home. Immunity, my friend! This shit and the capsule are totally connected to your brain, your auditory and visual systems, your coordination, your vital functions—everything. You now have direct control."

"Does it come with instructions?" Hoshito said flatly.

The Tentorians all burst out laughing.

"If you don't know how to use it, ask yourself and pronto, you'll know right away! Or, more simply, think of what you want to happen. It can be anything you can control with your body!"

"Careful what you wish for," Max cut in and started to laugh like a fool. "These primitives have no idea what's in store."

"Instead of laughing, you better make sure you keep a functional communication with Tentoria through this damned shield." Kaligor's reprimand came before he ceased laughing.

Still sporting a pleased expression, Max slapped a server case. "Boss, much work has gone into this. Communication between us, inside the bubble, and radio communication to the exterior. I set a little cyber-scheme into their frequency filtering system. Our small wide band sits beside their communications with the scouting ships. It's no wonder I come from the best."

"C'mon, now you're laying it on too thick..." Osman joined in. "A wimp specialization when it comes down to close combat. Then all you can do is run for it. You're no good at running either."

"So nice you have the brawns, man..."

"Enough!" Kaligor barked. "We are all Tentorians here. You may philosophically debate your origins all you want after we've finished our work here."

"Yeah..." Osman said grudgingly.

"Max, you'll go with our rebel," the Tentorian boss commanded. "Don't let her out of your sight. And you," he said to Claire bluntly, "you'd do well to help us. Otherwise I cannot be held responsible for my actions."

The young woman lowered her eyes as a sign of acceptance. *At least until I find a way out.*

Chapter 20

THE CONTROL CENTER

Several hours after the attack from the House of Security, night was about to replace day and tension in the Control Center reigned supreme. News of the massacre had injected everyone's minds with anxiety.

"That's the only person connecting us to the Tentorians," argued a woman with black, stick-straight hair flowing down her shoulders. "They left no one alive today, but out there in the woods he was left free."

"Why did Chris have to give him so many details?" the mustached man complained.

"Because the facts are hard to digest. Just look around you; look at the Island we live on. How is he supposed to believe something like this if not provided with the right data?"

"We certainly didn't need the fifty-sixth person knowing the truth down to that level. The system is based on total secrecy. It won't work otherwise."

"None of us knows everything, Arnar. We've sworn never to wish to know in the first place."

"We know enough...and now he knows too" the mustached man grumbled.

The woman looked away for no particular reason. She stared pensively, chin in hand, towards the only window in the office. The Center's courtyard was busier than usual and the alley drive where typically just one or two cars were parked was now filled with military vehicles.

"He wouldn't have been able to help otherwise," she reiterated. "The lad is already scared enough. How could we have asked for help unless we told him?"

The mustached man snorted. "Now he's spinning through the wheels of the system."

"What wheels?" her eyebrows furrowed. "Can't you see they aren't working as they should?"

"What do you mean?"

"The Tentorians made it through this shield surrounding us—which is supposedly one hundred kilometers in all directions and fully impregnable. Anything that goes past it without our authorization should be automatically pulverized, but they found a way in. Using our very ship for that matter."

"You're trying to accuse me of dereliction of duty too?"

"No, of course not! I'm only trying to understand how you could have handled the lad! In my view, he is the only link we have to the intruders. Besides, it was the Erudites' choice to contact him and tell him the truth. Their decision cannot be disputed."

Arnar growled. "Yes, sure, the supreme authority..."

The office door opened and all dialogue came to a halt. Chris entered accompanied by Cole, and quickly introduced the two.

"We have here with us the general of the House of Defense, Mr. Arnar Arnason, and his deputy, General Andreea Petrova."

The young man did not hold his hand out but merely addressed them respectfully from a distance with a simple, "Greetings."

He scanned them. The two wore similar military uniforms but without any breast badges, only five stripes on the general's shoulder and four on his deputy's. On the stripes he noticed the same emblem as on the place of worship he went to every Sunday with his family. He instinctively straightened his back and puffed up his chest. *What did I do that for?* he thought indignantly.

Petrova spoke to him first. "Mr. Williams, since you're probably asking yourself what's the matter with this institution you haven't heard of before, let me clarify things: the House of Defense is less known to the Island's population. I assume that now, after learning that we aren't alone on Earth, you also understand the reason why it exists. And to make speaking to each other easier, I'm Drew."

"I'm starting to get used to your little secrets," Cole replied.

Drew took the joke and flashed a phony smile.

Petrova was a sexy woman in her mid-forties, an impeccable demeanor and a military way of speaking every now and then belied by the elegance of her gestures and the still delicate features of her face.

"And I'm Cole," he added.

The general wedged in, wasting no time. "Okay, let's see how Cole can help us."

His stern tone and frown were befitting of his general status. The bushy moustache backed his rough way of being. *He is the Head of the House of Defense*, Cole reckoned. *Imagine that! Father could depict the smallest detail on any of the Heads in his sleep, from upbringing to height, voice pitch and so on, while nobody's heard of Arnason.*

He pointed to a map spread across the table. "Cole, let's see exactly where you met that Tentorian guy."

"Tentorian woman," Cole corrected. "It was a young woman."

The general shrugged as if the correction was meaningless.

Cole leaned over the map, placed his finger on a brown line, and followed it. "Here's the forest road. Here must be the cut off section giving way to the precipice...yes, right here!"

"Huh," Arnar snorted on spot. "There's nothing there save rivers, forests, and a precipice. What on earth was she doing there? I guess she was not out for a picnic. What the hell do they want?"

Drew leaned thoughtfully over the table. "Also, in the House of Security they went through all the files—what did they want with them?" Silence didn't help. "It might be worth sending him to the spot he saw her while keeping an eye out; she may show up again."

Chris had listened carefully, as always before making a decision. "This could be an idea," he said. "Although after the recent carnage it might be risky. You think they will stay as peaceful as before?"

The young man interfered, in great surprise, "Why do you think she might show up again and...what carnage are you talking about?"

Arnar rushed to answer, "This is the only lead we have. She may be looking for something in that area. At least we know she came up there twice so far."

"You didn't answer the second question," Cole pressed on.

"I'm afraid that information is going to remain classified, Mr. Williams."

"In a nutshell," Chris said, "the Tentorians attacked one

of the government buildings."

Arnar gave him an angered look. Seeing the general's reaction, the Erudite felt compelled to add, "We'll run this incident on news, too. It probably won't go unnoticed." He looked from one serviceman to the other as if seeking a consensus. "However, I don't know how we'll do it…"

Although concern was spread all over his face, Cole looked satisfied with the answer. "Okay, this may be a good lead. We can give it a shot. As far as I'm concerned I have nothing to lose; therefore I'm not afraid."

Drew took a step towards him. "For safety reasons, you'll be stationed here for a couple of days—at least until we understand what the Tentorians want. This center has already received reinforcements, and more are on the way tomorrow morning."

Curiosity twisted Cole's eyebrows. "Are you preparing for a similar attack here?"

"I'll speak my mind to you," the Erudite made it clear, "we've never had an event of this sort, nor any outside visits. We are a peaceful nation—no conflicts with anyone—so here everything is based on peaceful principles, the technology we own included. Nothing's designed to face such a situation."

"So, I take it you aren't ready," Cole concluded.

"Mr. Williams," Arnar intervened, "we honestly don't know if we are ready or not, as long as we don't know what they want from us."

The long silence stressed the cagey answer. Cole noticed the deep furrows on the general's forehead, trenches brought forth by too many similar expressions, the dull black rim around his orbits as the outcome of a time long gone; a man who has grown old with too many sorrows. *He's been through a lot, hasn't he?* he asked himself. *What conflicts had he been involved in when everything was peaceful on the Island...and what did he do to rise to this position? He must be carrying many burdens.*

Then Cole spoke, equally anxious. "I wish to call my family and tell them I am well."

"Fine," Drew approved before the two men, "but you'll have to find another explanation for not being home—not the truth, I mean. We don't know what's behind these events. You may put them at risk."

The young man weighed her words before consenting. "I agree, but I think they've seen my room already. They must have realized I went off in a hurry, with hardly a thing on me."

"We took care to arrange your room a little and took along a rucksack of yours as if you left of your own will."

"I get it. You're good at doing things to the smallest details."

Three inscrutable faces looked back at him.

"I'll tell them..." he pursed his lips and raised his pupils to the ceiling, "I left for the mountains for a few days...to regain my will to live. I meant to do that at some point anyway. I can handle it."

"Good," Drew agreed, faltering. She'd flipped through his medical record one hour earlier and wished she could console him but knew it was pointless. Many other people closer to him had surely done that already.

She went on confidently, "It's settled. Tomorrow morning we'll gear you up and send you into the area along with a surveillance team."

Chapter 21

Eight levels underground, completely cut off from the offices, was the monitoring and control room. Two Erudites were on duty that night. They sat in their large comfortable chairs. In line with them were ten similar chairs for each of the other Erudites, set in a circular arc. Covered in leather, personalized emblems sewn on each back, the chairs all had the same base mark: a star in the middle of a heart shaped corolla flower.

Although that day was unlike all the others, the Erudites monitored the activity calmly.

"I confirm switching to the maximum level of alert in the maritime perimeter too," one of them spoke as if sending the information to someone outside the Center.

"I confirm the flight over zone 100-200," the other said.

Behind the semicircle set of chairs, there were several workstations made up of a desk and an ergonomic chair; all of them for the Center's operational employees. Three of them were there at that time to back the activity of the two Erudites.

Today Leewana was at the rearmost desk, which meant she could see the room in its entirety. She was familiar with it down to the smallest detail and its design seemed to her just as strange as on the first day she had seen it: a mix of the futurist and the baroque. However, she admitted each time when reporting to work that it had the air of a sacred place. One reason for that were the walls, beautifully painted in the same symbols and slogans seen in houses of worship. At the same time, it served its primary function well: a fully equipped, ergonomic monitoring hall. At the front of the room hung scores of monitors that constantly scrolled data and images; some showed the state of the protection shield—a green hemisphere going around the Island—while others displayed images from the Center and various strategic points on the Island.

Like today, Leewana was entranced each time she thought about the way the Erudites controlled the system by way of brain-implanted technology. When she inquired about this, she was told they had an artificial synapse system implanted at the neuronal level which formed a bridge to the Erudites' visual and auditory communication centers. It was there to allow for a faster and more efficient control of the environment. *This technology is completely mad!* she told herself while looking once more at the back of the chairs where devices sat hat-like and extended several centimeters off the Erudites' heads.

She wished she could tell her husband about all these oddities, but she wasn't allowed. She had taken three sacred vows, each more serious than the one before: first when she joined the military twenty years before, the second time when she was recruited as an officer for the hidden House of Defense, and the third time when she received the invitation to join the small secret operational support team in reward for the devotion and reliability she had demonstrated over time.

She turned her sight again to the two Erudites. She was honored to be working with the only people who had control over the advanced technology on the Island. Every once in a while, the two glanced at the monitors to feel human—not that they needed it; the system along with the brain implant enabled them to monitor millions of devices at once: cameras, telephone networks, television, or the Internet. With just their minds, they could concurrently control scores of unmanned air and watercraft guarding the Island. Leewana liked to call that either "the Government's invisible eye" or "the invisible eye of the Island".

Chapter 22

The Tentorian Island base was getting ready for the assault. The military equipment was loaded into school buses to conceal the operation and one hundred Ragon allies equipped themselves with bulletproof vests, weapons, and ammunition before boarding. Claire watched them from a window in disgust. She knew she had no choice; she had to join them. In the room where she stood watching, the commotion was even greater; the Tentorians were also gearing up with haste.

"We must get going!" Hugh looked pleased by his freshly loaded weapon.

Claire loathingly assessed his headsman gestures. He was one of the Tentorians no one liked to upset. He would kill anyone without blinking.

The Tentorian woman moved imperceptibly, trying to keep herself alert and gearing up quickly with a harness, a pistol, and two magazines.

Max strutted around her. "You think you'll make it only with that?"

Claire barely shrugged. "Maybe. Perhaps I'll have to whack less people, won't I?" she taunted.

The man rolled his eyes, raised his shirt collar, and headed for the exit.

When boarding and seeing the other Tentorians' faces, Claire was awash with hate and fear. She sat like a stringed puppet guided by a trembling hand, and hurriedly used her device to text a message to her father: *Dad, leave the house right now! You're in danger! Stay away from any device that might recognize you and cut off any communication. Go to the old observatory. I'll call you there! I love y—*

Max sat down next to her. "What are you writing over there?"

Claire controlled every nerve in her body. "Nothing, just checking if everything was fine;" and she pressed "Send".

Max did not react but scrutinized her. The Tentorian woman felt him gazing at her without daring to breathe or blink. Her heart froze.

The man broke the silence. "You can give it vocal commands too, you know." He felt her uneasiness. "It'll all go quickly, sweetie. Don't worry!"

Claire kept on staring vacantly while Max raised her hair to expose the back of her neck. He was looking for the capsule that should have been implanted there. He shook his head, displeased, and sucked his teeth.

"It's my choice not to merge entirely with this technology." The young woman turned to challenge him. "It's always been my choice and my parents' wish. That's why we have these," she pointed to her hand device briefly, "to be able to keep it here too." She looked ahead and spoke softly. "I won't implant this in my brain just for one fight."

"That capsule held in the hand device is a waste of technology. You can't do all that much with it. You must give it vocal commands, or even worse I see...with your finger?"

Max waited for a reaction that did not come, then raised his hands in the air. "Okay, your business. Let's see how you manage."

The drapes covered the car windows and the convoy set itself in motion.

Chapter 23

About ten guards watched over the area in front of the Control Center, hearts harboring fear. Normally there were only two, the most important sticking closely to the boring military formalities. However, today the alert level had been raised to the maximum. Ten guards seemed too few and there was not a tinge of boredom in sight.

The young officer took the last drag of his cigarette that had turned to ashes faster than ever before. He had to watch over a strip of land several dozen meters wide along the fence surrounding the militarized area.

He had found out at the beginning of his shift about a certain incident at the House of Security. At first he didn't quite grasp what had happened down there, but a mate had told him people died there. *This could be something from outside the Island,* his mate had whispered, and goose bumps formed on his skin. A danger from outside the Island was something novel to them; they hadn't ever faced something like this throughout their careers. Their superiors had advised them to expect the worst and asked them to guard the area like their own home; whatever that might mean.

The visibility was still good; the late summer sun didn't yet dip below the horizon and still beamed its rays onto the coppice.

Reaching the filter, the man threw the butt on the ground and crushed it under his boot.

He heard a buzz and started at the sudden sound. He looked right, left, then up. Nothing. He turned swiftly. Three meters away, a mini-drone hovered in the air.

"What's—"

That was all he managed to say before a bullet pierced through his skull.

One hundred meters away, Hugh contently bared his teeth. His gun, equipped with a silencer, was still smoking in translucent spirals through the still leaves. The other guards were also mowed down. The hand of the Tentorian descended and countless inconspicuous shadows set themselves in motion through the woods. The Tentorians and their allies were ready to enter the base.

While silence reigned, two Asian people cut through the metallic fence to make room for the others to pass. After the first three went through, the alarm sounded. Orange lights spun and the entire base went into alert mode.

The seven Tentorians, along with Hoshito and his men, pushed forth through the militarized area of the Center. Neither the high pitched siren nor their detection was enough to dishearten them. Servicemen fell to the ground once entering the Tentorians' range of fire. The bullets they shot hit their targets in the head from dozens of meters away.

Hoshito watched in amazement the information provided by the new lens formed on his right eye: shooting angles, estimations of the bullet's trajectory, attack tactics, and data on the enemy. He fired his first shot and grinned after he took out his first serviceman from an almost impossible position.

After the fire in front of the building ceased, only a few Tentorian allies were down, whereas on the other side dozens of people lay dead.

Stillness seized the base. Nobody moved. A dense fog had settled over the Center's courtyard along with the fierce attack. It came from inside the cartridges, poisoning the air with an ashen tint, only to fade slowly away.

As soon as four Ragons lined themselves up in front of the main building, each with a rocket launcher on his shoulder, one of them snapped the order: "Fire!"

The two Erudites and the three officers watched the surprise attack from the monitoring room. There was little else they could do except transmit the received information to the people on the ground floor. To them, both the security of the Island and the shield was of utmost importance.

Leewana conquered her fear and arranged her military bonnet on her head. She liked to show it off even while at home. The rest of the suit she found too solemn and its blue too dark. But her husband would tell her just the opposite; he said she looked more sensual when dressed like a lady officer. Although finding it bizarre, she noticed her outfit made her feel stronger now.

The images sent by the cameras set in the courtyard of the Center vanished one by one from the screens. One of the Erudites looked over his shoulder to the back of the room. A long corridor ran lengthwise to the only access to the elevator and thus the ground level. Two back to back transparent walls separated the room from the corridor.

"Switch on the room shield," he said, gazing into the others' eyes.

He received a short nod, and the very next moment a blue, wave-like electric field enshrouded the two walls. By and by the wave faded.

"Good luck, boys," the Erudite whispered to himself. He stood with his face steadfastly turned to the corridor. He felt no need to convey the message through the station. It would have been of no use. The people above were doing their best to stave off the Tentorian attack. They could only pray and hope for them.

Todor, Chan, and Hugh were the first to set off towards the hole their rocket had blown through the building entrance, each holding two machine guns. They picked up the pace and started running shoulder to shoulder. Three mini-drones scouted through the smoke while the countless data received secured their danger-free advance.

The Island servicemen were waiting for the attack to come, hiding behind the corners of the hallway. They were in formation, ready for an ambush.

"The flying devices have cameras!" the station let them know when shots burst inside the building, too.

A mini-drone fell to the ground, hit by a bullet. One of its propellers had been destroyed.

"Oh my God, flying cameras!" The officer, nearing the device, stared at it, baffled. Mankind as he knew it could not imagine something like this.

He had no time to examine it because the drone tried to get up in the air again. He aimed for it and shot twice, this time hitting home.

One moment later, bullets flew right and left. The three Tentorians, followed by their allies, had entered the building. The servicemen were taken out before they saw their attackers. Tentorian rounds tore directly through doors and grenades were thrown into the servicemen's hiding places before they even suspected they'd been spotted.

Mini-drones spread all over the outer area, the main building, and its annexes. The bionic intruders made use of any scrap of information to evaluate the position of their targets and their battle strategy: shadows at great distances, light fluctuations, footsteps, even beyond walls. Only the Ragon mercenaries' encounters were fought on equal terms, but they were few and far between.

A sandbag barricade set up on one of the ground corridors kept the intruders at bay. The corridor, running the whole length of the building and standing four meters wide, had never been so crowded. Bodies robbed of souls or others shaking in pain were strewn along it, where only the white mountain flower patterned marine blue carpet had lain before. The heavy machine gun, mounted in the center of the bags, rattled on.

Chan's mini-drone transmitted that 14 servicemen were positioned behind the barricades, and a quick strategy took shape in every Tentorian mind. Behind the corner, Max and Hugh started firing their four machine guns into the ceiling above the 14 people until pieces of the falling rubble momentarily took them out of the fight. This gave Hoshito enough time to show up in the middle of the corridor with a rocket launcher. He got hit by three bullets, but the rocket went out before he fell to the ground.

The explosion in the middle of the barricade had come as an assault signal. The Tentorians, followed by dozens of allies, were now moving forward with their fingers pressed to their triggers, hot on the trail of the bullets now flying in only one direction.

When Kaligor appeared, Hoshito was doubled over in pain on the flower-print carpet, clutching the holes in his shirt and belly. The very moment he saw him, the Tentorian barked, "Use that damned technology I gave you!"

The look on the allied chief's face was strained; he wanted to stand the pain rather than use the device implanted in his head.

"Jackass," Kaligor barked again. "All you need to do is think that you want to be cured RIGHT NOW!" And on he went.

Hoshito's wounds suddenly began to heal, and a wild laughter roared distinctly through the whizzing bullets.

Claire crouched against a wall with her palms pressed over her ears, deafened by the endless onslaught. An incessant ringing reverberated through her head against the background of howls coming from somewhere...*far away*. An explosion shook everything around her while the rubble trickled into her hair, eyebrows, eyes, and mouth. *I am...lost. No, I'm not part of this fight!* She spotted Max dimly. He stood there, right in front of her, and called her at the top of his voice to follow him. She was in no mood to hear anything right now. Max turned his back on her and shot a burst of bullets towards a stray serviceman, with a malicious grin on his lips. A few bullets ricocheted near Claire. She was no longer capable of dodging them. *I am amidst a nightmare.*

"We are descending to minus one!" Max shouted at her. "We're done here!"

She watched him dissolve in the smoke, stood up, and made for the exit, disoriented and stumbling. She did not know what she was doing, feeling only the urge to leave. A new bang and her ears rang again. It was as if all her senses had been suppressed.

Chapter 24

"... T *oday's heinous deed at the House of Security has*
no explanation. The gang of armed people left no survivors
and now at least 36 families are in mourning..."

Jimmy's face was green. He turned his entire body to observe the bar crowd. He wanted to see their reaction, to make sure he wasn't the only one seeing the news on TV. They all watched, petrified, glasses in hands.

"This is the bloodiest armed episode in the last twenty years. Representatives of the House of Security have declared that the evidence collected points to the Shadow Ragons gang, a group known mostly for illegal substance trafficking. Although at this moment the connection between this gang and the murderous attack is unexplained, the Government promises more details as soon as the investigation allows for new clues to be disclosed to the public."

The Governor's materialization on the screen caught everyone's eye even more. Compared to the last time they had seen him, he appeared disheveled; now his shirt was not perfectly arranged, his hair was not perfectly combed. *"At the present moment, the reason why the criminals have taken so many lives is unknown. It all seems meaningless..."*

"The Governor," the gentleman next to Jimmy whispered pointlessly and left his pint of beer on the counter.

A drab-looking lady and another gaunt gentleman sitting

along the bar followed suit. The chubby young man stayed where he was, thinking a draught of beer went down his throat smoother than the lump forming there. He took a sip, but his face remained just as contorted.

"Earth is a peaceful place. Such deeds have no place and shall be harshly reprimanded. I am appalled and cannot understand what prompted these monsters to go as far as they did. The Code and the Government shall not condone any deed associated with this carnage. All those involved shall be brought to justice and shall pay for it. My mind now carries me to the families of the victims with whom the Government and its Heads deeply sympathize. We cry together with them...but we shall also support them with anything we are able to offer, from aid to investigations and answers."

Jimmy grabbed his phone and rushed to the exit. His call went straight to voicemail. "Cole, I know you don't have your phone on you, man, but who knows, you may listen to your messages once in a while. This morning I got a call from your folks...they know you're missing, but they don't have any other news. This evening we've all calmed down somehow. They told me that you called them and that you're okay, you just took a small break from civilization; no work, no phone. Why didn't you tell me? I hope you really are okay. Give me a sign when you can. I want to know how you're doing."

Chapter 25

In a dorm building several hundred meters off the main structure, Cole watched the lights of explosions and gunfire through the window. With each blast, the windows jiggled and so did his heart. Every once in a while, a group of servicemen would run to the main building while others covered them by shooting at the attackers' allies. They kept going onwards, but no one came back, and that intrigued him.

The door to the room opened suddenly. He stuck himself to the window with a resolute frown, prepared to face anything. Then he heaved a sigh of relief. It was Drew who came in with an officer, the young man he had seen several hours earlier in the interrogation room.

"You must leave! Martin will get you out through the back and take you to a safe place."

Cole stared at them inquisitively, giving the man standing at attention next to her a quick once over—a man younger than him with a frail body and a closely cropped military haircut. This man had served in the military, where he had probably only learned how to blink slower than most his age.

"Just Martin...alone?" he asked in surprise. He wiped his anxiety off his face and turned to the officer. "No offense, man, but—"

He left the last syllable hanging in the air, thinking he would be contradicted, but he read no trace of disagreement in Martin's eyes. What's more, they looked like they were just as nervous.

"You will go with a military group," she tried to reassure him, but she didn't look in control either.

"Hmm…how many men are in a military group?"

"Ten—good luck to you!" she added in a hurry before she left.

"Wait!" Cole tried to stop her.

He had many questions still gnawing at him, but Drew was already gone.

"Thank you…" Cole said to himself.

None of the Tentorians had been killed, while on the allies' side the losses were minimal. At the same time, they had managed to take out over a hundred servicemen in the Center.

In the main building, Chris, Arnar, and a platoon of officers and soldiers were at level -1, ready to face the Tentorian onslaught. Dozens of people were strategically scattered through the entire level. It was the only one that permitted access to -8, the level of the Island's main monitoring room. They had to defend it at all costs.

One, two, three…eight smoke grenades traveled from the service staircase to the corridor at -1 followed by the desperate shout of an officer.

"Masks!"

Arnar handed Chris a mask. The two waited together

with some servicemen behind a sandbag barricade erected in the middle of the main hallway. Twelve support columns, the same as the number of the Erudites, kept watch and soberly bore the still immaculate flags with the emblem of the Island. A star with a flower, artfully crafted in marble, spread at their feet and under the sandbags in the center of the hexagonal hallway. They had a clear view of the entire landing with the entrance to the elevator and the twenty men guarding it from behind another barricade stuck to the corner of the wall and close to the smoke filled entrance.

Silence went deathly. Strain turned into pain, and the masks tight on their faces became more and more difficult to bear. Even so, the men barely dared to blink. The smoke, which had engulfed the entire level, was the only thing that remained to be seen; visibility had dropped to under one meter ahead. Seconds of agonizing tension went by like minutes for some, while never ending moments of sheer fright passed through the others.

In the din, Chris noticed a continuous clang coming from the officer to his right. It was given off by the rhythmically shaking buckle of his machine gun's harness. His clasped hands shivered on the gun in spite of himself and only the officer's gas mask could hide his unstoppable tears. Chris gently tore the man's frozen fingers off the cold weapon and clasped them in his palms.

"It'll all be fine," he emboldened the man in a whisper.

He didn't need to shout; everything was too quiet for the slightest noise to go unnoticed. He put the officer's hands back on the machine gun and removed his fingers carefully, as if from a freshly smoothed sandcastle. The shaking ceased. Chris then turned his eyes upwards to think of a strategy, or maybe just to pray.

A few muffled noises came from the staircase. Then the buzz of the mini-drones suddenly cut through the silence. The sound came from right and left, humming an ever more threatening tune from somewhere behind the dense smoke curtains. The eyes of the servicemen went from one side to the other, chasing the strange noises until three hollow-sounding shots muffled the buzz. They glanced at one another, at a loss as to what to do. From that moment the shots resumed to a heartbeat pace and kept on getting closer. One of them stood up and tried to find a target. He came back immediately, baffled; visibility was too poor.

"We must open fire," Arnar prepped them. "On my signal you stand up and—"

A powerful explosion at the base of the barricade cut his speech short and threw everyone several meters away. Bursts of bullets ensued and Arnar was hit in the stomach of his bulletproof vest. Chris, too, suffered a bullet in his shoulder. Instinctively, he turned around, pain drilling through him. He then felt Arnar's hand clasping his shirt, dragging him out of the line of fire and behind a column. He allowed himself to be guided with a blank stare, unable to conceal the bafflement of defeat, blinking heavily and quivering as if electrocuted with each thump of metal hitting the bodies of his people. Their fight was all but lost.

Todor and Max had made it to the door of the elevator leading to the -8 level. The cunning IT specialist laid a hand on the elevator's control panel and a stream of nanobots flowed into the electronic device.

"Yo," he said, "I need more processing power here!"

The information captured by the nanobots instantly went to all the Tentorians. The control panel decryption program now ran into each of their capsules.

After a short while, the panel screen displayed in green letters: `Access granted.`

The doors opened automatically. Todor, Max, and five of their allies stepped into the lift and pressed the "Underground 8" button while several allies remained behind with Hugh and Hoshito to guard the access point. The doors hardly closed, and Hugh took out two foil wrapped sandwiches from his chest pocket, opened them, and laid them on an officer's bullet-riddled body. He took the top sandwich and sank his teeth in greedily.

"Mmmm...this stone age shit is seriously good!" His eyes brimmed with satisfaction as he took in the shape of the bite.

A jumble of jangling sounds strangled the silence in the elevator. It came from magazines mounted on firearms and bolts pushed up in the firing position.

Another clink and the doors opened. Two mini-drones went out scouting while gunfire hit the wall in front of the elevator. No one met them; no riposte, no armed men, only a long corridor leading to the main monitoring and command room.

Set at the rear end of the room, two transparent walls separated them from the two Erudites and the three operational staff officers. On hearing the firearms, Leewana got up from her work station and scurried to the middle of the room to join the others. She instinctively searched each wall's door. Their sturdiness reassured her.

The stillness was broken by the intercom relaying the sweet, fiendish sound of Max's voice. "Knock, knock, anybody hoooome?"

None of the five spoke back. They only looked at him, disgusted. There was nobody left to protect them, save the secured windows. Two Ragons grinned diabolically while pressing their faces against the glass.

The failed rapper laid his hand on the electronic panel in the first wall door and sent a stream of nanobots through. Save the panel, the door was as translucent as the wall. Then he waved to a Ragon, who began mounting a device on the panel. He pressed a few buttons and gestured to everyone to move away. For a few split seconds an electric field radiated one meter away from the device—an overcast night's full moon-like glow. When the halo died down, the entire pane of glass gave off a gauzy, greenish hue.

Suddenly, hundreds of sweat beads appeared on one officer's face. Leewana clasped his hand and before she knew it her eyes were swimming in tears too. The first wall's securing field deactivated. The same Ragon now took out an explosive device and set it on the edge of the sliding door. Impatience could be read all over the hellish wry smiles spread on their faces. The deafening blast of the explosion threw the three officers down to the floor. Despite silence descending upon them again, Leewana's hands were still clasped over her ears. She was afraid to get back on her feet. She had seen on monitoring screens what the murderous beasts behind the glass were capable of.

The first transparent wall was shattered, and the seven people hastily prepared the same procedure on the second one.

There was no doubt left in the Erudites' minds: The odds were overwhelmingly against them. They turned to the screens and quickly programmed something in the system. After a few seconds, all screens displayed one single message:

The Central System control room ready to self-destruct. Confirmation needed!

"Erudites," the system articulated, *"please confirm self-destruct vocally and by means of an intentional thought."*

The two people stood up and straightened their grey tunics carefully, bracing for the big moment. Leewana, too, mustered the force to stand. She wanted to add something but was content just to read in the Erudites' eyes—a glimmer of hope and fulfilment in compensation for an entire lifetime of achievements and love. It wasn't hope for their own lives, it was for the Islanders'. They'd come to terms with their own deaths. They did their best for the good of the Island. She knew that because she stood by them during the last years. They hugged and shook hands, standing up one in front of the other, ready for an honorable death. They also looked at the other officers one by one, seeking to see on their faces reconciliation as to what was to happen, and forgiveness, too. An officer with tears in his eyes bowed an approval. The other man followed suit. Leewana found the strength to smile at them and she, too, bowed her head, at peace with herself.

Just as the five people joined their arms in a prayer circle, the electric field enveloped the second window, which soon turned green and vulnerable.

"Computer, destroy the central system and the command room," one of the Erudites uttered clearly.

"Why are you moving so slow for, sow asses?" Todor's deep voice thundered through his men. "They are going to fry us in here!"

In a frantic gesture, he aimed his weapon at the partition wall and began firing one shot after another. Rabid with fury, he watched his bullets flatten with thuds against the still withstanding glass.

The system speaker went on for the last time. *"The*

system operation has been transferred to the backup unit. The central unit is being deactivated. Self-destruct will initiate in five seconds."

Stillness followed. The monitors turned black. The Erudites and the officers held their hands tighter and closed their eyes.

Leewana thought of the fragrance of the redolent wind wafting by her front porch, the entrancing shimmer of the northern lights during heavy winters, the hill in front of her bedroom window covered in a carpet of blue bellflowers in early spring, and the image of her husband waiting for her between the warm sheets while she stared naked out of the window. She would have liked to tell him she loved him one more time. She had lived a fulfilled life with him and she wasn't at all ready to put an end to it. She cried through her tightly shut eyes for the last time.

The desperate dash of the seven intruders along the corridor was to be the last motion ever made at Level -8. An utterly soundless blue flame turned everything standing between the walls and up to the elevator to dust in no time at all.

At Level -1, Chris, Arnar, and a handful of servicemen fought to hold their last defensive position sheltered behind four supporting columns in the hexagonal hallway. They had been cornered there by ten or so Tentorian allies, positioned behind a freshly captured sandbag barricade. The flags attached to the columns were no longer proudly watching, instead hanging dejectedly, burned, blackened, or holed.

An officer emerged from behind the column and sprayed the intruders with bullets. The fire grazed a Ragon mercenary, but before he had time to take a step back, a stream of bullets had already filled him. Each hit pushed him back, inch by inch, until he fell down. The ugly, satisfied look of the enemy wielding the smoking machine gun in hand was the last thing that remained imprinted on his retina.

Chris yelled furiously, gripped at his shoulder wound, and came out halfway from behind the column where he stood to fire his gun at the barricade. He did not have a precise target, doing it rather to quench his anger than anything else. Arnar pulled him back immediately.

"Are you out of your mind?"

He came upon a face twisted with hatred as he had never seen before. He unclasped Chris' bloodied hand from his wounded shoulder. It was serious. He squinted and turned on his heel to one of his warrant officers.

"Hand me two grenades!"

"They are too far, General!"

"I didn't ask for your opinion!" Arnar snapped, hand held out. "After the explosion, fire at will at the barricade! Attention: fire above head! Understood?"

"Understood!" the officer answered curtly.

"Now duck!"

Unflinchingly, the general took the pin from the first grenade and threw it at the enemy close to the stack of bags.

"Grenade!" came a howl from the other side.

All the enemies huddled tightly behind the sandbags. The

explosion shook the walls but moved not a single bag from its place. Against the deafening sound of the fire coming from the Island servicemen, Arnar set off on a mad rush straight to the barricade. He ran with no weapons save the second grenade he'd already taken the pin out of. He dove on his stomach, raised his hand off the lever, counted, and lobbed it over the stack of bags.

"Damn!" was all that ever came from the other side.

A bang rattled the dorm building just before Cole and Officer Martin could exit. Martin took out his pistol, swallowed the lump in his throat, and cracked the door ajar. Several servicemen lay dead in front of the entry while others ran aimlessly in the direction of the main building. A round of machine gun fire and they, too, were mowed down, executed behind their backs. He withdrew right away and closed the door, then he pressed his back to it, terrified.

"What?" Cole asked, eyes wide and popping out.

The answer came in one shaky breath. "They are all dead."

The unwilling guest slammed his palm violently against the wall. "Damn it! We have a plan B?"

"No," the officer snapped. "No," he repeated, seized by panic. "No."

Cole cracked the door just enough to peek around. He saw Drew ten meters away in front of the building, pressed against the wall of a storage facility. She clasped her gun tightly and her right foot was bleeding. She saw him and waved for him to stay inside and make no noise, raising her palms once, lowering them, and raising only one palm again to indicate there were 15 enemies to the right. They were keeping watch close by, ready to take down the servicemen rushing to back those in the main building; they fired at anything that moved. Cole scanned the dismal scene shortly, stretched out a hand, and took the gun of a fallen officer before he warily stepped back.

"There's someone in that building—at the entrance!" one of the Asian men yelled, pointing at the closing door.

A minute later, two of them approached the building with grenade launchers. They loaded and braced themselves for shooting.

"Step away from the entrance!" Drew shouted desperately and pulled herself up, aiming the gun at the two Ragons.

She shot five rounds and took them out. Scores of bullets were shot instantly at her from somewhere on the right side of the building. A bullet skinned her neck and a lock of hair fell to her shoulder. *They are too many,* she assessed briefly. She turned on one foot and jumped on her stomach into a small ditch. *Way too many!*

The bullets hit the ground around her and dirt rained on top of her. She raised her eyes to look for a place to hide but another round shook the earth. *I am trapped here*...in a ditch that was growing smaller and smaller as the storm of bullets grew denser. The bullets whizzed closer and closer to her body, the sound of death humming in her ears, the dirt showering upon her thicker and thicker, making its way into her mouth and eyes. With each passing second, she felt closer to death. *There's no way out for me. I must get out and fight to the last breath.*

The edge of the tiny dirt ditch protecting her was eaten up as if it had never been there. A bullet took a piece of her coat followed by another one. There was no room left for her to huddle.

She yelled savagely. Air in the lungs, the weapon loaded...*I'm ready to face them.*

"On the count of three, Drew, three!" she whispered to herself. *One, two...*She raised a hand and pointed the gun at the enemy.

The machine guns stopped short. Befuddled, she stared ahead and then back. Only three meters behind her, she saw a redheaded green-eyed young woman pointing a pistol at her. She looked into the green eyes and understood it was time for her to think of her loved ones. She shut her eyes and waited for the final fire. She opened her eyes again. The young redhead was frozen with her finger on the trigger. Her eyes were misty with bloodshot capillaries while a tear was about to trickle down her cheek.

The sound of the first shot hit with a sinister pitch. Instinctively, Drew brought her eyelashes together. Another shot and another.

"Claire, what the devil are you doing shooting at us?" a man from the Tentorians' ally camp bawled. "It's *us!*" the voice insisted.

The hand on Drew's shoulder pushed her away from the spot where she had seen her end coming; she could no longer walk. Gunshots began again from the Ragon side. She swung to them and shot along with the redhead. They were moving too slowly and standing within range. The Tentorian women grabbed her by the collar and piggybacked her to the barrack's corner, shooting rounds behind her all the while.

Although puzzled, Drew quickly understood she was saved. When eased down behind the storage facility, she saw a tattoo at the base of the redhead's neck: three star shaped T's. She had never seen anything like this before. That was probably the Tentorian "T" and the grimy girl may well have been the same Tentorian Cole Williams had told them about. They stood a meter apart, staring at each other, not daring to blink. They remained motionless, face to face, clasping their weapons.

A huge blast shook the earth. The door of the building Cole and Martin were in had been torn down.

"They're coming at us!" The shout from the officer froze Cole's heart. "There are six Ragons," he whispered and rushed to cross from one wall of the hallway to the other. "Cover me!"

That was all he managed to say. A downpour of bullets mowed him down on the spot. He lowered his chin and looked at his bloodied, bullet-mangled body. He seemed unable to understand what was happening to him. Through the last pulsations of pain, he turned to Cole and tried to tell him to run. He knew, however, that even if he could summon the strength to tell him, it would make no difference. The attackers were way too many.

"Murderers!" Cole blew his top, watching him collapse.

Horrified, his eyes stuck to the blood dripping onto the floor and the hand that was still moving; he had never watched anyone die. *Pull yourself together, Cole,* he braced himself, *and fight with dignity! I was to die anyway; at least now I am doing it right.* He filled his lungs and examined the pistol in his hand: *safety catch, sight, trigger...it can't be that difficult! I only need to hold it tight and not shut my eyes.*

"I love you, Mom, I love you, Dad, I love you, Mathew!"

Howling indistinctly and firing at the first enemy popping up in his sight, Cole exited the building. He aimed just at him, blinded by revenge, but others started to fall too. Claire's weapon was also hungry for revenge.

Some long seconds had passed since the six hit the ground, but Cole kept on pulling the trigger, driven by the adrenaline invading his body. His pistol's firing now gave off only hollow clicks; it no longer fired bullets.

The same beautiful red haired creature he had met in the forest now grabbed him by the hand. "We must get out of here!"

He pulled himself together. "Yes."

The strange shudder gripping his mouth would not let him say anything else. The deafening sound of machine guns and the two bullets that hit the Tentorian's hip would have cut him short anyway. Claire gasped briefly.

"Down!" he said and threw her to the ground. Another volley of bullets whizzed past their heads.

Some seconds later, the guns fell silent. It was Drew's turn to save their lives. She waved them to withdraw to the back of the garrison. She would stay behind and provide cover.

The sun, halfway below the horizon, beamed reddish rays over what was left from the Center, when Cole grabbed Claire by the armpit and began pulling her, squatting, towards the back of the building he'd just exited. As soon as he set off, the beautiful Tentorian pressed the device at her wrist a few times and leaned her head back. Her eyes were closed but still twitching slightly while healing. They had barely gotten around corner of the building before her wounds vanished.

"Wonderful," he said dryly. "I expect you can take it from here."

"That's unless you want to piggyback me," she retorted in the same vein. Both their faces were half twisted.

From the place they were in, the whole back side of the unit could be seen. They looked right and left then ran to the surrounding fence.

But several meters away, Cole slowed and held out his hand to stop her. A parked off-road vehicle looked like it was winking at him. "You wait here!"

"Do you need help?" the woman asked.

"That's my line of work," he boasted before skulking to the car.

He climbed in and quickly took off the cover below the steering wheel. Thirty seconds later, the sweet sound of escape roared full-bodied from under the off-roader's bonnet.

"Wonderful," it was Claire's turn to say as she climbed into the car.

The young motorcar aficionado floored the throttle and drove the beast into the wire fence.

"Damn it!" her voice sounded again when the car flattened the fence and made for the forest.

Cole's gleeful yell made the Tentorian woman smile briefly. She forgot for a moment all they had been through. The forest road loomed ahead and the off-roader evened out. The Command Center vanished farther and farther behind them.

"*Intruders leaving the base!*" speakers blared.

"To all units," Chris broadcasted, "do not engage in pursuit! I repeat: do not engage in pursuit!" He lowered his voice. "We already have too many losses. Over!"

Kaligor, Chan, Hugh, Osman, and Hoshito were running along with roughly 20 allies towards one of the buses while covered by the others in their camp.

Their vehicle was the first to roll away at full speed. Inside, the painful moans of one of Hoshito's men, muffled the sound of the engine. He had been seriously injured in his arm and stomach. Three seats away, a few scratches mended themselves on Kaligor's neck while he provided some explanation on a call to Tentoria:

"No, we didn't make it. They activated self-destruction before we could do anything."

"Was I wrong when I trusted you?" Nemilo's words fell ruthlessly.

The bald man cursed to himself. "I apologize." He paused. "The bright side is that the main Monitoring and Command Center has been completely wiped out and two Erudites are dead; few losses from our side. It looks like they only have the Backup Center left."

"Good. It took us a while to find out the coordinates of the Main Center; how will you find out where the backup one is located?"

Kaligor straightened his upper back, sure of himself. "I have an idea, don't worry."

"I trust you can finish what you started."

"I will," the bald man concluded, ending the connection.

He was seething. It hadn't exactly been the kind of conversation he would have liked to have with Nemilo. He turned to Hugh.

"Isn't it jarring your ears?" He pointed at the suffering Asian man, who was groaning loudly. "Help him! We still need him in shape."

Hugh got up and planted himself with a malicious grin in front of the wounded man. "Do you wanna be fixed?"

Chapter 26

The two young people had already been driving for half an hour, crossing wild grass, overgrown coniferous forests, and meadows. The grey copper sky was perfectly clear and the road was lit by the almost-full moon and the red sun setting on the horizon. They said nothing to each other since they'd left, still silent and staring ahead.

Claire remembered asking herself when setting off, *Where are we going?* Since then, she'd forgotten to ask that again out loud. She couldn't care less about anything anymore. All she wanted was to be somewhere far from those places. Less than one hour ago her entire existence had been questioned. She was ashamed of her own race, of what it could spawn. She felt guilty of all the harm done by her fellow people and wished to think of home, of her father. She had lost her mother consequently to a medical error, in a fight for everlasting life—for perfection. Her mum risked and failed to win it. She lost her sister too, who had been heartsick and driven by technology to take her own life. Her father was the only one left, only wishing her to live like a real human being, to face the ups and downs of life as they were with their rights and wrongs, with no state-of-the-art technology to improve her. *Perfection does not bring happiness*, she managed to think, almost daydreaming in a last ditch attempt. She closed her eyes and fell asleep.

Cole was lost in thought too. Only the road markings and the speedometer needle kept part of his mind in the present.

As for the rest, he was overpowered by recollections, sequences, and experiences he'd lived through. He was trying to find meaning behind the events in his life, searching for elements he'd overlooked. Many things made sense now, though most were still meaningless. Thousands of questions rattled through his mind, thousands of memories pointing out the naked truth. *We are such small creatures in such a large and mysterious world.* He wished he could forget everything and return to that innocence that had been stolen from him.

He looked at Claire. She was sleeping like an angel, a Tentorian angel. He brushed her hair away from her forehead and gently touched her cheek with the back of his fingers. *What a pleasant...thrill...*

One hour later, the duller sound of the killed engine woke Claire so suddenly she grabbed her weapon and made Cole cower.

"Sorry!" she said, still befuddled.

"Okay...it's okay." He drew a sigh of relief and pressed his hand to his heart.

"Where are we?" Her voice was numb.

"In the middle of the forest," Cole answered simply. He pointed to a glade. "Do you see that little wooden cabin?" The redhead rubbed her eyes. "That's the place where I go with my folks from time to time. They keep telling me that's the ideal spot to make peace with nature; to rediscover ourselves as a family, away from civilization."

"Charming. It looks so...natural." She got out of the car.

"I hope that at least it looks safer."

"Right...uh...I'm Claire." She only raised her hand.

"Cole," he answered in kind on the other side of the car. "Let me show you something."

He came close and took her by the hand. He led her down a path, through a thicket, walked a bit more through the forest, and stopped in front of a mist-enveloped lake.

Claire cried out in wonderment. The moon, mirrored by the lake, conveyed a fairytale appearance. A wondrous peace ruled over the entire place.

"It's a thermal lake. I love this spot," Cole added, heading for a large boulder on the shore. "I used to sit here for minutes on end, contemplating the Universe."

Claire drew a breath, closed her eyes, and tilted her head back. It was a moment she relished for long seconds.

"And...you bring all the girls here?" She turned to him and wrapped an inquisitive look around him, smiling.

Cole lapsed into a smile as well and turned to the lake, face awash in the moonlight. "Only those from outside the Island."

The girl tittered. "That's perfect then."

She came and sat next to him on a rock while carrying on looking at the lake. The moon's reflection melted in wafts of steam, and the water looked like it dripped skywards. She turned her head towards him, admired him for one more instant, then returned to the dreamy view.

He broke the silence. "Why did you save me?"

The young Tentorian woman faltered a bit. "Because... I did not want to support an unfair action."

"Then why did you start such a battle?"

"It was all...'thought through,'" she found the right words at last. "I had no idea—although I should have figured it out. Our mission was a scouting one, and perhaps we could have entertained a peaceful communication with you; nobody said anything to me about an attack. We didn't even have fighting gear on us, and it was the wrong team for this kind of mission. On that last point I tend to think I was mistaken."

"And what happened? What do you want—what do *they* want from us or from our Government? Or from the Erudites?"

"They want to conquer the Island."

The answer came like a high-speed train shooting out of a dark tunnel. The Islander's face went suddenly white.

"And...what will happen to us?"

Claire felt the pang of guilt weighing down on her even harder as she focused her moist eyes on a remote line separating the forest from the sky.

"I don't know...I don't know what their plan is. What's sure is that things are very serious and grim."

The way she said it sent a chill down Cole's spine.

"It's all so very strange. My world could collapse any time now. My family, my friends..."

"I couldn't stop them. I had to look like I was on their side. I'm a small cog in a big mechanism. They could have gotten rid of me in no time at all. They are very dangerous, Cole. You cannot even imagine how dangerous."

"And what should we do now?"

"I don't know. I'm still thinking."

The Islander went silent for a few heartbeats. "I want to wake up from this nightmare. I want to forget all about this war."

Claire followed every word leaving his lips. A pleasant shiver ran through her body. *I want to forget all about this war, too.*

"You know what?" she broke off the discussion. "I've always wanted to go into a lake with clothes on. Besides, dusty as I am, I think it would come in handy."

Cole burst out laughing and kept on watching her beautiful green, almond-shaped eyes. The Tentorian stared back at him while a delicate shudder took hold of her body. A stray thought running loose took her aback.

"Without shoes though!" she added quickly and flashed her teeth to bluff it out.

She took off her boots and ran to the water.

"You're mad!"

"C'mon, jump in," she tempted him, already neck-deep in the water. "It's so warm!"

"The hell with it...why not?"

He immediately took off his shoes and dove into the water. He came out just two meters away from her. "Wow, it is quite warm!"

"I told you." The beautiful Tentorian waved her hands like a wallowing child. Then she raised them to the sky and shouted, "Look, I am standing here!"

"Be careful, you've climbed onto a monster fish!"

"Whaaat?"

Cole laughed his head off. The mysterious being entranced him more and more. His smile, previously hardly sketched, was now unruly, betraying him.

"Thank you," she said a few seconds later.

"What for?"

"I feel like I'm really living now."

"Me...too," he stammered, hot with the blood rushing into his cheeks.

Claire wavered at first and then she found herself mumbling a futile question, "You too... thank me?"

"Me too. I feel that I'm alive...truly..."

Truly? Seriously? What did I say that for? I'm behaving like a schmuck...in love. She may have referred to the landscape, to the nature...

"The lake, the forest..." Claire listed.

"Course, not me. how could it—"

"You," she interrupted. "Everything's charming. And maybe it's especially...you."

And maybe it's especially? Claire reproached herself. *What's wrong with me?*

Cole's heart was beating harder in his chest. He closed one meter from her in awkward gestures as if he'd forgotten how to swim. Silence fell back over the lake; only their increasingly deeper breathing could be heard while they drew closer to one another. Her green eyes lingered on him and her lips no longer touched each other. They longed for another touch. *I am throbbing with all my body...and I was just getting to know him.*

Droplets were still dripping off his lips and down his chin, dissolving into the smooth surface of the water and rippling towards the Tentorian's superbly curved shoulders.

*I am floating so high...*a breeze-like thought delighted him. *And I only got to know her.* He raised a hand from the water and caressed her silky cheek. *So fine.* A droplet fell from his forehead onto her lips, and she welcomed it like a drop of rain in the desert. They were both shaking. He closed his eyes and kissed her.

The forest around them murmured with its seemingly alive leaves shimmering under the moon, but there, between them, only their increasingly fast breath could be heard, betraying the deceptive serenity of the kiss. Claire pushed him a few meters towards the shore, then wrapped her arms around him as his lips trailed down her chin and neck. Her blouse, slipping off her body with the water, allowed him access to her bare shoulder among red strands of hair caressing his cheek. Another kiss touched her naked back, and another one lower, and another one, like the wet petals of a flower scattered on a sultry summer day. The buttons of her blouse seemed to unclasp themselves. The two shoulders, now fully bare, made the Islander lose himself in mad thoughts. She turned to face him again; he went dumb. A bare breast demanded to be touched.

"Mmm..." she sighed without knowing.

She kissed him on the neck, letting her hands rest on his chest, and hugged him. He carried her in his arms and lay her gently by the shore on a soft, mossy forest blanket.

The slippery warm skin, tender lips, the touch of palms, the deep quiet...everything was divine.

Chapter 27

The Control Center looked like a battlefield. Ambulances never ceased rolling in to provide emergency care to the wounded. For many of them it was too late, and they were already covered in plastic sheets. Others were whisked away on stretchers and put into ambulances, their cries louder than the intermittent sirens.

Chris was heading towards an ambulance as well, leaning against Drew, who was doing her best to limp no more.

"We must seal this place," he directed her. "Set up a meeting with all the Erudites at the Backup Center. Only those on duty must attend; the rest we will communicate with in a conference call to avoid unnecessary risks. We should leave here at once."

Drew stopped him. "You must go to the hospital. You must get some rest!"

"I guess I could tell you the same thing."

"I'm fine. I only have a flesh leg injury."

"No. We are going there! We have the best doctors with us."

They sat down on a stretcher while a doctor and a nurse rushed to aid them.

Chris stifled a moan when his shoulder was touched. He crushed his lips between his teeth, then looked at Drew and made his point: "So...after we're done here, we'll go to the Backup Center. If that makes you feel better, we'll ride in the ambulance; that way we can get care on the way as well."

Drew approved. "Where is Arnar?" she wanted to check.

The Erudite grimaced at the antiseptic compress on his shoulder and said between clenched teeth, "He's regrouping the forces."

When the collar of his completely unbuttoned shirt was let down by the doctor, the same tattoo Drew saw on the back of Claire's neck was revealed before her eyes. The woman went completely silent, heart stopped and gaze frozen.

"Are you okay?" Chris asked.

"Yeah." Her lips barely moved.

Chapter 28

Cole sat in front of the cabin barefoot, wearing only a pair of jeans. Next to him, Bon Jovi's "It's my life" could scarcely be heard on a CD player as he stared ahead.

Claire came out of the cabin wearing one of his short-sleeved shirts.

"That tune," she said, "is vintage 2000 from something in no way related to the Island." She handed him a T-shirt too. "Put this on. It got a bit chilly."

"Thanks. I've been listening to them since I was young." He slipped the T-shirt over his head and brought his eyebrows together when he noticed his old short-sleeved shirt shaping itself so lovely on Claire's body. He smiled slightly but didn't speak his mind. "It looked to me that band was too cool for the 90s and our Island."

"Maybe the Erudites enjoyed it enough to have it make the top 10 Island hits."

Cole laughed. He looked her over again and decided he liked also the frayed jeans he ceased wearing more than ten years ago from the moment his folks brought them here. To her, they suited perfectly.

"You know," he gazed at her through hooded eyes, "you look...some way."

"Some way...?"

"So very good."

"You flatter me. If you're interested, it was Mother Nature's doing. At least that's what I was told." Claire straightened and smiled as if posing.

"Duly noted." He smirked.

"But you...you clearly ran off the Island and had a few aesthetic medical interventions."

"Ha! You got your compliment right this time."

Claire briefly closed her right eye as confirmation.

"Interesting!" he said some moments later admiring the tattoo at the back of her head. He noticed her feigning a smile and failing to conceal her sorrow. "Does it mean something?"

"Yes. It means..." she pondered. "All of us genuine Tentorians have it."

"What does that mean?"

"All those brought to life at the very moment our nation was created—along with the 22nd century World War, and us, their natural descendants."

"Am I to understand there is another kind of Tentorian, too...the artificial ones?" He frowned, but quickly got back to the topic at hand. "I don't want to know," he concluded dryly.

After putting their shoes on, they seated themselves on the only step at the cabin's entrance. Claire checked the 'watch' on her arm for a while before she pointed it at him.

"Do you want to know how this cool technology works?"

"No—well, I mean yes. Sure, tell me!" He sat up taller to see.

"This contraption was created for special missions." She looked him over to make sure she had his undivided attention, like a little girl pleased with her toys. "It's a pretty rare thing, especially having so much technology concentrated into such a small device. Few have laid their hands on such a thing."

She raised her eyebrows proudly. The Islander bowed.

"Otherwise," she carried on, "the technology is on the market anyway. Everything you have seen out of the ordinary is pure nanotechnology and artificial intelligence." Cole frowned inquisitively. "That means the technology developed through many centuries—intelligent machines smaller than the molecules in our bodies acting on a microscopic scale."

"Now then," Cole mumbled. "How's that possible?"

"Well..." The redhead stumbled. "Pay attention. Just imagine some bulky robots standing several meters tall arranging a heap of boulders. With the technology known on the Island it might be possible, or at least imaginable."

"Okay."

"Now, imagine that advancement over hundreds of years makes it possible for such a robot to be smaller, more intelligent, and move better year after year." She took a deep breath. "Progress has made it possible for us to incorporate ever better technologies and improved artificial intelligence—initially into computers, then into telephones and devices that grew smaller and smaller." The young Islander was entranced. "At long last, sticking to this trend towards ever smaller and ever more intelligent devices, you end up having this."

After touching the screen of the device on her wrist a few times, she pointed at him. She missed not the chance to ogle him while staring at his inquisitive face and sketching the smile of a child in love.

"Are you showing me something...besides the tip of your finger?" Cole checked it out while smiling in turn. "I can't see a thing."

"Kiss me before I explain."

"Well, that's easy."

He moved closer and gently caught one of her lips between his teeth. He kissed her and caressed her thighs, then suddenly missed his old shirt and found himself checking its texture over a larger area. He was pushed forth and before making up his mind as to what he wanted from her, he received only the explanation.

"Here we have a nanorobot with an impressive processing power; what's more, it's specialized in anatomy," she pushed her chest forward as if showing the little robot respect.

Cole peered at her with one eye "Processing power? How large a fraction of what our computers have?"

She found the question funny and laughed out loud. "Fraction? It's many times more intelligent than your computer at home."

That can't be true, Cole wanted to say but kept the futile line for himself. "Still, so small..."

"You can't see it on my finger because 'nano' in 'nanorobot' is a billion times smaller in gauge. But it's there—take my word for it—just because I asked it to be there."

She finished by pursing her lips, in an effort to avoid the corners of her mouth arching with the inertia of her petty boast.

"You're so clever," he penalized her in a suggesting intonation.

"Hey!" She gently slapped his belly. "See here what it looks like."

On the device screen now popped up the image of a tentacled robot—a squid and cargo ship hybrid.

"Yikes." Cole frowned. "I don't know whether to be disgusted or amazed. Is this for real?"

"Certainly." She allowed him one moment more to examine the image on the screen spinning around an axis. "They can penetrate, walk, or swim through all kinds of microscopic elements; they can hack and transport anything."

"Of course, only a teensy little bit in line with their teensy little size," he finished just to crack a joke.

The green-eyed young woman showed her milky white teeth. "Something like that. For instance, they can transport some kinds of stem cells, from which other cells can be built, and then later on build tissues. They can reconstruct molecules, structures, or elements in our body up to anything the savviest doctor may imagine. And they can do that by way of their processing power or artificial intelligence in the field of medical interventions."

"And where do they draw their energy from?"

"Energy and other substances they also get from the body. They know how and where from."

Cole was amazed, besieged by murky thoughts.

"How many of these tiny robots would you say I have in here?" She tapped the rectangular watch with her finger.

"Hmm, I could only guess...a million, a billion?"

"I think there's a bit more, but you're close. Just think of the processing power they have together, and the coordinated impact achieved when communicating one to the other and with the so-called central mini-system here." She tapped the watch again.

"I suppose they...hibernate when not at work," Cole ventured his opinion like a student paying attention to a lecture.

"You could say that."

They took a break, allowing the stillness of the forest to surround and seep inside their bodies anew. For a few moments, they got lost in each other's eyes. Suddenly, a high pitched, penetrating sound sprang from the dark forest. The Tentorian woman was startled, she frowned and stopped breathing. Cole squinted and pursed his lips, struggling not to laugh.

"Cricket," he pronounced professorially, "the technology of the 2000s: short, wide bodied insects with long antennae, large eyes, and jump-adapted hind legs with two elytra that rub together to give off piercing sounds."

"Hah. Wise guy." Her expression lightened.

They smiled at each other.

"Tell me more about the little robots. Considering their smallness, how come they had...the force to put the flesh of your leg back together?"

"They come in different sizes, not just nano. There are some much larger ones, which can physically reconstitute body parts, weld them together, and repair them. There are, however, also smaller ones—the pico sized, for instance. Picorobots are up to one thousand times smaller and have functions specific to their size." Cole listened carefully. "Particle interstices much smaller than cells are boulevards to them. They can control even the information transmitted at brain level, down to the neural sensors. Connected to the brain, they may increase one's intelligence level, calculation ability, be part and parcel of one's thinking—you cannot even imagine how well they can integrate."

Claire took a conspicuous pause. She ran her thin fingers over a freshly fallen birch leaf. "Did I bore you?" she asked.

The young man snorted loudly. "With that? Not a

chance! I realize how many things I didn't know."

"Good." She raised the wrist where her watch was secured. "Let's return to them. Now imagine me ordering them to change or reconstruct tissues and organs any way I like. I send them into the body and play the Creator game."

"This doesn't sound right."

Her green eyes approved. "I'm no expert in sciences, but believe me, with their size and some chemistry, medicine, molecular control, and a great deal of technology, they can do anything. You just give them a command and they would know how to translate it in medical terms; they know how to act."

"That's..." Cole stumbled. "You mean you can use them if one body part grows sick or old, and...how long do you live?"

"You can practically trick fate indefinitely and live forever."

One part of his mind spun while the other could only think of his disease. Without knowing why, he suddenly felt more relieved.

"That's truly a very cool thing!"

"It depends. Consider that everybody has access to such a thing—good and bad people alike. If they're able to control brain cells and the information travelling through you, they can control thoughts, feelings, pain, pleasure, what you see, what you hear. Sometimes you cannot even be sure you're experiencing the real thing because someone may take advantage without your knowledge or permission."

"Then certain practices should be forbidden. There should be some kind of firewalls or protection software, like a computer's antivirus."

"That's being done too, but as long as this technology's around someone may be able to create even better viruses."

"True," Cole murmured.

"Even more terribly, imagine an evil-minded person getting 'connected' to the entire population that owns a similar device. The consequences may be devastating. If you use such a technology only once, you are exposed. However, if you don't use it, you still live in a world that does. Someone may employ it against you like a weapon, whether you want it or not."

The young Tentorian sighed and placed her index finger to the wrist device.

"Even from this very device one can send a number of nanobots to wreak havoc in a defenseless person's body. It's a good thing that here, in a less interconnected world, they must have direct physical contact. Otherwise you'd have seen the Tentorian team committing real massacres." Dejected, she stopped short and looked up at the starry sky. "In my world," she said, dejected, "some people are willing to do bad things for power or just for entertainment. It's pointless to even make love for real—you can cheat your imagination by way of technology. You may have someone deeply fall for you by briefly applying a technical 'recipe'. You can trick perception to the point where you are no longer able to tell the difference between reality and fiction because this technology can work down to the very last detail. What you think you feel, see, or hear is what matters."

"This is an ethical issue. A big one."

Claire wavered. "Sadly, it is. Hundreds of years back, one could control the sex of children being born. One knew down to the smallest detail how healthy the newborn was going to be. Now we don't even need that anymore because we can practically change the children into what we want after birth. They are all perfect now."

She exhaled then lowered her voice and uttered, "What on earth is the point of all that? I don't get why that's not more than clear for some of the Tentorians."

"It means everything that defines the human nature, everything we call a soul, has been lost. That's the saddest of all."

"Even worse…" Claire observed despondently, "you can't even tell whether there's not some kind of machinery out there, some sort of intricate software that has everyone under its full control."

Cole stroked her hair tenderly, kissed her on the forehead, and hugged her. "It'll be fine." He decided to switch to a safer topic. "Tell me about invisibility."

The corners of Claire's lips arched again. "That's easier, and not so sad."

"So there's a better part to this future—uh…present," Cole tried to hit the mark.

"Yes. This technique was developed in a form close to what we now have in the early 2100s and was steadily improved since. It's a trick; it's a very thin extra layer, like a suit shaping itself in a matter of seconds over my body and clothes and concealing them."

Ever the technology buff, Cole turned his whole body towards her, all eyes and ears.

"This suit is made up of practically millions of…how should I call them? Tiny cameras and millions of…LEDs. Does the word LED mean anything to you?"

He smiled. "Yep, it comes from our age."

"Good! The cameras on one side of the body send the image to be displayed in real time to the LEDs on the other side. I don't know the suit-shaping mechanism very well, nor how the cameras and the LEDs are built, but what's sure is they're in sync with the LEDs to convey a flawless image behind me regardless of the onlooker's position. And lo, we eventually got this!"

She pressed the touch screen several times, and some moments later her right arm became invisible from elbow to fingertips.

Cole drew back, slightly scared, yet he couldn't look away. "Wow, this gives me the creeps!"

"Actually, what you see," Claire explained, showing off her wrist, "is the image behind the hand, captured, as I said, by mini-cameras then processed and retransmitted on the side you can see."

"Hmm...that's some wicked trick."

He studied her hand from various angles while she moved it.

"If you look carefully," he remarked, "you can see small shadows at the edges. They aren't easy to spot, but...well, it's not perfect."

She raised her chin to him. "Ha! Behold the technology critic! They are working on that too." She kissed him. "I can also turn it into a more advanced television screen to take the shape of my hand. I can project any image here."

She pressed the rectangular watch again a few times and a recording appeared in her palm of Cole sleeping in the woods. The images showed him sobering up, sensing her still invisible presence. He listened to himself mumbling then rubbing his eyes vigorously in an attempt to see better. The recording went on, shot from the Tentorian's perspective, while she was running through the woods. The last frame froze.

"It looked to me like there was something there...and you recorded me, too!" He eyed her tenderly.

"I couldn't help myself," she admitted, which made him smile. "You looked so...lost. And at the same time so likeable. I had to film you."

Cole was entranced by each sound undulating on the flawless line of her lips, the tip of her tongue shifting leisurely over her teeth with certain consonants.

"Maybe that's the best way I used this device camera so far," she concluded.

He felt thousands of butterflies in his stomach. "You're even sexier with all these gizmos on and after seeing that video, I guess it's safe to say you rather like me."

Claire blushed and stopped the projection. They took each other by the hand, poring over each other's lips, cheeks, eyes, foreheads, and lips again, saying no words. A few seconds elapsed before they broke apart to catch their breath and come back down to earth.

"And...what else does the cool girl from another world have in there?"

Claire feigned laughter.

"You can take that as a compliment," he tried to mend matters.

"Fine, fine..."

A child-like curiosity seethed inside the young Islander. "So?"

"All right. There is also the tiny flying devil; that's what I like to call it. Or the third eye."

Cole noticed the grey device Claire wore on her left wrist looked somewhat like a larger watch or a matchbox clasped by a rubber-like strap. Its touch screen had a mirror reflection, and thus he saw a few stars glimmering on its surface. The Tentorian woman pressed the device sideways and the thin tinsel-like screen withdrew completely as if vanishing. There were two compartments. She pointed to the square shaped left one, about three centimeters wide with a mini-drone inside. The right compartment contained a beautifully polished river stone-like black capsule with a T shaped red sign lit up.

"T?" he asked.

"Stands for Tentorian."

Claire took out the mini-drone and with a flick of her hand, threw it upwards. The mini-drone stopped in midair, hovering with a fan-like delicate buzzing sound.

"Huh?" Cole was enchanted. "That's a devil, all right!"

"It's a built-in camera mini-drone. It was especially designed for scouting missions, but it also has other options." Cole gaped inquisitively, begging for details which were long in coming. "Well...strong discharges of electric impulses, object emulation for the purpose of transportation or control...and so on."

"This *contraption*," he emphasized the last word, "is really cool!"

He reigned in his fascination at seeing the uncanny device.

"This small thing can carry up to 20 kilograms. Can you believe it?"

"Not really, but you're the owner; I should take your word for it."

"You should," she recommended with a smile.

His attention returned to the black capsule. "And I guess this tiny barrel is accommodating the nanobots you told me about."

"Yes, among other things. You're catching up quickly; you're not as daft as I thought."

"Heeey!" Cole lightly smacked her leg, taking up a serious

mien.

"I take my words back. You are a genius!" She kissed him on the forehead.

"You won't buy my forgiveness that easily, Miss!" His voice sounded momentous and patronizing on purpose.

She grinned.

"Nope."

Their peals of laughter resounded like music in the stillness of the night.

"I still cannot believe what I'm going through," Cole said after a while in a flat voice, eyes wandering towards the lake.

"Sadly, that is the dire reality."

A tree branch cracked in the forest, to the right side of the lake.

"Shh," Claire whispered tensely.

"That may be an animal. Or is it possible someone followed us here?" He also whispered his question.

"I don't know, but I'd rather find that out a little later."

She took her drone from the air in one move and put it back in its tiny chamber, which closed automatically. "Hide! I'll try to create a diversion."

A brief look right and left and she crouched down. She searched the dark forest, creased her forehead, and inhaled. After concentrating for half a second, she broke into a run through the trees, to the other side where the noise had originated, jumping over shrubs and dry leaves. A few moments later, something gave chase. She then sensed more and more shadows parallel to her. The increasingly alert rhythm of her breathing betrayed both her strain and fear. She had to find who or what was out there, so she moved her hand to the device to send the mini-drone scouting, but she didn't get the chance. A luminous electric impulse hit her back like an arrow. Her own speed threw her inert body into the rough branches of the trees and then to the ground; she grazed like a misfired shell.

She woke up motionless at the root of a tree. She tried to turn her head and look back, but it was weighted. Blood oozed from the scratches on her face. She raised her left hand to check her device when a shot popped in the quiet of the forest. Fire smacked into the middle of the 'watch,' the bullet piercing it completely along with the Tentorian woman's wrist. A sharp pang shrilled her voice into a grating yell. She did not have the strength to look back. Blood now poured from her hand too. Suddenly, she found herself exhausted. *So exhausted.* Meaningless images popped into her brain. Her eyes closed in spite of herself.

Cole was lying on his stomach between burdocks. He had been brought there by the sound of heavy boots treading the floor of the wooden cabin, rooting hastily around for something. He realized in anger how hard it was to breathe silently. *Stay in control and listen!* he thought, his face tense and his gaze alert. Someone was running through the forest, rushing fear through his body. He felt his heart beat so loudly.

"Claire?" he called out in a whisper.

A noise came from behind him and he turned. He succeeded in making out an object barreling down on his head before it struck him.

Chapter 29

Damage assessment was well underway at the spot where, just hours ago, the Island's monitoring and control center had been working. Ambulances sped off one after another, ferrying the wounded away to hospitals while the few servicemen still standing were rushing to the cargo trucks leaving that area.

An officer jogged up to the two, adjusted the cap on his dusty hair, and straightened his posture. "Mr. McCain, we have to get going!"

"We'll be riding in the ambulance; we still need some medical care."

The officer nodded slightly. "Understood!"

The Erudite stood still for a while, watching him running to a military vehicle, his mind wandering elsewhere. He breathed in the stifling air and rubbed his eyes as if trying to wake from a nightmare. Shortly afterwards, he turned to Drew and the doctor. "Let's go."

Drew was watching him in stupefaction while he climbed into the ambulance. She didn't move.

"Are you coming?" Chris asked.

She braced herself, climbed in after him, and put one chair between them as she sat down. No longer hesitating, she looked straight into his eyes and told him resolutely, "I've seen the mark on your neck."

"What?" he asked softly, taken aback.

Drew's face darkened. "Do you want me to say it again?"

The man talked to the nurse getting the ambulance ready for departure. "Can you excuse us for a little while, Miss?"

"Certainly."

They watched her step away, then Drew resumed unflinchingly, "That same mark you have at the base of your neck I saw a couple of hours ago on the Tentorian girl. You're a Tentorian, aren't you?" Chris avoided her gaze. "Please..." she pressed on, "you know what I'm talking about!"

"Drew, you have to trust me. Please!"

He stretched his arms to touch her, but the woman pushed them away and blurted in the same low tone, "Are you or aren't you a Tentorian?"

Although silent for a while, in the end he caved in. "Yes, I am—I *was*. I've nothing to do with this."

The lieutenant general sank her face into her hands. She sat motionless for a few moments then took her hands away from her face just to make herself heard. "Are you the only one among the Erudites? Are you the only one in the Island's leadership?"

"Yes. No."

The woman gestured her despair as if screaming but keeping her voice even. "Yes or no?"

Silence.

"Chris?"

"No. There's one more person in the leadership."

"Who?"

"I am sworn not to tell."

The woman turned around and bumped her head against the upper storage panel of the ambulance. "Damn it!" She felt a hand trying to touch her shoulder again. "Keep away from me," she whispered. Chris carefully withdrew his hand.

"Then what the hell is this? Why are they attacking our territory? How can I trust you? How can we—the whole nation—trust *you*?"

The man shook his head, unhappy with Drew's way of seeing things.

"Government people," she continued in a low tone but not mincing her words, "are talking round corners about us not knowing for sure how we got on this Island. They rightly fear they don't know everything."

"I knew nothing about what happened. You must trust me!" he repeated just before Arnar appeared by the ambulance door.

"Can I ride with you two?"

Drew watched Chris apprehensively then she looked back at Arnar. "Yes...yes of course. Hop in."

As he shifted into the vehicle, he threw each of them a searching look before sitting down between them. The Erudite glanced at Drew and then looked down. They all fell silent.

The ambulance left the Control Center heading for the Backup Control Center, scattering the hungry ravens by the unit's exit.

Chapter 30

A spider climbed down the red disheveled hair and crept on the rough cement to the center of the room. The young woman lying on the floor, her clothes muddied and ragged, still had fresh scratches and dried blood on her face. Her hand was completely covered in blood, but it had ceased flowing; it had clotted around the wound for some time now.

She opened her eyes, hardly seeing something through heavy lids. She dimly made out a metallic door and a gritty floor once sloppily cemented. The smell of mold and the coldness of the cement against her cheek woke her further. The first survival instinct made her raise her left hand to her face to check her portable device. It wasn't there anymore. She gnashed her teeth and moaned quietly, terrified at what she saw. She immediately felt all the pain in her hand and body, not knowing whether the pangs running through her were due to the wounds or the missing healing device. She couldn't remember the last time she'd taken it off. In its place, she now had only a nasty wound, outlined by a mix of dried blood and grit; her hand was outright numb from the elbow down.

She got up and let her eyes wander. Her body was so heavy—heavier than any time before; pain sapped her strength. She found herself in a deserted basement, lit by a bulb fed by two wires dangling from the ceiling. In one corner of the room there was an old closet. In another, Cole lay with a fairly large gash on his forehead.

She stumbled her way to him. "Cole," she called out in a whisper, but got no reaction. "Cole!" she raised her voice a fraction and shook him.

The Islander woke as if from a bad dream, frightened, shielding his face with his hands.

"It's me."

For an instant, he did not react, made no sound, and then he breathed a sigh of relief. "Oooh, I hate Tentorians!" he moaned with his hands still against his face. He sounded half hateful, half mournful. "Why do they love being such bastards and shitheads? Aren't they getting enough entertainment with their technology? What else do they want?"

Claire took one of his hands in hers. "Maybe it's because... they don't know what it is to be human."

She wished she could say more, maybe even apologize on behalf of the nation she was part of. Her cheek received the stroke of Cole's fingers like an absolution.

"Don't worry. It looks like you know all too well."

She liked that. She tried to put a smile on top of her pain-induced grimace; she moved her cheek closer to his palm, shut her eyes, and a few seconds later relished his touch. It made her forget her stinging pain.

"Thank you," Cole said after a while.

"What happened there...it's me who should apologize."

"It's not for yesterday I'm thanking you."

She hesitated. "What for then?"

"For that day I met you in the forest. You saved my life when I stopped the car and started chasing you."

"What are you talking about?"

"I was driving like hell, wishing to kill myself. I was flooring the gas, aiming to hit the car against a boulder, to end up in a ditch or something like that. I'm going to die anyway, no matter how this story ends." Claire looked him over in surprise. "A few days ago, I was diagnosed with a rare type of cancer. I was told I had less than a year to live...and that soon I was going to be progressively affected by the disease and, at a later stage, I'd...be paralyzed." His throat turned heavy. He hardly breathed. "I don't want to live like that. Not even for a week. I'd rather die." He felt relieved. "Everything that had brought me here next to you is this disease." Now he seemed to hate it less. From that moment on, fate could have carried him anywhere. *That's odd*, he thought. He felt fulfilled dispelling some of the haunting thoughts the disease had caused in favor of something much more complex. His fate had taken an unexpected turn. The present time, family, nation, the Island—they all sounded different now.

Baffled, Claire ran her eyes over his face then looked down to the floor. She wished now more than ever she had that tiny barrel to cure him, *but would he accept?* Cole's voice brought her back into the cold room.

"Some time ago I thought I was invincible. But I am...nothing."

Claire caressed his cheek. "You are the best thing that's happened to me. You are alive and know how to live better than anyone else I know." Her words lit up Cole's face. "Do you fear dying?"

"Probably not as much as I fear eternal life, but I don't want to die now—by a wretched cancer!"

Claire hesitated. "You know, it doesn't have to be that way. You can be healed with the technology we have—"

The remote laughter of a man interrupted her. It came from somewhere behind the door and sounded as if it was travelling from the end of a hall. Again, the same laughter, then two people talking. They could hardly hear them, but the slightly staccato Mandarin accent was unmistakable.

"...You owe me a beer," came through.

They froze, listening intently. It was hard to make out much, but they were able to decipher a trivial discussion on who was the best boozer. Their steps went upstairs. A door, probably somewhere at the end of the hall, slammed shut, and they looked at each other, dumbfounded.

Claire's mind suddenly returned to her last statement. She wanted to understand more about the danger awaiting the man she had opened her very soul to. *Disease?* For long that word had not been used in Tentoria. *Still, it's so widespread here.* It was so tempting for her to resume the conversation. The thrill of playing God took hold of her. For a brief moment she saw herself sitting before a kids' puzzle she could crack at any time. *Can it be so simple? And what if it's not? Who am I to try such an experiment? On a real human, an Islander, the man that I...fell for. And what if I fail?* That last thought stopped her breathing short.

Cole broke the silence. "Where on earth are we?"

The Tentorian put off answering. She wished not to spoil the moment. *We'll have time to broach this when all is finished—if it's finished. If we make it out alive.* She swallowed the dryness in her throat. "I suspect we're in the basement of our Island base, in a disused power station."

"Oooh, wonderful! I'll get to meet all your friends now."

"C'mon, shut up. Don't be a jerk."

Cole raised his palms in the air and bowed his head.

"I miss my bracelet," she said, looking at her left hand again. Pain made her clench her teeth.

"We must get the hell out of this basement! What do you

think will they do to us?"

Claire snorted and shook herself. "Honestly, I don't know and I don't want to find out. I must be a threat to them. I don't even know if we can get out of here."

Cole checked the door and walked around the room, feeling walls.

"So...we're stranded here." He opened the metallic closet in the corner of the room and rooted around. It was full of farming utensils and fertilizer. He started counting by throwing them down on the floor. "Brushes, hoe, saltpeter...hmm, fertilizer, a lawn trimmer...with a gasoline engine!" His voice undulated with pleasure. "And many paint cans. I think I have an idea!"

Chapter 31

Trucks ferrying troops rolled off the forest road. First, they entered a junction arm no more than a hundred meters long, then fanned out onto a wide lawn hemmed in by tall firs and spruces. They were followed by heavy weapons provided armored vehicles and the ambulance carrying Chris, Arnar, and Drew. A concrete fence ran along the entire area while at the entrance the large board attached to the post by the two metallic gates warned in capital letters:

GOVERNMENT PROPERTY!

NO TRESPASSING

BEYOND THIS POINT!

And below, in small letters:

Please report on the spot any unauthorized

presence in this area to the Government

Inspector you are assigned to!

If you fail to comply with this obligation, you are in violation of Law 24/1968, which is a first-degree offence.

The Backup Center was a smaller but well run military base. Three long ground floor buildings sprawled on both sides and behind the main building. Asphalted alleys delimited through white borders of the neatly mowed lawn between the buildings. Arnar was surprised to see the parking lot at the center's entrance so overcrowded. He noticed it hadn't been designed to accommodate so many vehicles. He checked the proper position of the guards and the heavy weapons in the defense positions strategically set on the four cardinal points. Everything was according to the instructions.

In the corridor of the main building, the officers met them, standing at attention and saluting in perfect sync like the servicemen manning the entrance of the garrison had when their ambulance rolled by the gate. Contrary to her habit, Drew did not smile at them when she entered, nor did she take time to admire the mountain landscapes painted on the walls or the sculpted obsidian half-pillars bedecking them. Her limp leg hurt enough to push every smile away. Chris didn't seem as curious as usual either.

He drew close to one of the officers and asked formally, "I need the Backup Center operational status. Who's monitoring the Island?"

"In the monitoring room we have a minimum presence of three Erudites and five assistants, appointed 24/7, Mr. McCain. There is no unusual activity outside or around the shield at this time."

He noticed the officer hardly refrained to react when he took in the sling immobilizing his arm, but he kept talking nevertheless.

"Good. We'll have a meeting as soon as everybody's ready."

"They've all been alerted, sir. The Governor is due to arrive too. The others are on the way or are going to connect to us via teleconference. The other six Erudites will specifically not be present in the Center at the same time, keeping with the security protocol."

"Very well. We're maintaining that protocol. We're

---

heading straight to the conference room; we'll be waiting for them there."

"Understood, sir!"

Arnar intervened, "Any idea where Mr. Cole Williams and Martin may be?"

"Martin..." Drew said in a small voice, "didn't make it."

"Damn! And Cole?"

"I believe he saved his skin along with the Tentorian girl." Chris looked inquisitively. "Yes, the girl saved him—she saved us both. I believe they got away, but we don't know where they are."

Chris' healthy hand went to his chin. "Interesting. Very interesting. At least it seems the girl is on our side."

Chapter 32

Hugh gulped down a sandwich in the main room of the Tentorian base.

"Theoretically," he said to one of the hosts, "I shall enjoy this grub just for being natural on the Island of 2000s. But I'll be damned if it doesn't start to taste funny to me; it tastes chemical and, I dunno, like it's missing some ingredients."

Osman admonished him in a deep voice, "So why do you keep eating sandwiches? Since coming to the Island that's all you eat." He didn't look at him at all. He just kept on clenching a rubber ring and admiring his arm straining with each grip. "Suddenly you don't like it no more!"

Hugh did not bother to reply but rolled his eyes.

"Talk to the kitchen!" a Ragon suggested in a broken accent.

"You see," Hugh answered, chewing, "that's the problem here with you; that I have to talk to the kitchen when things could be solved so much easier by changing a thought or a sense of perception. All I need to do is wish it has the ideal taste and there you are: the perfect sandwich!"

"Then do it and cease complaining! One thousand!" the hulk finished counting his rubber ring practice.

Hugh's loud disapproving burp made the Asian guy burst into a stupid laugh. None of the others budged.

"I don't get how you guys put up with this disgusting life," Hugh insisted, "when just a shred of technology is enough to turn everything into a dream." He swiveled in his chair to watch a series of data scrolling on a monitor but quickly resumed his monologue directed at the Asian man. "You know, my friend, you can simulate any dream your heart desires to make everything look damned real. I was once the President of the world!" After saying that, he burst into a moronic laugh.

"And the world came to nothing the next day," Chan butted in.

Hugh gave him a bored look, took another bite, went back to the monitor, and cried out through more chewing, "Snap! Boss, I think I came across a list of important addresses! I still don't get whether any of them belong to the Erudites or which ones."

Kaligor's mouth widened. "Good! Send them to the base for analysis. They can check them faster. If they belong to the Erudites, we'll hunt them down one by one."

"Done! In the meantime, let's have a word with our Island boy fooling around with Tentorian girls. With as long as he was in the Command Center, he must know something."

Kaligor signaled Hoshito to handle that, and the latter wasted no time. He went to a drawer and took out a case of lances, tourniquets, and pliers of all sizes, which he opened leisurely on the table.

"Can I help you with this?"

"Hmm," Kaligor reacted, "you people are so backward here. There are less painful methods in my world. Why should we make the guy suffer?"

Hoshito flexed his voice. "Don't worry, it'll be my pleasure!"

"If you must." The Tentorian leader let out a sardonic

laugh.

All the men in the room followed suit. He stopped abruptly and ordered one of Hoshito's subordinates, "Bring that lousy primitive over here!"

"The floozy too?"

"I think not. We don't need her services any longer. She's a traitor; get rid of her."

He lowered his chin as if saddened by the decision so that the Asian man kept his eyes on him and waited.

"Now!" Kaligor roared.

Brought back to reality, the Ragon stood at attention and took his weapon out of its holster.

"You there: you're coming with me!" he ordered another man and they both left the room.

A hinge creaked and the door to the basement opened. The two Ragons stepped into a corridor dimly lit by a yellow bulb and slammed the door behind them. A sharp solvent odor hit them as soon as they entered. One crinkled his wrinkled nose in a more horrid visage than usual. The other, puny and with a head wide enough to see his sideburns face-on furrowed his eyebrows. The corridor led to just one door, which opened to the basement room where Cole and Claire were kept under lock. They could see the big padlock keeping the door shut, still untouched, but something had changed in the corridor. Two steps later, they gave it a more careful look over: down on the floor, on the side from the locked room, a greenish liquid reflected the pale light. Edginess took over their faces. They cocked their pistols and pointed them ahead, ready to shoot. They stepped warily halfway through the hall, and once they neared the liquid, the punier and the higher ranked of them carefully touched a finger to it and smelled the substance.

"Gasoline, paint—what shit is this?" He wiped his finger on his pants, got a good grip on his weapon, and pointed it at the locked door. "Do you wanna mess with us?" he barked at the room in broken English.

No answer came. The two looked at each other, visibly tense, and started cautiously through the sticky liquid. The little one stopped one meter from the door and aimed at it, ready to pull the trigger. He signaled to his subordinate, who drew close, took out a key, and slipped it carefully into the lock with his left hand. His other hand was on the gun and one of his cheeks twitched with excitement when he turned the key slowly. He looked back one more time, making sure he had cover, then lightly pushed the door so it was partly open. There was no sign of anyone inside.

The two stared at each other, at a loss.

The noise of an engine cut through the silence without warning. The lawn trimmer in Cole's hand showed up from behind the door at ground level with sparks shooting from it. The mixture of gasoline, paint, and saltpeter caught fire at once. Little seeped into the room, most of it having been carefully shoved into the hall from under the door. After Cole jerked the door back, the hallway went up in flames along with the feet of the two Asian men, the thick smoke of the burned saltpeter rushing through the corridor. Terrified, the little superior fired two shots at the door then both began to draw back.

"Bastards!" he yelled.

The same door suddenly opened and Cole ran through the smoke, a shovel in his hand and a rag over his nose and mouth. A shot, discharged instinctively from the ugly subordinate's weapon, whizzed only a few centimeters from Cole's hip. The very next moment Cole struck the Ragon's head with the shovel and knocked him over into the fire. Cole vanished into the smoke.

On the other side of the building, in the main working room, a third gunshot was heard. Kaligor frowned.

"What on earth are those two doing there, killing them both? Hugh, go and check!"

"Okay, boss!" And out he went.

The puny superior had managed to wriggle himself out of the fire. The entire corridor was enveloped in smoke; he could barely see half a meter ahead. He coughed in panic, tightly gripping the weapon and pointing it in the direction he thought the basement room was located. He sensed something behind him and turned abruptly; then he spotted something from the corner of his eye and turned again, quivering with fear. He realized shortly he could no longer find the exit.

"I'll have your skin grilled and enjoy it with salt, you filthy bastards!" He spat the words in his peculiar English. Then he coughed hard.

From behind, a rake wedged itself deep into his throat, and, half paralyzed, he wanted to kiss the ground at once.

Claire tore the weapon from his hand, but the puny guy let out a cry of despair as he grasped her by the wrist. In the end, his hands wound around her neck.

The Tentorian woman dropped the weapon. Overcome by the terrible strength, a tear ran down her cheek. Then the shovel smacked the Ragon right on the crown of his head and knocked him flat.

Cole emerged from the fire, shovel in hand. "Are you in one piece?" No sound came from Claire's mouth. He let the shovel fall to the ground and leaned over her. "Hey, are you okay?"

A coughing fit covered her throttled voice as she struggled to get up. "I'm... trying..."

Footfalls from the other side of the door interrupted her.

He pointed to part of the wall beside the door, about to swing open any moment now. "Over here!" Cole grabbed her hand and drew her to him.

The two hardly breathed. There was no other way out. No noise from the other side, and the door didn't open. In a desperate move, Cole picked up the shovel and came back to Claire. The door opened.

"What...?" The corridor filled with smoke, to the surprise of the Tentorian who'd just entered.

Claire's eyes closed in fear. She made out Hugh's voice, and stories about him flashed through her mind. When he first joined the team, he was introduced as the robot-like thinking man, the Tentorian that went through way too many "alterations"—so many that he even managed to survive for a period without a heart. During the war, he was many times crippled but making it through anyway. *That's our end!* The thought made her squeeze Cole's hand.

Cole sensed her fear and tightened his grip around the shovel. He was ready to wage a fight. Never-ending moments went by and still no sound came from behind the open door. Hugh was up to something.

Out of nowhere, the cold buzz of a mini-drone was heard. Claire had always loved that sound but now it spelled death to her. The drone flew forth into the corridor; it went off without "looking" back, then vanished, engulfed by the smoke. Silence returned. Their hearts beat hard enough to rip out of the chests they struggled behind.

The smoke in front of them cleared, blown away by the propellers of the mini-drone. It was one meter away; it seemed Hugh could see them now.

"Hoooo-ha...get out of there, kiddies! What are you doing with that shovel, you backward little boy?"

The Islander was almost suffocated by hatred. Although a door stood between them, virtual lines superposed the image running across Hugh's red eye lens, showing him the angle between the drone and Cole's hand gripping the shovel. Another imaginary line set out from his weapon, calculating possible bullets ricocheting off the door towards the shovel's virtual shape. It was exactly what Hugh needed. One shot fired through the wooden door into the shovel's handle sufficed, and the implement fell to the ground. They held each other like two death row inmates.

With his weapon aimed at Cole, Hugh snatched the shovel from the floor. "What did you want to do with this, smarty-pants, hit me? You, hit me? Huh, Island boy!"

Cole sized him up, while Claire pulled him to her. He stood in the open before Hugh's weapon but he couldn't care less. The shovel hit him hard on the head and he slipped out of Claire's tense arms. His eyelashes came together, and he went away, beyond death. Sun beamed its shining rays through the swaying trees, his chum Jimmy was laughing at him from a passing kart, his mom served him the flapjacks he liked most, his brother was running through the house with a model boat while his father watched him tenderly. Claire looked into his eyes and kissed him ardently. And she shouted for him. Her yell woke him from the dead. *I cannot open my lids...my body is paralyzed*. He struggled hard to open an eye wide enough to hazily make out Hugh two meters away with a hand stuck into Claire's red hair and the barrel of his gun propped under her chin.

"I'm sorry. I really liked you." He licked her cheek. "All the time I kept thinking how to have you."

"Go on, kill me," she goaded, disgusted, "you stinking soulless piece of garbage! You should have died in the war! You are the exact opposite of a human and you got everything wrong about our meaning here on this planet."

"Good. It seems we understand each other. Now you have to die and the Island boy comes with me for a little chat." Claire shut her eyes, waiting for the liberating bullet. "But first, I wanna have you. Can we do it quietly please?"

The girl felt tears welling in her eyes. She squeezed them and the moisture ran down her cheeks. *Stop, keep your head clear!* she told herself and put all her pain away. *I can take him out*. She opened her eyes and let Hugh relish their vibrant green closer than ever before.

"If you promise to let him live," she said, "you'll enjoy it, too. He knows nothing."

The Tentorian grinned. "Hmmm...yes, I promise."

He pulled his hand out of her hair and slid the gun down her body. First, he dragged it over the buttons of her shirt, blackened by smoke and mud, then pressed it with all his might against the studs of her jeans, which began to slip down on their own. Claire followed the weapon's descent, concealing her terror. Taking advantage of Hugh's lack of attention, she pushed the gun aside with a simple gesture.

When outside the weapon's range, she jammed her knee violently between the Tentorian's legs.

He groaned in a hollow voice and was suddenly only able to crouch. That was when another blow of the shovel struck him.

Cole held the implement in a white-knuckled grip, watching him breathing. Before long, he would come around, so without wasting any more time, he hit him once again in the head, and again, and again. A minute later, a pool of blood spread in front of him.

"I must borrow this for a little while," Claire spoke to Hugh's body. "I don't think you will need it anymore."

Shortly afterwards, shivering with hate, she held the capsule from his squashed head. Then she took off his hand device and positioned it with difficulty, now drained of all strength, at her limp hand. She pressed sideways once to take out the display and put the pod into its compartment; the mini-drone also came back to the device. After pressing the screen several more times, she heaved a sigh. Her wounds began to heal. "I've missed this!" She leaned back, eyes closed, like a junkie getting his long-awaited dose.

When her eyes suddenly opened, she uttered, "Let's go. We have no time to lose!"

Cole raised his palms into the air. "I'm fine, thanks!" He followed her. "No, no...don't worry!"

They crossed the whole length of the building. They were still underground so they had to climb the stairs to level zero step by step, they could increasingly make out the Tentorians and their allies' voices.

Claire drew close to his ear and whispered, "The only passageway we can walk through to the exit is past their room. There's another passageway leading to a hall, but as many as a hundred people may be there. It's way more dangerous."

"Just tell me there's another way."

The Islander disliked the denial he received. Only the slightly ajar door at the end of the stairway stood between them and that passageway. He cast an eye through the crack of the door and withdrew his head at once. He pressed his body against the wall.

"It's difficult, if not impossible," he murmured.

The passageway leading to the exit stood about two meters wide and had one room on the right side with a wide open door: the main office all the Tentorians and their high ranking allies gathered. From his position, Cole stole a glance and saw two men with dragon tattoos on their necks standing in the doorway, chatting and smoking.

"There are two Ragons in the passageway," he whispered. "What should we do?"

"Now it's my turn," Claire said. "Let's try the 2500's way!"

The young man frowned then smirked. "Okay, your turn."

She kissed him quickly. "Don't forget that I love you."

"Saying it now doesn't sound right to me."

"Let me put it another way: why don't you pray to...your Governor and let's just go through this miserable corridor undetected." She threw a swift look through the crack in the door before pressing the device twice. "Give me your hand!"

Claire grabbed his left hand with her right and inched through the door. Her left hand turned slightly invisible, then her body, her right hand and his left hand. *What?* Cole's lips hardly formed the question.

"We must find that darn place!" Kaligor's unmistakable voice bellowed from the main office.

Claire could also make out Chan's voice, seemingly trying to simmer down the leader but failed to understand one single word.

"At least we have all the Erudites' addresses," he said. "If we get rid of them, there won't be anyone left to control the Island shield so effectively. From then on it would be only a matter of time before we took out the shield."

Kaligor's blunt wheezy pitch charged, "But I don't have time!" He mused a while, looking down to the floor, and in the end he agreed. "Still...I don't think it's a bad idea. Let's see what our primitive gent knows! Are they bringing him over here or not?"

Claire and Cole were no more than dim outlines walking the corridor. The lighting was a stroke of luck: a pale yellow neon lamp. The hum of voices in the room was also helpful. Passing the office door, they slowed down and glided painstakingly to the exit, almost one with the opposite wall.

One of the two allies standing in the doorway startled. He turned towards them and took a deep breath. The escapees froze. They were facing the enemy, now looking their way. Claire gripped Cole's hand and pointed her invisible weapon at the Asian man's head. A moment later, he turned his eyes to the basement door, saw it open, and took another heavy breath. Then he looked at the other end of the corridor, towards the building's way out, and then returned his attention to the basement.

"You smell something?" he asked.

The other inhaled through his flared nostrils. "Yup. Paint...gasoline."

Driven by curiosity, he made for the stairs, passing inches away from the Tentorian girl's pistol. She kept her focus on him for another five meters. Claire was trapped in her own hatred. She would have targeted him on and on if not woken up by Cole's hand gently tapping her on the back. They had to resume their journey towards the exit.

"Scumbags!" came the ally's baffled shout from the basement.

Claire stilled with her hand on the exit door handle when those in the room rushed out of their office, loading their weapons and surging down to the basement. At that very second, they were out, breathing the fresh air.

The purple twilight stole past the few trucks aligned in the makeshift parking lot. A gust of wind coming from the same direction brought a weak whiff of sulfur from a spring nearby. Claire hated it from the very first day they had set up base there, but now it seemed like the finest smell she had ever experienced.

Once the invisibility cloak started pulling off, they looked for a getaway vehicle. A few cars and motorcycles already beckoned them.

Cole gave them a thorough look over. "I think I prefer..." He stopped at a garage taken by a vintage sports car. *From the times they were still building good engines,* he thought as he neared. "That!" He jumped in, followed by Claire. "The key's in the sun shade. Like in the good movies!"

The threatening sound of the powerful engine tore through the silence reigning over the base. Those inside turned their eyes to the way out while two of them, closer by, dashed to the door.

"Ahhhhh," Kaligor howled, "that's my best car!"

He shut his eyes and kicked the wall as hard as possible. After briefly assessing the situation, he reached two conclusions: from where they were now they could not catch up with the fugitives, and the hole he made in the wall had wedged his boot inside.

The redhead pressed the device touch screen in a hurry. "Wait a moment!"

"What are we waiting for?" Cole hastened.

"Let's do a top ten of the engines inside the yard." And the mini-drone set out on a brief assessing tour.

"Are you kidding?"

"Not at all." The pictures of two motorcycles flashed on the screen. She took her weapon out the car window and fired several shots at them. "Now we have the fastest one. Step on it!"

A flat-out start glued them to their seats, and the sports car became lost into a cloud of dust.

"Yes!" Cole shouted as he floored the gas to freedom.

Chapter 33

"You must follow my instructions strictly," Chris demanded.

"We're listening," Cole confirmed.

Although nobody had tailed them, the gas station and attached motel was the first stop they dared make on their way to the capital. They managed to contact the Governmental Inspectors and later Chris on the phone.

"First of all, stay off the road," the Erudite went on.

"Okay, understood."

"We'll send men to pick you up from Central Park by the big clock. Be there one hour from now. Keep your heads low! We'll find you."

"Okay."

"Don't talk to anyone. Don't stray off your path!"

"Understood."

"The girl must get rid of any device the Tentorians might use to track her."

Almost stuck to the receiver, Claire's eyes widened. "Let me talk to him, please!" Cole handed her the phone. "Hey," she said in the receiver, "I can't let this device go—not now when things are out of control." She hesitated. "That includes you!"

"Are you using it for communication?" came Chris's measured voice.

"Among other things."

"They will track you."

"For the time being, I unhooked it from any connections to our temporary base or other devices."

"They will find a way eventually."

The young woman leaned hard against the phone booth window. Lost in thought, she breathed in the smell of the freshly painted wooden frame. Although underneath the paint she could see the wood was affected by time, she thought the new painting gave the booth a fresh look. She came back on the phone right before the Erudite's patience ran low.

"Not if you send me a good program. Something to block any communications from outside."

The seconds of stillness were stressed by the Erudite's deep breathing.

"Hey, are you still there?" Claire rushed him.

"Yes."

"And?"

"I agree. I need more data on your device."

"Good. What do I do?"

"Jot down this Internet address and connect to it through a computer in no more than five minutes. I'll see then what we can come up with."

"Hey," Claire added, "take care in what you send me. I'm trusting you."

"You have no choice. By the way, you'll have to leave the place you are now as soon as possible."

"I know."

"And get rid of the car you took."

Cole's lips took on the shape of a conspicuous "*Damn!*".

Two minutes later, the two entered the motel. A chubby youngster was sleeping in an armchair behind the check-in counter. From a carefully organized shelf, the picture of the

Governor smiled down at them, encased in a silver frame. Almost all the keys were in their expected place, hanging from a wooden panel; hence Cole reasoning that the motel was empty. He squinted and cleared his throat noisily.

"Yes...yes," the lad started groggily, "you want a room!"

"No, we don't want a room. We'd like to use the Internet for a few minutes," Cole said kindly and pointed at the computer in the corner of the tiny lobby.

The boy rubbed his eyes, still drowsy. "The Internet..." he repeated. He gave a shy smile to Claire, glanced at their grungy clothes, and puffed out his chin and nostrils. He carried on some seconds later: "...is only for those lodged here."

"And what can we do about it?"

"Well, the easiest thing would be for you to rent a room for one night; I'll put your personal data on record and the computer is yours."

"I have no documents on me..."

Alarmed, the chubby youngster drew back as if witnessing a crime and sharpened his voice in revolt. "That's against the Code!"

"And I have no money to pay for a room either," Cole added.

The plump lad's expression turned stolid. "I cannot help you," he finished drily. "Anything else I can do for you?" He did not wait for an answer. "If not, I'd like to go back to my pleasant dream."

"No. I only want to use the Internet and it is a very important matter...please."

The failed receptionist plucked up his courage and puffed up like a turkey. "Let me explain—perhaps you don't get it: without an identity document you cannot even identify yourself to use the Internet, as both of you well know, I hope..." He glanced at Claire, drew a breath, and took an authoritative stance. "The Constitutional Governance Code—more specifically in article 204 of 1990, if I'm not mistaken—decrees that any use of the Internet must be assigned to an identified person. I-den-ti-fied," he spelled out with gusto. "And you may also be aware that, in accordance with Decree number 11 on 1991, Governmental Institutions have the right to monitor any use thereof. And guess what? Governmental Inspectors put the said Decree to extremely good use and visit us on a monthly basis. Welcome to Planet Earth. *Duhhhh!*"

The chubby kid, pleased with his thorough explanation, put on an idiotic grin. "Is that clear to you now?" He once again waited for no answer. "If yes, is there anything else you want?"

Cole was close to flying off the handle. Claire pushed him delicately to one side, undulated her way closer to the counter, and bit her lower lip incitingly. "Look here...Chanté," she said, reading his name on the badge. The boy gave her an awkward smile, then resumed his manly stance and acted as if paying attention. "Me and my friend would like to use the Internet for no more than five minutes. We are kind-hearted and civilized people, and that's the only reason we ask nicely. Otherwise—and you can take my word for it—we could use it without asking for your approval." The plump fellow raised an eyebrow, but then smiled again. "Now, you see, I care about my friend very much and I appreciate him for the civilized manner he tried to negotiate this issue with you." The Tentorian woman's hand put the weapon down on the counter in full view. "But, honestly, we are running out of time and—if at all possible and wishing your humble life doesn't come to an end this day—I would like you to ask my friend nicely to use your own Internet account and give him a hand getting connected."

Chanté tightened his lips to keep them from trembling and swallowed hard. Then he tried to crack another smile. "Yes, sure, definitely!"

After few minutes online, Claire read on the screen, "Application downloaded. Wonderful!"

"Perfect, let's go!" Cole said.

The redhead went back to the lost receptionist and kissed him on the forehead. "You see? It wasn't that hard. By the way, in accordance with article 97 of 1930," she taunted him, "you are under obligation to report the incident at once to the Governmental Inspectors. Tell them we send our greetings."

Cole also drew close, just one step away from him, and smirked. "And tell them to put this Internet use on Chris McCain's tab."

The joke was lost on Chanté. He stood frozen next to the computer, gaping at the two people heading for the exit.

"And one more thing," Cole addressed him from the doorway, "as far as I know, we need to comply with the Government's requirements to the letter, right?"

"Right."

"Well, the Big Boss with a capital B has ordered me explicitly to borrow another car." He gave Claire a solemn expression. "Isn't that so?"

"Exactly." She used the same tone.

"Mmm...tell me, Chanté, that red car outside—a beauty with a capital B—is it yours?"

"Who else's?" Claire butted in. "You think there's anyone

around checking in at this dump?"

The youngster stood agape, caught between stupor and his failed attempt to retort, and puzzled by their dialogue.

"You know," Cole said, "my friend Jimmy wants to have a dead replica of that, save a way sadder color than this cool red." He winked at Chanté, who stood dumb like a wax statue. The door closed with a dry noise behind them.

"Listen," Claire said as Cole slipped behind the wheel, "what about telling him he can have the supercar we're leaving?"

"Mmm...nope!"

A red car rolled closer to the corner of Central Park. It slowed down, and its lights went out. In the stillness of the night, the only thing that could be heard were the mellow purr of the engine and the nipping sound of tiny gravel crushed under its wheels. The car came to a halt. After a quick check of the deserted street, Cole and Claire summoned the courage to get out of the vehicle.

The park alley was dimly lit by increasingly sparser lampposts. As they advanced, Claire found the alley more and more bleak.

A beggar sprawled on a bench caught their eyes. Although he looked casual, the two of them watched as he reached into his breast pocket. He watched them listlessly through one half-closed eye, took out a liquor flask, and threw it back. Claire was the first to release the air she had kept anxiously in her lungs. They walked away carefully, and soon focused on the darkened alley. The trees' contorted shadows danced in the grey-yellowish radiation of the pale bulbs, painfully swirling through their optic nerves. They crossed a small footbridge; one look behind them and they made sure the alley was empty. Dead ahead there was the clock, a glowing cube on a pole whose hands ticked almost past the hour mark since they'd talked with Chris.

Suddenly, a pungent smell invaded their nostrils. Claire glanced over her shoulder; the beggar was one meter away, ragged and with jagged shadows sprawled all over his face. She pushed Cole hard and pulled out her gun, aiming at the intruder.

"Poor me!" the drunk got scared and hid his head between his elbows. "Can you spare a penny, please?"

"Scram!" Cole snapped at him in a whisper. "You scared the pants off me, man!"

"Wretched bastard!" Claire added.

She stood still, pointing her gun at him until the man got lost in the dark, running like hell on the park's twisted alleyways.

"Ugh!" breathed Cole. "I'm going to die of a heart attack before anything else." He wiped the sweat off his brow.

"It's me who did most of the scaring. I'm sorry! When you're coming from a world where danger lurks at any step, any face may be hiding a monster."

"It's fine; you did right. We can never know who is what." He turned to the clock, gesturing with his chin. "Let's wait there behind those shrubs."

"I agree."

They went round the timepiece and sat on the grass,

raking out the surroundings for a while.

A man in a military uniform ran to the clock and set his machine gun in firing position. Another one showed up and installed himself similarly, back to back with the first. Three more were already strategically placed at the corners of the alley; another one had settled on the footbridge.

"Psst!" came from behind them.

The young Tentorian put her hand to her heart and peered back, intrigued. "Please don't do that again!"

The man, armed to the teeth, looked like he hadn't heard her. "Follow me."

They complied and soon fell into step with the soldier as one by one the Special Forces men popped up from side alleys and between trees to regroup behind them.

Three black cars waited for them in the street. They got into the middle one, accompanied by a few members of the Special Troops, and set off in convoy. Through the dark window, Claire noticed an old woman closing the shutters in a hurry. She raised her cheekbones and rolled her eyes as if stressing she couldn't care less about what was going on in front of her house. The young woman smiled. She enjoyed this all-natural behavior of the Island people; even the weird ones.

A few turns, several more streets, and the speed increased.

"We got on the highway," came from one of the soldiers' radios. *"We confirm there's nobody tailing us."*

"Good. We'll be waiting for you at the Center."

The cars kicked up dust by the sign at the Backup Command Center entrance. *"Going past this point is strictly forbidden..."* Cole read silently. *As if this is the first forbidden point I've ever entered.* Passing the barrier, they received the guards' salutes.

Claire found the unit similar to the first Center, but it encompassed a smaller area with lower buildings and a yard too narrow to accommodate so many pieces of heavy artillery or defense posts needed to cope with the situation.

Servicemen scurried between buildings or the manned security posts while the two of them were escorted to the main building. They entered the corridor and stopped in front of a door that read "Deputy General".

The serviceman straightened his back, pulled his waistcoat down in an attempt to line it up perfectly parallel to his belt, and knocked on the door. "They're here, ma'am."

"Show them in please!"

"Andreea Petrova," she introduced herself politely, holding her hand out to the young Tentorian woman. I am the Deputy General of the House of Defense.

They shook hands. "Claire."

Although slightly taller, Drew did her best not to appear as though she was looking down on her. She bowed her head respectfully, letting gratitude show in her eyes, and added, "First of all, I thank you."

Claire quickly understood that she was talking about their first encounter. "You're welcome."

She then spoke to Cole. "We've met before."

He bowed his head in salute. *You are my new family of sorrow*, he thought mournfully.

"Thank you. You're dismissed," Drew said to the officer. Then she turned her attention back to them. "We're happy to have you here." She swiftly examined the scratches on Cole's neck and hand as well as the contusion on his head. "You probably need medical care."

"There's no need; I'm okay. I'll die soon anyway. Why make a fuss?" he threw in with irony, "I think a hot shower and some new clothes would do us a lot of good though."

Claire cast a furtive look to her wristband and wanted to say something, but hesitated.

Drew was also looking down at the impeccably military style polished wooden floor, musing. She didn't want to say she'd checked Cole's file. She then turned to face Claire, giving her a brief head to toe once over.

"And you..." She stared at her left arm. "Are you okay?"

There was dried blood and no visible wounds, yet the dirt and the burn marks still told the tale of her last few hours. For all her damaged clothes, the redhead raised her arms in a demonstrative gesture while smiling awkwardly. "Like new."

"I don't want to know," Drew concluded. "Let me show you to your rooms! You'll probably be staying here for a few days until things calm down. I wish you could choose between staying here or not, but unfortunately, I don't think there's a safer place. I suspect you haven't remained on the best of terms with the Tentorians." She looked at Claire. "I mean those on the Island."

Claire blinked her confirmation.

Once they reached the military dorm buildings, the deputy general showed them the rooms.

They'd walked one hundred meters from the main building, and on their way, Claire admired the contrast between the asphalted alleys, their freshly painted white curbs, and the natural green of the turf on which they tread. In Tentoria, none of these colors would have been natural.

"I'll send somebody to bring you several changes of plain clothes. If you're lucky, you may even find something you like. Anything else you need, use the room phone. Don't fight over the rooms," Drew joked. "They're both the same."

Cole was pleased by the commiseration in her voice.

"I've started getting used to military lodgings," he said, throwing a glance toward the cold corridor awash in shades of grey and crammed with dozens of dormitory doors.

The deputy general let the remark slide with a slight bow and tactful smile. Without wasting any more time, she turned around and started down the corridor.

"Thank you, Miss Petrova!" Claire did her best to finish in a warmer note. The host stopped and turned her head so Claire could just make out her closed eyes. "Call me Drew...and you are *very* welcome."

Chapter 34

Crisis meetings were held continuously, and the boardroom felt more crowded than ever to the attending Heads, generals, and Erudites. Tension was in the air while the hard working brains gave off heat, mist floating over the bulbs in the crystal chandelier. The glistening candelabrum commanded from high above the center of the huge oval table, while on both its sides the refreshments had remained untouched in their coolers. Some other time they would have been already half empty, but now nobody even thought of having a drink. Around them, paper rolls, notebooks, pencils, wide open maps, and defense plans were scattered in disarray.

"To announce the population," Arnar went on, addressing the Governor. He took a small pause and corrected himself. "To tell the population the truth is out of the question. What can we gain from that? Nothing but panic. The population cannot help us. They'll very likely need several weeks to digest the facts."

"The ten Erudites have also voted for that unanimously," Chris concurred. "The secret shall be kept." *What's more important is we are unable to call on such short notice for the help of any other power from outside,* he thought, but could not say it out loud. "We are sworn—God help us—to keep everything as it is. We shall keep the same Code and the same rules. All that can be done is in the hands of the people at this table."

The Governor contemplated the only wall with no paint, draped with the colors of the Island equally surrounding its plainly framed photo. He returned to Chris and confirmed, lowering his eyelids. Then he turned around with his whole body to the Head of the Security House.

"Sir, can you give us some details about our attackers' allies?"

The tall, gaunt man with a receding hairline took a deep breath. "Our analysis of the attack on the Center was confirmed by the information provided by the young Tentorian woman. It is now clear that the only help they have comes from the gang of the Shadow Ragons. They had prepared their arrival, and now are hosting them; providing them logistics, armaments, and more. We do not yet know how this association started, what their true objective is, how they communicated with the Tentorians before their arrival—we have many unanswered questions. There aren't many illegal activities on the Island, but ninety percent of them are done by this gang. After all that's happened, the suspicion of them being involved in the weapons robbery at our eastern warehouse last year is now confirmed. That is where the weapons used in today's attack came from."

"And why did we ignore this until now? Why did we neglect them? Who's responsible for this?" the Governor interrupted. "I've been telling you forever they look more dangerous than some petty smugglers."

"Now it's of less consequence as to whom is responsible, Excellency," Arnar subverted the conversation. "Now we must have a constructive approach."

Chris backed him, too. "I agree. Let's be constructive! We'll ask such questions another time." He hesitated. "Perfectly valid as they are."

A short break dispelled much of the tension in the room.

"*Sirs,*" an Erudite spoke through the audio-conference system, "*we must also pay attention to press management. Until now, the population has been duly informed in relation to the Security House incident, but we also need to inform them about the Command Center attack. No matter how secret the site was, it'll certainly leak that we lost two hundred men in there.*"

One of the Heads straightened in his chair. "We'll handle this! We are contacting the families and we're working on a press release. The Center shall be presented to the population in terms most people working there were already familiar with: they'll know it was part of the House of Security. The Shadow Ragons will be the only ones blamed—again."

Chris's saddened voice interfered, "Unless the population wonders how such an insignificant group has gained such power or why they attacked a Governmental institution…" He looked up and resumed in the same deep tone, "Should someone up there see us, we ask for forgiveness!"

"Chris, you know we're doing the right thing," another Erudite soothed his apprehension. "It's for the good of the Island people."

The door opened and Cole and Claire came into the room escorted by an officer. They were all watching them. Claire felt like she was a leopard with the way they looked upon her in fear and curiosity.

Although never a real supporter of the idolatry created around the Government, like most of the Islanders, Cole couldn't help himself and instinctively bowed to the Governor. It was the second time in his life he saw this man in flesh and blood. The first time was when he was nine and been conferred a "Falcon of the Island" title, a symbolic gesture given to all the third graders. It was that one extraordinary moment in the life of every child of the Island and his family. At that time, Cole had been part of the Governor welcome brigade: ten children, each holding a flag with different symbols. Since then, he had seen him almost daily, but only on TV or in public institution paintings.

Arnar scowled upon seeing Claire. "Who the hell invited *her* to our meeting?"

"I did." Drew stood. "We need her."

"A Tentorian? Isn't it enough we let her into the Center? Now we're inviting her to join strategic meetings!"

The silence in the room made the fancy mustachioed man's breathing increase. "My good men," he said, all wound up, "she and her brothers are all behind this!" He pointed at the redhead.

Claire's tongue was tinged with a harsh reply, but she refrained. She answered composed, albeit a bit remorseful. "They are not my brothers. I had but a sister who died during the last so-called 'technological world war'. All she wanted was to avoid connecting to any device for as long as she lived. She only managed 19 years. She committed suicide after a chip was forcefully implanted in her brain to protect her against a possible drone invasion. But you can't naturally know all this, Mr..."

"Arnar," Cole whispered.

"Mr. Arnar, because you more likely than not have no idea what's going on outside."

The general pressed his lips into a thin white line. He looked around for another opinion, begging for someone to back him, but everyone was waiting for the Tentorian woman to resume.

"If I wished to fight you," Claire went on, "I wouldn't have put my life on the line and I wouldn't be here now. I believe we all share the same desire: to get back to our families—or what's left of them—and live as human beings should."

Chris intervened. "Regardless of how much I would like to agree with you, Arnar, we need her. She provided us data we knew nothing about."

Arnar swept his eyes over the room. *So be it.* He waved to the officer who had escorted the newcomers to meeting that he was dismissed.

"That being said, let's get back to our point," Chris attempted to ease the tension.

For the few moments silence reigned, Cole noticed the monotony of the single colored suits strewn about the room: the Erudites' all-grey tunics and the Heads' black ones were donned over white shirts. But the navy blue of the generals' outfit and the flowery patterns painted on the walls somewhat enlivened the gloomy air.

The Governor made up his mind to take the floor. "Then I'm for backing the first proposal. We set up an army to strike them before they attack us. Now we know where they are."

Claire approached the oval table and leaned in so she could fix the Governor's eyes in a stare across from her. "With all due respect, what military technology is going to support this army? Besides the state-of-the-art shield and the monitoring system, you are way dated. You have nothing." Although spoken in the same key, the last word rang caustically in everyone's ears.

A murmur broke out in the room, but nobody dared raising his voice.

"On top of that," Claire added, "They've recently done a

highly accurate assessment of your forces. Does anyone care for a presentation?"

"How dare she?" the Governor found himself speaking to himself.

For the first time in his life, Cole entertained an outright different image of the system and the Governor in particular. That aura of deification melted with each word Claire spoke. He looked like all the others. The young man found himself in another world, one outside the known Island, in another reality, in a hall where a different truth and perspective held sway. It looked like nobody needed the image of the Governor as it was forced into Cole's world. The year 2500 sat at that oval table while the Governor still ruled the 2000s world of genuine Islanders. A strange pride soared into him as he imagined climbing the ranks and the system, bettering himself. However, in no time at all he realized it wasn't so much that he was rising, but the pedestal of leadership that had leaned on him so long was crumbling before his eyes. Another childish feeling also taunted him: he would have wanted his father here, the one for whom this power aura of the Governor was more dazzling than to anyone else. Cole would have liked to see his reaction or at least one day be able to share all this with his family or friends. He would likely never have the chance. Cole swallowed the lump in his parched throat.

Claire's voice abruptly scattered his thoughts. "Or maybe you'll be sending peace-loving Erudites?" She looked at the Erudites, save Chris, who she didn't dare eye. It wasn't hard to tell them apart since they were all wearing the same kind of tunic. They watched her, slightly baffled and hurt, but nobody contradicted her. "I beg your pardon," she said, lowering her head as if before some noblemen, "but against these mercenaries, the army you have won't do. You had one in the main Control Center and you lost it. As you've seen, they are supported by their pals that have an entire arsenal within reach while the Tentorians proved many times way more dangerous and efficient in battle than anyone here."

Chris' calm voice permeated the room in an attempt to raise their spirits. "We have to fight. We'll get reinforcements soon."

"You can try." Claire took a positive view. "Your army could be above their allies." She pondered. "You might even take them by surprise, but for that you must plan your approach to their base well without being noticed."

"We can conduct an air attack with the two fighting planes we have," Arnar offered. "We'll use land forces at the same time."

"Don't forget we've—*they've*—deployed surface-to-air missiles and sentries over the entire area," Claire reminded him.

Cole gave all those assembled a thorough once over. He felt the lump in his throat growing larger when he saw fear on some of their faces; he had also noticed the general had begun to stutter his responses, unsure of their strategy. Claire's last line seemed to have glued everyone's mouths shut.

"You must admit," she pressed on, "you've never prepared for an attack from outside the Island. The only danger you've seen was the breakout of an inside uprising. You're living in a quiet little world enforced by strict rules devised for law-abiding people. Those on the other side have the mindset and the strength of a war machine. They have nothing to lose while you're only...humans."

Silence ruled and no one dared to speak. Arnar rubbed

his eyes and glanced at the others, all stumped and lost in thought.

"Miss," the mustached man dared, "these are Government secrets. You can't know what we're prepared to do and what not—"

"Drop it," Drew cut him short in a whisper.

"All right..." Chris looked up at Arnar and Drew. "How much time do we need to prepare this attack?"

Arnar was about to reply, but then cleared his throat and took his time before answering. "Keeping in mind that part of our forces will stay to defend the Backup Center, we also need time to track the sentries and the anti-aircraft artillery...maybe between 12 and 24 hours."

He looked to the deputy general and other commanders for advice. Drew blinked and nodded her approval. Whispers surged between all who'd gathered, but in the end, they each agreed with the plan.

"In that case, gentlemen," the Erudite said, "I suggest we all get down to work!" *We have an Island to defend*, he dared to add only to himself.

Chapter 35

Her whole body shivered with fear, heart clenched in a knot. She had managed to get a secure connection to outside the Island for a few minutes, yet as she did so, she couldn't help but think she had turned against her own team. She strode toward the exit of the main building of the Backup Center and then onto a paved alley lined by chipped but carefully cleaned, whitewashed curbs. After a few meters, she slowed down. She sensed all she had learned in her tough training sessions, her commonsense, and her Tentorian instincts fading. *I must call him!* That thought whooshed through her mind. What she wanted more than anything was to know that he was fine. Each cell in her body vibrated in sync with her heart. *I am only human. I have a soul...it's normal for me to feel that way and that's what I love most about humans.* The sun hid for a long time below the horizon, casting a vibrant cherry hue on the faraway clouds. She watched them for a fleeting moment, drew a breath, and pressed the buttons of a mobile phone.

"Claire!" a warm voice came through from thousands of miles away.

"Dad, you have no idea how glad I am to hear you!"

"My dear girl, I was worried about you." His voice was feeble. "Just tell me that you're all right please!"

"Dad, things took a turn for the worse here. We've been so wrong about these people. What's going on back home is totally wrong."

"Just tell me you're okay!"

"I'm okay, Dad," a tear ran down her cheek, "but I felt so...lost there and I've found myself here. We're not human there. We're—"

"Don't talk like that! Of course we are." He paused. "I wanted to know you're fine...and that you'll be coming back home," he said awkwardly.

"I'll come back. I'll come to you as soon as I can. For the time being, I need you to stay away from everything we know as civilization."

"And I want you to stay out of harm's way."

"I love you, Dad. I'll..." Her voice died. Words grew gooey as she wiped her tears and cleared her throat. "I will come after you as soon as things are mended here. Right now, I'm trying to stop them, but I don't know exactly how to—"

"I don't want to know, Claire!" he cut her off. "Don't put your life on the line!"

She admonished in a whisper, "Dad, how come you don't want to know? Why are you talking that way?"

She got no answer and murky thoughts took hold of her mind. In the background, she could make out what sounded like a faint moan she hadn't heard since the day she lost her sister. On that very day they'd both decided to stand out from the other Tentorians, to live as unhooked from technology as possible.

"Dad...?" she pressed on, trembling, "are you alone there?"

"My child..." An even fainter cry.

Beside him, another man's voice sent tremors throughout her body. "Claire, could you please return to the base and stop helping the enemy?"

Her heart froze on the spot, her legs gave way, and tears

ran down her face. She went breathless, unable to utter a single word.

"Mr. Nemilo," the same male voice said, speaking to someone else, "we and our host have received the long-awaited call. I'm putting you through."

"Claire," a different voice said, "the interim Tentorian ruler speaking. Don't be a turncoat; we have an objective to fulfil over there."

"Bastards," she retorted. "Our leader is Xilo...and the enemy is yourselves. That's no objective to fulfil!"

"Xilo *was* our leader."

"Was"? A fleeting thought she cast aside.

"What do you want from my father? What does he have to do with any of this?"

Nemilo's tone turned menacing. "You thought you'd be able to hide him? This is my turf! You think there's anything moving here without me seeing and feeling it?" His words soared into a howl. "I am in each of your minds. I am everywhere!"

"I don't want to join your mission!" Claire cried.

Nemilo's voice sounded low and cold this time. "Hmm...but you can't side with the enemy either, Claire."

The thorn in her throat wouldn't allow her to say any more words.

"Let me put it otherwise: you report to our Island base before tomorrow morning at 9 o'clock or your father won't be around anymore. Goodbye."

"Hello?" Nothing else came from the other side. Claire sat on the curb, buried her head between her knees, and made herself as small as she could.

A few minutes later, Cole showed up at the building entrance, searching for Claire. He hurried down the alley after spotting her in the semidarkness. The young woman gave him the cold shoulder as she past him, wrought with that blind, lost look that demanded no one stop her.

"Claire!"

She entered the building resolutely and went straight to the door of the deputy general's office.

"Come in..." Drew's voice came from the other side of the door. Claire stepped. "Nobody sleeps tonight, I see."

"I need your help." Claire wasted no time. "Please."

Claire splashed cold water onto her face to hide her angry tears.

"If you go there, I'm coming with you," Cole said from the bathroom doorway, one eyebrow pressed against the frame.

"Cole, *I* have to go," she stressed, "for my father...and because I have to mend things. It's my fault; it's the Tentorians' fault."

"Okay, but you still need someone to watch your back...and a good driver."

Claire turned her head without looking at him. "Don't insist. I'm going alone."

"Hey," he said in earnest, "for once I can try to do some good for my family, for you, for my friends...for the Island. You know too well that I'm going to die anyway."

"No...!" The Tentorian plunged her head into the sink. "Cole, before I leave I want to do something for you." She turned to him, hair disheveled, and told him in one breath, "I want to use this technology to cure you."

Cole had no reaction; he looked through her without uttering a sound. He ran his fingers through his hair. "You'll think I'm mad, but the way the situation looks right now, with the probability of being killed any one of these days at..." he lifted his eyes to the ceiling as if making some quick calculations, "over 90%, I think I'd rather stay as I am. I don't feel ready to let billions of robots run through my body, defying the laws of nature—at least not now. I want to live, but now I must do something else, which is fight by your side."

"No, that's stupid! You'll stay here and be safe...and healthy."

"Safe?" Cole rushed out. "Can't you see there's an all out war going on?" He flung an arm to the window. "What will you do out there all by yourself? I'm coming with you—I told you! Maybe you stand no chance with me either, but all by yourself makes those odds even less likely. If we fail, then this Island—me, my family, everyone—will all end in the same fate."

A brief knock stopped him short and Drew came into the room. "Sorry to disturb you, but I don't have time. Listen to me carefully," she addressed Claire. "This discussion never took place! A car has been authorized to leave and is waiting out front. Once you're out of the unit, you may gear up. You'll find everything you need in the boot."

"Thank you."

"You'll also have a mobile phone in the glove compartment. I'd like..." excitement flooded her voice, "keep in touch. Good luck!" She turned on her heel and headed for the exit.

"Wait!" Claire stopped her. In five steps, she caught up with Drew and gave her a hug. "Thank you for everything. I hope to see you all soon."

Drew patted her back, and Claire got swept away by a feeling she'd only experienced when her mother was still alive.

"Me too." Drew hugged her like a daughter. It felt like she wanted to add something else, but her strength failed her. She exhaled and stepped out of the door without looking back.

Half an hour later, Claire rushed towards the car parked in the garrison courtyard. The revving engine shook her from her thoughts. The side window came down and Cole sat behind the wheel grinning.

"Well, well...I was just wondering where you were!" she said.

The young Islander leisurely slipped a cap on his head. "You can't do this alone. And anyway, what can you do to me now? I'm stuck to the wheel."

She shook her head but still threw her arms around him, keeping him close for a long time. Off the top of her head she found herself saying, "What the hell? As I like to say: step on it!"

"All I wanted to hear." He shifted the car into gear. "That's the green-eyed redhead I fell in love with."

The sun had risen hours ago, but the entire Island was still asleep.

The car moved cautiously, as if trying to not break the peace. The same peace prevailed inside the car. The two of them were quiet and Claire found the road much longer than it looked on the map; it seemed as if it would never come to an end.

They slowed near a recess on the side of the road. "I'll stop for a few minutes," said Cole.

He took the mobile phone from the glove compartment, climbed out of the car, and gazed at the red sphere rising in the east. He took a deep breath, closed his eyes as if in a brief meditation, then stepped several meters away and dialed.

Minutes later, he leaned his head against a utility pole, ear stuck to the phone. "Stop crying, Mum. I'm fine—I just told you!"

"We miss you," Christina's spent voice managed to say.

"Mother...you must know that I love you. Give Mathew a big hug for me and tell him I can't wait to see him and start tinkering again with the car engine together."

Only sobs reached him now. His mother sniffled and gulped down some of her tears. "When are you returning home?"

"I'm coming, Mum, I'm coming! First I have to get my thoughts in order, and my life. And I need to help a good friend out of a mess."

"What friend? What mess? What are you talking about?"

"It doesn't matter. What's important is I'm fine; that I'm finding myself again. I keep thinking more and more about our existence, about humankind...and it does me good."

Matthew's light, dear voice could be heard in the background: "Mother, why aren't you asleep? Who are you talking to? Is that Cole?"

His longing tore Cole apart.

"We...love you." Her mother's words came amid sobs. "You should know that."

"And I love you too..."

Although she watched from where she was by the car, Claire could feel his grief without hearing a sound. It was in the way he strained his features, lips trembling and eyes searching as if he was lost for good this time.

When he was done, Cole took a deep breath and dialed another number to check his voicemail.

"*You have 14 messages! First message: Where are you, Cole?*" His mother's voice.

He pressed a key.

"*Next message: We are very worried! You took your backpack and left without a sign. Get in touch with us!*"

One after the other, the messages told him how important he was to his family and friends. He would have liked to warn them out loud about the danger they were all in, do something to protect them. He drove that thought away and turned his eyes back to the fireball above the horizon.

He took the phone away from his ear, ready to shut it off, when his voicemail announced, "*Last message.*"

"*It's still me, man,*" Jimmy's plain, upbeat voice filled the air. "*I've been told you left for the mountains. You mustn't be afraid of the disease. It'll be okay; you'll get the best of it somehow!*" Cole's eyelids came together to relish the bolster. "*I just found out that another incident happened at a research base of the House of Security outside the capital. They say a lot of people died there too. Strange. Very strange. I hope it's in no way connected to the experience you went through two days ago. All kinds of scenarios go through my head..."*

"If only you knew," Cole muttered.

"Now to another matter: the boss doesn't seem mad at you for giving him the slip like the slacker you are. He said he understands you need some fresh air without exhaust gases..." he sensed the smile in Jimmy's voice and could picture his mouth stretched over his chubby face, *"and that he's waiting for you—anytime you want to come back. I can see him in my mind waiting for you the way we were waiting for that slick snail to cross the finish line."* Despite the bitter taste in his mouth, a slight curve appeared at the corners of Cole's lips. *"Do you remember back in college, when we both skipped the architecture class to go to that idiotic snail contest? How foolish we were! Well, no more of it...I'll hang up so I stop going on and on all by myself like a fool—not that it would be the last time."* Cole smiled. *"I'll be waiting for you to have a beer together. Take care and don't do anything stupid!"* The voicemail ended with a beep. *"To save this message, please press..."*

There were no tears on his face, but his eyes had turned ruby. Cole remembered where he was and missed his loved ones more. He pressed the phone against his shoulder and glanced at Claire. His back straightened, he breathed deeply and made a beeline to the car trunk.

"Let's see what we have here." His forehead became smooth with delight. "Phew!"

The boot was packed full of weapons, ammunition, bulletproof vests, holsters, and other military accoutrements.

"Mmm, not bad!" she approved.

The oval capsule coldly reflected the hot sun on Claire's face. She kept it tight between her fingers, above her head, and sized it up hatefully against the violet-blue sky.

"You know, I thought I'd never have to implant this in my head." She sat on the side of the same road with her heart in her throat, as if bracing for an important exam. She never felt the capsule so cold.

"You're the one who said 'this is for a just cause'," Cole encouraged, "along with many other very good arguments."

"It's just...like most of the technological advancements spelling doom on us."

The Islander refrained from replying right away. "I'll leave you alone to do that. I'll be waiting by the car." He rubbed her back before he stepped away.

The moment Claire would have liked to postpone indefinitely had finally come. She squinted, shooting fierce eyes at the horizon, then raised the hair above the back of her neck. She closed her eyes, inhaled, and stuck the capsule to her nape. Its root-like pivots started sliding off to perform their tasks, pushing and inserting the capsule into the base of her skull. The pivots turned into wires, then into ever smaller ramifications, down to nanoscale connections, and further on to even smaller pico-ones, a billion times smaller than the millimeter roots they had sprung out from. Millions of connections allowed neuronal networks to become one with the foreign body; the capsule was becoming part of the young woman's brain. A few seconds more, and it was completely inside. Her pupils dilated, and a spasmodic, excruciating pain seized her body. Instinctively, Claire dug her hands into the grass and gripped as hard as she could.

Shortly afterwards, the blood around the capsule vanished, and only a T shaped red LED glowed through her red hair as she let it fall back into place.

Everything in her head spun at dizzying speed. Thousands of calculations flooded her mind. *One hour, 54 minutes, 8 seconds and 22 thousandths of a second*, she found herself counting, *that's how much time I have before 9 o'clock. Still 29 kilometers and 850 meters to go I reach the base. I must get to the base!*

The seconds of pain dispersed quickly. The device which before she had only been in control of via vocal and tactile commands was now part and parcel of herself; her mind and her body functions. *What a strange feeling!* she thought. She felt the mini-drone the same way she sensed the movement of her fingers, the same way her eyes could see the landscape around her. It was as if some part of her could take to the skies. *That's the evolutionism we support.* She realized she could look anywhere around, behind some tree or into a thicket of grass. She likewise felt she could control billions of nanobots in the capsule eagerly awaiting any thought she ordered. Hundreds of other new functions— *inhuman abilities*—were also ready to be activated on the electrical impulse of a thought.

She couldn't help herself and cast her eyes over the sweeping green field ahead. The mini-drone relayed images of grass blades it flew over with only the power of thought. She noticed a flock of birds. *I want to be up there with you for a moment!* and she soared next to them. *I envy you for your view!* She took a deep breath, wishing to feel the air from such a height, but she was down on the ground. All she sensed was the smell of asphalt.

"I'd love to let you gaze around all day," Cole interrupted, "but it's time to get going."

She looked at him, closed her eyes for a moment, and

nodded. "You know, I have an idea of how to put the little devil to better use." The Islander raised an eyebrow but said nothing. "And it's time for me to teach you how to use these stupid weapons; I'm gonna need your help."

Chapter 36

The car pulled into the parking lot of the former power plant. Claire assessed the courtyard of bustling bodies, from the rusty fence running along its entire length and up to the peeling, weather-beaten walls of the building. She spotted trucks and buses with Ragons swarming around to get them ready as well as many off-roaders with mounted machine guns and launchers. Everything was prepared for an attack. She wondered again how the allies succeeded in concealing all this since they'd arrived. Some had known about the impending attack—if not all of them. *I was blind.*

Alone in the car, she looked at the sky in silent prayer then put her sun glasses on and opened the door. As soon as she was in the open, she was already being examined by two allies wielding semiautomatics and ready to fire. One of them looked like he was undressing her with his eyes; he gaped at her black tight-fitted jacket, eyes lingering on her black and grey trousers, while almost entirely missing her military-issue boots. Claire couldn't do anything but ignore them as she walked into her former work accommodation.

A bossy voice greeted her as soon as she stepped into the makeshift office. "Well, well, what do you know? It's you at last!" Chan articulated. He sat comfortably on a chair, full of himself.

Claire paid him no mind as she scanned the area. The main office was unchanged, although it was strange to her only one Tentorian would be here.

"Where are the others?" she asked.

"Does it matter?" He pressed a button on the desk console. "Boss, the missus is here."

"*Wonderful!*" Nemilo's voice blared from the loudspeaker.

"I've kept my word," Claire said before Chan could reply. "Now leave my father alone!"

"Fine, but first take the device off your hand and put it on the table." Chan's order came in a staccato English.

Her heart pounding harder. She faltered for a split second, casting suspicious eyes around; she counted eight allies in the room. She looked defiantly down on Chan and took off her wristband while glancing at the others. She abandoned the device on the desktop.

"Thank you," Chan said before he pulled out his gun and fired right into her chest.

The shock surged through every inch of her body. Then the humid warmth of the blood gushing under her clothes stunned her. Claire collapsed, her puzzled expression fastened on Chan. Unfortunately, her most pessimistic scenario had come true, and reality was grimmer than she'd hoped.

A bad tune played in her eardrums. The voice was Chan's, accompanied by the murmur of her own blood flowing tumultuously out of her chest.

"Now, if you really wanna know where the others are I can tell you. Most of them went hunting down your friends, the Erudites. After finishing them, we'll all go to the Backup Center and wreck it for good. Simple, isn't it?"

His diabolical laughter resounded like an echo in Claire's head.

"That's some plan," she clenched her teeth, "but I wouldn't say it's as simple as that!"

On her last legs, she took off her sunglasses and let Chan see her eyes. The red right eye contact lens displayed a fierce thirst for revenge before she closed her eyes. It was the last thing the triple furrowed chin Tentorian would see.

"Dirty bi—"

A bullet shot him from behind and traveled right into the nape of his neck where the implanted capsule was located, ploughing through the brain. Chan collapsed with a hole in his head, his mouth frozen on the vowel "i" and his blood spreading in a puddle on the floor close to Claire's.

The levitating weapon on the Tentorian woman's mini-drone hovered over the spot where Chan's nape had stood just some seconds before. Scared and utterly baffled, the allies could see the impending danger of the object ahead and started firing recklessly at the flying weapon. After eight brief moves of the drone and eight gunshots, silence blanketed the room. All nine people lay still on the floor, each with identical holes in their heads.

"What is going on there? Chan? Chan?" the loudspeaker conveyed Nemilo's puzzled voice.

Claire took a deep breath and opened her eyes wide: a blend of green and red portended storm. Offensive tactics flew through her head, weapon and hand to hand fight strategies flooding her neural network. *Hmmm, the things I'm capable of!* The gurgle of gushing blood ceased; the hemorrhage stopped. Her chest was healing.

"*Chan!*" the loudspeaker buzzed again.

"Chan is no longer with us," she said. "Listen here, Nemilo, I know you weren't going to keep my father alive; he knows too much about you."

"You bastard!" the Tentorian leader growled.

"Instead, think well about what I'm going to tell you—you look a smart boy to me! If you kill my father, I'll rip through your people sent here to the Island worse than you ever thought possible. Then I'll go back to Tentoria and inflict ten times the pain you've put me through."

"You really see yourself capable of doing that? How can you be so sure I wouldn't sacrifice my people or position just for good old revenge?" The ice-cold question had a deadly ring to it.

Claire mulled it over a moment. *There's no turning back. Otherwise he'll crush me.*

"Because you're not stupid enough to spit on your own blanket. Are you familiar with that expression? It comes from a time you thought primitive. But wait a minute! You are a thoroughbred Tentorian. All information is available to you in a split second. You must be familiar with it! My father will be your insurance policy as long as you keep him alive. I know too much about what you people are trying to do; with that alone I can destroy you as soon as I return to Tentoria. Keep him alive and you still stand a chance...and my desire for revenge might wear off."

She seethed with rage. This was a most treacherous game and she was playing it against an intelligent beast. *Why isn't he answering? Wait for him...wait for him. Don't say another word. He'll give in.*

"Bastard...bastard!" Nemilo took to mumbling again.

"Nothing better to say?"

Time dragged on, pushing Claire's anxiety overboard.

Nemilo calmed down. "You're a smart scumbag; you play dirty."

"I haven't got time for your profiling."

"You're as good as dead! That's going to be a very short-term insurance policy. But after whacking you, you have my word your dad will kick off too. You got it right, I won't need him anymore. I'll enjoy doing it; he helped bring you to life and you're nothing but an example of how evolution has gone astray. Your gene pool must be wiped out!"

"You're dead wrong. I'm coming after you, you bastard!"

"Wow, should I be shaking in my boots? We're coming to the Island, don't worry!"

On Claire's lens, the gun aimed at the communication console. "Good bye."

A fire echoed in the room; then she aimed at the Tentorian communication server and shot it twice.

"Hello?" Nemilo reacted in sheer surprise. "Hello! You scumbag!" he spat, disgusted by his word of choice before turning to a subordinate. "How many Tentorians are left on our Island base?"

"For the time being, besides her, none. Instead we have about one hundred allies armed and ready to set off to the Backup Center."

The shaggy-haired thug swore and cursed, rolling his eyes. "How can we stay in touch with our men now?"

"Just a moment, I'm checking." While waiting for an answer, Nemilo restlessly paced the room. "There can be a way in. We could send messages to their mobile devices."

"Good. Make sure they have someone capable sent back to the base to scatter her brains!"

Claire slipped off her jacket and revealed her concealed holster. A walkie-talkie, two pistols, and many magazines were attached to her vest and belt. When she held out her hand, the mini-drone carrying the gun levitated into her palm. She pulled a magazine off the holster, replaced it in no time at all, and then let it hover.

The special material incorporated into the drone gripped the weapon like a hand. Claire thought of putting the ferrying and handling function of the tiny imp to good use. The black matte fabric had been transformed into a living tissue structure. A tongue-like extension of this artificial "tissue" closely fit the trigger. It was coordinated by nanobots the same way a living muscle was coordinated by nerves. *I feel the pistol as if I'm holding it,* Claire thought in amazement, *looking through the sight and aiming at the target.*

She also pulled out the two armpit-holstered guns, cocked them, and spoke in a low voice while leaning over the walkie-talkie.

"Blow'em up!"

"Alright, boss!" Cole's care-free voice came through. The boot of their car opened and the Islander appeared with a missile launcher in his hands. He yanked it onto his shoulder, sighted the truck exit, and...*Fire!*

A powerful explosion shook the building. A few Ragons fled, yelling through the blast-blown hole. Some were crawling, others scampering around, ablaze. A luckier one, who had been in the place where the projectile had made contact, wanted to see the yard from above and got a free ride over half of its width.

The Islander swapped the missile launcher with a rocket

propelled grenade and took to firing aimlessly at the trucks ready to roll away from the front of the building.

Both guns in hand and the mini-drone's weapon levitating one meter behind her, Claire walked the twisting hallways of the former power plant. She moved unflinchingly as her brain and the contact lens provided the tactical attack data she needed.

"I'm off to the large hall," she spoke into the transmitter. "You just keep the yard exit hot to make them all stay in the building. I can handle things here."

"*Whatever you say, dear*!" Cole answered.

"C'mon!" Claire rebuked him.

Two more corridors to the hall, and the allies' footfalls resounded in her mind. *Four average weight men,* she processed before she saw them. When a shoulder appeared from around a corner, one bullet left Claire's weapon and shot directly to the edge of the wall above it; straight into the enemy's head. He didn't live to see what hit him. She could hear alarmed Mandarin voices not far from the same corner, but no one showed themselves. The mini-drone affixed with the gun flew to their corridor while both the kick and the pistol weight were mastered by the powerful mini-drone's propellers. *Such high fidelity; like a clear thought,* she reflected. One, two, three shots, and silence was regained. When she passed the four fallen bodies, Claire stared ahead. She did not dare to look at them.

The metallic door she kicked slammed against the wall of the large hall. She did not know the hall too well; usually she didn't have business there. Tens of pairs of eyes watched her from the shadow. The rusty boilers and pipes projected shades of gray all over the moldy floor, while the dark walls framed the landscape. She hardly scanned the sweeping room more than a few milliseconds before the three guns started firing. The enemies fell from the suspended footbridges running along the hall while Claire scurried in sync with the automatic fire.

"*I can hear gunshots in the hall*," Cole's voice came through the transmitter.

When the levitating gun was empty, she dodged and ducked behind a boiler and answered: "*Dear*, are you bored?"

"*Why are you mocking me? I just wanted to know whether you're out there and that...you're okay.*"

"These guys thought it might be interesting to start shooting at each other."

Cole laughed. "*I'm glad you're all right.*"

Claire took out a holstered magazine and cast it in the air to the mini-drone. A living tissue-like fabric strip shot off the magazine's release catch while the gun set the fully loaded into its slot. It was already late when Claire realized she hadn't asked the drone to cock the weapon into the firing position. She only heard a click and knew the pistol was ready to spew bullets again. She did not let the thought go. She was bothered by the technology being so advanced as to prevent routine tasks from exhausting her brain and instead being *instinctually* coordinated by the capsule. *But what if the bullet was fired by the same instinct?* She gulped and reached the same opinion as before: *This technology is hell on Earth, but I need it now.* She loaded her two hand guns as well while she resumed firing the airborne weapon.

She did not linger there too long. She needed a better angle, so she took the stairs up to the upper catwalks, stopping at the highest one.

Twisted steel pipes wound between large rusty aluminum

boilers under her feet. None of the corners of the hall were more than 50 meters away from that point, thus providing a perfect bullet range. Targets fell again one by one. *My weapons are extensions of my body*, she kept repeating to herself. She sensed each of their movements at micron length scales. Adrenaline had long made her forget the difference between her eyes and the mini-drone camera locking onto targets; *my...lethal visual extension.* Attack tactics merged with her thinking and reflexes; time seemed to pass much slower in discernible thousandths of seconds.

Claire had never entertained the ambition of becoming an elite fighter. She joined this special department only because it had been created for missions outside of Tentoria. All she wanted was to know another kind of world, another kind of people. As a researcher, it had been promised that she would stay out of the fight. Still, she had been forced to go through weekly military training. Now she appreciated it more than ever.

Machinegun fire called her back to the present. A bullet hit her ankle.

"I liked those boots," she said mostly to herself, and a bullet flew back, straight into the shooter's head.

When two grenades were lobbed at her from below, their trajectories immediately showed up on her lens along with possible impact points. She took a deep breath, following the two grenades with her arms, and gunshots fired from all three pistols at once: two shots from the mini-drone at the grenade throwers, and four from the weapons in her hands aimed at the grenades themselves. Bouncing twice, they exploded somewhere in the air, under the catwalk. Claire took shelter and watched scores of splinters spewing around the borders of the catwalk like iron snowflakes. She thought she could count or gauge the size of each and every one of them if needed.

"*Claire*," the transmitter blared while her crushed ankle healed, "*they are starting to leave the building. I'm going to need you here!*"

"I'm coming!" She sprinted to the next catwalk, firing bullets. "From what I see, they were ready to attack the Backup Center."

Cole stood motionless behind a smoking truck. His bulletproof vest seemed too tight on him, the pistol too heavy. Nonetheless, he thought he'd done a pretty good job so far. He succeeded in wrecking enough vehicles and hide from those who'd seen him lobbing grenades.

The gunshots ceased inside the building too. *Such a sinister silence,* he thought.

Eventually, several voices could be made out in the distance, getting closer and closer. A group of Ragon mercenaries were loudly looking for him among the destroyed trucks.

"There!" one shouted.

Cole gripped the weapon even harder, ready to fire. Bursts of machinegun fire came from all directions, but no bullets hit his truck. They were aiming at Claire, not at him. Slowly, each machinegun barked less and less, stopped by her pistols fires.

"*Behind you!*" he heard from the walkie-talkie. "*Just come towards me; I'll cover you!*"

The Islander threw a glance behind the truck wheel and a red splotch heartened him. It was the young woman's hair. She stood her ground, arms flung open, controlling all angles. After Cole ran to her they stood back to back in the same position.

"I've seen it done in the movies, but honestly, I'm not convinced this is right. Are you sure we're safe?"

"Dunno, but I like it too."

"*What?*"

"It was a *joke!*"

Cole grunted in response.

"Right now, I'm like a human scanner, Cole; two eyes and a camera on the mini-drone. I can see all that moves. Can see them before they see me."

"Then let's stand like this a bit longer. We sure look good."

With that, he managed to make Claire smile.

"It seems the Tentorians are gone," she let him know. "I think Osman, Kaligor, and Hoshito plus a small army are going to waste some Erudites."

"How do we find them?"

"Let's check inside; we may discover something. I think we're done here."

On seeing the nine of them in the makeshift office, Cole straightened his back and whistled brazenly. All were frozen in strange positions while looking downward for some object. Anyway, none seemed to be just sleeping, the Islander reckoned after spotting the hole in each head.

"I see you can be very upset sometimes," he joked.

"Careful," she answered in kind while looking for clues around the room.

Everything was unchanged except for the blood-soaked bodies. Even Powalski's dried blood was still there, on the long-since emptied weapon case.

Claire used her drone to scan the papers in the waste bin. Nothing.

"It can't get any simpler than that." Cole looked at the

monitor he had switched on.

Claire came up behind him. "Let's see...what do we have here?"

"It looks like the addresses of some private homes..."

"And the Backup Center."

The Islander placed his finger on the display. "Look here; it's Chris McCain! One of the addresses is his."

"These are the Erudites' addresses. That seems to be the plan; they are taking them out one by one and will later attack the Backup Center." She blurted a curse and furiously kicked her boot against the computer case. "If they whack the Erudites, there would be no one around to secure the Island properly."

Cole sank his head in his hands, rubbing his forehead. "We can try stopping them," he urged. "I hope they haven't been gone long."

Claire took less than a second to analyze. "Let's go," she agreed, and took another glance at the display. "I've memorized the addresses."

"Good. We'll begin with the closest."

They rushed into the hall and headed for the door.

"Aaah!" A Ragon's angered yell hit their ears.

Weapon in hand, *he had come out of nowhere*, thought Cole.

Two shots went off, but Claire continued her beeline for the exit as if nothing had happened. She turned to Cole. "Are you coming or what?"

Dazed, he turned his head towards the Ragon, still standing but with two holes in his head. Neither those, nor his rotten teeth, nor the thin, bristly moustache, nor his pointy sheepdog's ears were sufficiently repulsive enough to make Cole take his eyes off him for an instant. He collapsed under Cole's gaze. Only when the still smoking levitating gun whizzed past him following Claire did Cole press his hand to his heart and heave a sigh.

Hurrying to the car they'd arrived in, the almost imperceptible sound of an engine struck the air. Claire closed her eyes and stopped breathing.

"What is it?" he asked.

"It's a truck...the same kind we used to have here at the base. It's...nine hundred meters away...eight hundred and fifty; the engine is running, so it's full. Load your gun, ready the launcher, and let's get behind the car," she ordered curtly.

The truck stopped just one hundred meters away from them, and about fifteen well-armed Ragon mercenaries along with Osman jumped out.

Claire peeked around and whispered, "They sent back a truck full of pissed off men."

"And? A piece of cake, no?"

"Hmmm, not really. There's a Tentorian with them." Cole picked up the rocket launcher, but she stopped him. "You won't have time; don't even think about it!"

He dropped the weapon and clenched his fingers around the pistol.

Osman, the two meter tall man designed from wrestlers' genes with a body and fighting spirit befitting a Tentorian, paced sluggishly like a goliath to the main entrance. The ground trembled with each footfall.

The mini-drone whizzed ahead of him, buzzing above their car. *Damn it!* Cole's lips silently mouthed. He looked to Claire, ready to run, but she didn't move. A machine gun burst hit the car and countless shards flew over them. A few seconds later, the car was a goner, completely riddled on the side Osman was coming from.

The giant allowed them a brief reprieve, no more than needed to shake off the empty machinegun and hoist a grenade launcher onto his right shoulder.

"Inside!" she shouted at Cole. "*Now!*"

Everything went by as fast as the two Tentorians' head implanted technology could master. While Claire and Cole ran towards the entrance, the weapon on her mini-drone flew at Osman, firing in rapid succession in the direction of his face; once, twice, and then he was riddled with bullets. Shaking under the molten metal blows, he threw his left hand to the weapon at his waist and, in a split second, bullets started flying towards Claire's mini-drone too. They zipped centimeters away of each other, perfectly parallel and in opposite directions—some towards Osman's face and others towards Claire's weapon. *It must buy us a little time,* Claire reflected, *to get us inside.*

Osman let the grenade launcher fall off his shoulder and used his right hand to pull out a second weapon from the waist. This time he shot straight at them. A single bullet was well on its way towards Cole's head just as they took cover in the building. From behind the door, Claire gritted her teeth while watching her slowly reconstructing hand. She'd flung it in front of the bullet one inch from Cole's temple to protect him. He now stared at her, voiceless.

"He destroyed my flying devil, the wretched bastard!" she mumbled.

"Do I have to start praying?" he stammered a joke.

"Shut up! I think my friend Chan may lend me his." She went straight into the main room to Chan's body, where she pressed his wrist device several times. The drone ejected itself and flew into the air. "Thanks!" she said cynically to the lifeless corpse.

"And here's an accessory for it." Cole handed her a weapon.

"Good. Let's go; we can get out through the hall."

"I hope you know the way."

"This used to be my workplace. Remember?"

The Islander put two fingers together and raised them to his temple.

Once inside the power plant lobby, they made for the truck exit. Each of the bodies lined up along the catwalks turned Cole's face to stone for an instant.

The sound of a mini-drone woke him completely as it flew across the hall some small distance away, and he was sure it wasn't Claire's, which he could see flying in the opposite direction. The heavy steps of the two-meter giant confirmed it. They were fast closing in, thumping on the passageway like a trotting stallion.

"We can't run all that much," Claire noted. "I must go to him. Get behind this boiler and shoot at everything that comes through that hole." She pointed at the breach in the wall he had made earlier with the rocket launcher. "Take care of yourself!"

She hugged him as if reluctant to let him go. *I don't want to lose you,* she said, but only to herself, and looked one more time into his soothing eyes. *A thousand chips can't give me the strength you give me.*

"One more thing," she said. "I would borrow a machinegun if I were you." Her chin gestured at the people taken down a short while ago.

"I guess it's you I'd worry about more, now that I've seen this pissed off dude."

"Thanks for cheering me up," she added ironically. With

the three weapons pointing ahead, she ran to the entrance towards the giant.

Osman's trotting became louder and louder, the metallic doorframe rattling when he appeared down the hall. He'd just spotted her when he started firing. Claire found it hard to force her way through, but nonetheless in no mood to duck or take a defensive stance. The capsule conveyed that. The giant did the same, trying to dodge her bullets, yet he was far less nimble. He had not expected to find her running at him.

Projectiles buzzed dissonant notes past their heads when Osman's left ear was hit. Immediately, another bullet nipped Claire's neck. A full blow into the thug's shoulder and one into the young woman's hip, then in the other one; the thug's heavy leg also received a full hit. The dry sound of the five firing pins came as a rather sophisticated intermission gong. They had all run out of ammunition.

As if signaled, Claire and Osman rushed to a boiler nearby—they had both eyed it at the same time. Claire was the first to hide behind it. The two-meter tall giant took cover on the other side. They both needed some time to heal their wounds and load their weapons. Claire decided not to load the one hovering in the air; by calling her drone she would lose sight of the enemy, and that could cost her life.

"I see you couldn't stand the temptation," Osman broke the silence, "and got the device implanted into your head...and with it our redhead has acquired a load of abilities overnight!"

"I guess I learnt from the best, huh?"

The flying devils danced in a circle above the boiler, analyzing each movement of the adversary.

"And...do you enjoy not being human?" he persisted in

the pointless discussion.

"Don't worry, it's only temporary," she answered and threw herself laterally on the floor to get a shooting angle.

Osman noticed the move. He was already waiting and pointing his weapons at her when bullets were fired towards his massive hands. He had, however, adopted the same strategy, and he was likewise a good shot. Suddenly, they felt their fingers crushed while the bullets hit their weapons and they fell out of their hands. Osman sprang towards her like an eager fisherman rushing to unhook his catch right on the shore. He caught her by her feet, then by her arms, and thrust his bullet-shattered hands to her neck. They gradually rebuilt themselves around her neck, becoming stronger and stronger.

"Die!" he bellowed.

"It's not as easy as that," she managed to say.

The pistol on the mini-drone slammed him on the head once, and then again and again until his grip slackened. It was enough for Claire to catch her breath and crawl from under him behind the boiler as she searched for a weapon.

On the other side of the hall, a burst of machinegun fire echoed through every nook and cranny as Cole encountered the Ragons who had arrived with Osman. He preferred to lie low and fire only now and then to keep them at bay. A direct encounter would have tipped the scales in their favor. They were much better prepared and outnumbered him.

An arm's length away, Claire's mini-drone suddenly appeared, pointing its gun at him. He was startled at first but understood quickly what to do when he saw it released an empty magazine. He took another one from his belt and loaded the levitating gun, which took off and flew towards Claire.

"You've acquired abilities, but you haven't implanted muscles too," Osman bragged after coming round.

Then he let out a barbaric howl and with all his might, pushed the immense boiler sitting between him and Claire. He was shivering like a lunatic, straining each muscle until the base the boiler was set on gave way and the huge object bent like a straw. He lost no time admiring the collapse, but sprang at Claire again, who managed to narrowly avoid the falling boiler. Two brawny arms were again around her fragile throat, squeezing.

"My best ability," she said in a faint voice, "is that I'm human."

"So what?" Osman spluttered. His droning turned into laughter while his hands applied more pressure to her windpipe.

Claire looked over his shoulder, took a last breath, and concluded the lesson she thought the thug was never going to learn. "When you're human, you're making true friends."

Three bullets left her levitating pistol towards Osman's nape. He collapsed loudly with that inane grin still spread across his mug.

On the upper catwalks, the Ragons shot at Cole from two directions. A bullet nipped his boot. *Damn! I have to get out of here.*

He fired his way out and darted up a catwalk's metallic stairs. A grenade thrown by a Ragon at its base shook the entire structure, and the rust covering it became more visible. The blast made it glitter in the light slipping through the hall. It had the shimmer of black reddish clouds fluffed around welded metal pieces, and the clouds expanded when they were released into the sky. For a moment, Cole's mind escaped far away, to the white clouds of flour he saw in the kitchen every time his mother made pancakes for him. He missed them so badly. He missed everything back home.

The structure was leaning sideways, pulled down by gravity. The stairs collapsed under his feet and dozens of bullets were in search of him. Cole jumped to the other side, away from the falling staircase, his hands thrust forward as if diving into water. A few meters in the air, a bullet almost grazed his shoulder; Cole felt the heat of the hot metal tearing away a fragment of his shirt. Unexpectedly, the levitating weapon went by close to his face, then under him, aiming back at the enemy. In his mind, time froze. There, in the air, everything unfolded in slow motion. He could have sworn he was sensing each split second, the weapon passing beneath him firing shot after shot, and the bullets hitting the enemy's body, who in the end lost control of the machinegun and stuck lifelessly to the catwalk handrail.

Cole rolled over to cushion his fall and found himself lying on the floor, completely exposed as he looked up to the ceiling. There was only one thing he could do from where he was: empty his magazine firing upwards to the enemies targeting him.

Claire fired some more shots in the direction of the higher catwalks before she managed a 270 degree back flip. She leaned on Cole when she landed, face up, back to his chest. At the same time, two bullets pierced her body. They were less painful to her, knowing she'd stopped them from hitting Cole.

Four gunshots and the two sharpshooters high above were sent straight to the floor.

The first flattened bullet fell to the cement with a sharp clink. The second left Claire's body with another while the Tentorian woman resolutely stepped toward the exit. The spots she'd been injured some moments earlier were now two self-closing scabs. Her skin repaired itself to perfection.

When Cole walked past the two bullets lying on the floor, his mouth twisted into an astounded *"Damn it!"* He looked at the beautiful redhead and saw a fierce fighter who no longer had anything to lose. Maybe under other circumstances he wouldn't have liked what he saw. Now, however, it suited him, just like the air he was still able to breathe.

A frenzied man came from behind the corner with a machinegun in hand. The Tentorian immediately recognized her number one fan, the Ragon always saying she was the most beautiful woman he had ever seen. One morning a week earlier, she suspected his wife had somehow gotten wind of that view, for he reported to duty with two swollen eyes. She took pity on him because even without them, his eyes were usually the largest, bulging from his face more than any of the others. She remembered feeling guilty enough to ask him for the first time what his name was. Now she no longer could recall his name, but she didn't even want to, as the man ceased beaming smiles at her and turned into a venom-withered being even uglier than when his wife had beaten him.

He managed to fire a missed short burst before the redhead's leg struck his weapon. It was the closest he'd ever been to Claire since meeting her, his terror laced expression conveying to her how he'd never wanted to move farther away than at this moment. Nonetheless, he looked like he didn't love her so much anymore, Claire gathered. Suddenly, he got to his feet and tried to run away—perhaps he missed his wife. She forgave him for the change of heart and taught him a lesson less harsh than his wife's. She punched him hard in the throttle and launched her foot into someone else's face before he was ready to fire. As she fell, Claire borrowed a grenade from his chest and lobbed it at an ammunition loaded truck.

"Take cover!" she told Cole in a steady voice as if everything was under control.

Boom! She remained upright, unflinching, confidently tracking the splinters as they rushed past. Her fan wasn't so lucky.

Some jerky sounds could still be heard in the hall. From where she was, unblinking for several more shots, Claire floated her gaze over to the levitating weapon as stillness claimed the entire base.

"Whew," Cole exclaimed. "I like you when you're angry."

"Mmm, that's good, because I intend to stay that way for a while." Frowning, she checked the road at the base exit. "There are still some bad boys to get."

"By the way, I spotted a fast motorbike while playing the shootout game." Cole nodded to a building recess. "I hope it's still in one piece."

As they climbed on, the saddle was soft and as comfortable as it could be between his legs, while the handlebar fabric made him feel whole.

"If you please, Miss, take this helmet," he said tactfully, "climb behind me, and hug me tight to your chest as if you're very fond of me."

"I could be," she answered, beaming. She watched him run a hand through his hair and throw her a macho look. Although awkward, she liked the gesture.

"Well then, just enjoy this wonderful ride! Now it's my turn to show off."

The motorcycle drove away at breakneck speed, leaving

behind only the smoke curling up from the wrecked trucks.

The peace of the small, European-like residence block promised another quiet day. A car was just speeding away from a house when Cole's motorcycle slowed down.

"Here's the first address." He pulled over nearby. "Nothing fishy about that car?"

"I don't know, let's check inside."

The only sounds that broke the idyllic scene were a lawn sprinkler and a child laughing inside an adjacent yard.

The two of them drew near the alleyway leading to the house's porch.

"Maybe we should get in touch with the Center first," Claire advised, "to call and make sure everything is fine here." She read the name on the mailbox set at the end of the thuja hedge. "He lives here. Tell them to warn the other Erudites. If everything's okay, we'll leave for the next—"

A violent blast shook the entire block and the blow knocked them to the ground. The Erudite's home went up in smoke. Baffled, Cole and Claire stumbled to their feet and pulled each other toward the motorcycle, which was now leaning sideways.

"Are you okay?" Claire shouted.

Cole found the strength to answer. "Yes..." He rubbed his waist and straightened his back. "Warn the people at the Center." He handed her the mobile phone. "In the meantime, we're chasing that car!"

They struggled to pull the motorcycle upright and sped in the direction of the vehicle they'd seen drive off when they first arrived.

"It's the road leading to the next address on the list," she said in his ear. "I'll guide you. I want to speak to Chris McCain, please," she then said into the phone.

Several minutes later, they spotted the runaway car on the road. It was the other, uglier model Jimmy hadn't chosen—black with sharp edges. They gained on it and flashed the high beams, but the vehicle sped up and, without checking, overtook a freight truck.

"Damn it, it's them!" the Islander realized.

From the oncoming lane, another car avoided a frontal impact at the last moment. They saw it leave the roadway and bounce across the furrows of a ploughed field into a dust cloud. The truck driver's horn blared far behind them while Cole rotated his wrist on the throttle.

When only ten meters behind the car, Claire pulled out a gun and fired two shots into the left side tires. That was enough. The car skidded to the left, jerked to the right, and then backwards. The attempt to redress failed. The car ended up crosswise on the highway, spun several times in the air, then plunged into a parapet.

The wheels of the overturned car were still rotating while the eerie thud of a tire hitting a piece of iron could be heard with each spin. Against that sinister background, the two of them approached warily, weapons at the ready. Claire was the first to notice Hoshito's blood-stained nape sticking out from the horribly twisted body of the car.

"Why am I not surprised?" she exclaimed.

He was alone, seriously wounded, and too entangled in

the wreckage to wriggle himself out. However, his wounds were already healing; he'd gotten the hang of that quickly. He watched her through the blood trickling down his face as he coughed out a jerky laughter.

"You bastard, I saw you blowing up one of the Erudites," Claire snapped, "and from what I gather from the Island's leadership, it was the second on your list. Why are you doing this?" Hoshito stopped laughing and a smile spread across his face. "Where is Kaligor?"

"Too late," came a sneering mumble. The Ragon tried to laugh again. "If I were you, I'd stop worrying about the Erudites."

"What?"

"You'll be saying hello to your Tentorian folks very soon." He pointed to the sky. "They'll all be joining us and we'll be *one biiiiig happy family* reunited on this pretty Island...taken for a little while by these primitive mortals."

He stood still, pointing at Cole while trying to reach the weapon that had fallen to the inner roof of the overturned car with the other hand.

"I think you've forgotten where you came from," Cole admonished him.

"You...primitive man. You know nothing! I know very well where I come from. You see this big scar on my left cheek? I found out a few years ago where it was truly from." He broke into a sickly cough. "More importantly, there was a message that came along with it: The payment for any mistake could be dire!"

The next moment he stretched out his hand and succeeded in grabbing hold of the gun.

The noise of the shot fired from the Islander's pistol muffled the sound of the tires revolving while Hoshito's blood gushed out of his chest and the weapon slipped out of his hand.

"What a jerk," Cole said. "Where does he think he's coming from?"

The Tentorian woman wanted to reply but she was running short on time. "I feel like they changed the plan and left with all the men for the Backup Center." She leaned over Hoshito. "That's what they did, didn't they? They've left just you to deal with the Erudites all by yourself?"

The scarred man breathed heavily then burst into a roar of laughter. The Tentorian woman leaned even closer over him and said in a poised, clear voice: "Now it's time to say goodbye, but first let me tell you who the primitive is. Everything out there you're drooling for makes you a primitive. Out there, we've evolved only to return, bit by bit, to the most basic instinct of animal survival. And we can't even do that on our own; we're using technology and robots. We no longer strive for feelings of any kind—not even happiness. When you implanted that device in your head, you gave up the most precious of all rights: that of being *human*!"

For a moment, Hoshito's expression froze as if he'd missed her point. Finally, he rolled his eyes to show how unfazed he was.

"You had the chance to be human," Claire went on, "and you missed it."

The wheel stopped spinning. Silence fell again.

The two of them turned their backs on him while the mini-drone left the device at Claire's wrist. Hoshito watched them moving away and wanted to seize the opportunity. He did not hesitate and tried again reaching the pistol. He grabbed it and pointed it at the young woman.

The echo of a gunshot broke the silence again. The still-smoking barrel of Claire's gun floated in the air behind the ally leader's head. The T of his capsule that had glimmered there just a moment ago shattered into smithereens upon contact with the flat tip of the fatal bullet.

They both got on the motorcycle.

"We must warn the people at the Center," Claire said.

"It seems no one is answering." Cole pressed the phone to his ear. "We're going there. Hang on tight, I'm going to go as fast as I can!"

Chapter 37

Several thousand kilometers away from the Island, in the heart of the small Tentorian city, the air base was bustling—Nemilo included. He was circling the presidential office like a caged lion.

"Yes, I want the first squadron to take off," he snapped at the hulky commander, large as a mountain.

"Still no sign from the Island. The shield is still there. If we hover too close, we'll draw even more attention on ourselves. Are you sure?" For his size, the man's voice was squeaky with anxiety.

Nemilo clenched his teeth. "You're taking me for an idiot; you think I'm not able to think? You have ten minutes to execute!"

The longhaired man blocked his hearing, controlled through technology, and did not listen to the reply. He shut his eyes to focus his mind on the city landscape. Seen from the surveillance devices high above, Tentoria looked even smaller to him. Too small. The building style of the 2000s was nowhere to be seen, and that pleased him. The white-grey hue of the metallic material and the cube structured modular architecture prevailed instead. But even this new style looked dated; the buildings hadn't stayed in a pristine condition for long and now they appeared frowsy and dilapidated. He gave it a thought and found he wasn't bothered at all.

The military air base spread imposingly in the middle, evenly distanced from the one hundred meter tall wall surrounding the city and glimmering like a ring of fire in the sunlight. It had been built there rather symbolically to send a blunt message to the Tentorians: here is the border of your nation; outside of it you must uphold the rules the other nations live by. Nemilo scrutinized it again and laughed inwardly. *A monument of stupidity; as if we'd give a shit about symbols!*

"Sir, the first squadron is taking off right now," the commander transmitted.

I can see that, too. What an idiot!

He grinned in awe when he looked upon the air base. Hundreds of fighter planes, the four giant cargo aircrafts, and thousands of troops were on high alert, ready for the secret mission. Troops rushed along underground corridors, heading for their aircrafts and blindly driven by the prospect of a new conquest. The black protective suits hid their faces while the grey protective lenses covering their eyes conveyed a messenger of death appearance, concealing the long-forgotten face of humanity. Through underground tunnels dozens of meters wide, huge containers were routed to the large cargo ships while whole divisions of troops ran alongside them.

Stingray-shaped airplanes rose vertically into the air as if thrust by an invisible force. A cargo ship also went up sluggishly, and Nemilo's grin took over his entire face. His Tentoria was planning a great invasion for an island to match.

GOVERNMENT_.
__SPASSING
BEYOND THI__

It had been almost an hour since that panel, half-torn and riddled with dozens of bullets, had stopped conveying the whole interdiction message in front of the Backup Center.

The stifling smoke and the smell of burning entirely took hold of the military unit. Every now and then a howl of pain and a fire burst could be heard from the rather shallow trenches hastily dug by the Island servicemen, often accompanied by the flapping wings of feasting ravens. The bullet riddled buildings also spoke of a tragically ended siege. Countless lifeless bodies of governmental soldiers, along with just a few of the enemy's, were strewn across the path into the main building. The door was hardly held in place by one hinge; wrecked offices and dozens of Islanders taken out by a single headshot indicated a fast and uneven fight concealed only by the thick smoke trying to find its way out.

Underground, in the monitoring and control room, the bodies of three Erudites lay beside their seats while the operative staff was scattered throughout the room, breathless. The main screen displayed three simple messages:

```
Access denied to all users.
All interfaces to the system are blocked.
Self-control mode active.
```

Kaligor sat in one of the kingly seats, squinting from one monitor to the other. The Island's protection parameters and the shield system were still running. His face wrinkled with hatred. He took a military laptop from a backpack, opened it, and connected it through a cable to a monitoring system console. Just by thinking, Kaligor gave it a few access commands, which were immediately displayed on the laptop screen. The result was not long in coming:

```
Access denied.
```

His voice grumbled full of impatience. "Comrades, I'm physically connected and still nothing! All I got is just a connection with you, which I had anyway until a few hours ago...when the traitor woman destroyed our communication system." A mere sigh left the other end. "You must give me something quickly, or I cannot enter the system. These fuckers have installed new technologies—here at least—just to fuck me up!"

A wounded officer lying on the floor raised his head slightly and aimed his gun at Kaligor. The deafening sound echoed off the walls and the piece of lead slammed into the intruder's back. The officer strained his finger on the trigger to fire once more when, in a split second, Kaligor flicked his wrist and a bullet suddenly hit the officer's head. The man went down in a pool of blood.

"*Everything okay there?*" came the reaction from Tentoria.

Kaligor's hoarse voice went on taunting, "Yeah, nothing to worry about! Tell me, any luck with the data I sent?"

"*We're analyzing it. We're trying to find a breach in the*

security system, a loophole, anything like that."

"I can't wait for years in here! I'm only equipped with measly, primitive weapons."

"Understood. The upside is that no matter how new the technology, the system doesn't have the latest security updates."

"All right, but you need to find something faster!" He reached behind him, grasped the flattened bullet, and stared at it with one eye closed. "I hardly have any more friends left around here."

"We're ready for an invasion with a whole army."

"Yes, yes..." *But all that force and technology will be for nothing,* Kaligor thought. *Kept at bay by a wretched shield.*

"The champagne's ready here," Nemilo stepped into the conversation from somewhere in Tentoria's presidential building. He sounded more irked than cheerful. *"I want you to rid me once and for all of this shitty shield,"* he roared, *"so I can lay my feet again on our land! I want to go home in the new Tentoria!"*

"I'm waiting for you, my brethren!" Kaligor gloated.

Under a staircase, not far from the main entrance, two people sat on the floor leaning against each other. Their faces and clothes could barely be made out under many blood stains and grime.

"Chris, you have to hold on!" The cramps in her bleeding

leg stifled Drew's voice.

"What's my life worth now..." he spat his words through blood-coated lips. His bulletproof vest had been pierced by large-caliber bullets; they'd gone straight through his abdomen. "Where is Arnar?" he mumbled.

"I don't know. I lost touch with him. The last time I saw him he was going down into the monitoring room."

"I hope he's fine," he said, clenching his teeth in pain. "I'm sorry...sorry for not doing more...I was naive!"

"It's not your fault, it's the Tentorians. And we...we all did our best."

"Yes, but I was a Tentorian too, Drew. I was..." He gnashed his teeth again. "I could have had all the technology we needed to defend ourselves had I known it would come to this."

"But why did we not have this technology just in case? Why just a shield and the monitoring system?"

Chris was silent. Drew had never seen him so vulnerable, and now, all sorts of scenarios burning like torches in a dark cave slipped through her mind. *Why does he keep asking about Arnar? Arnar may be the other Tentorian...* She frowned. *But no, he didn't seem to know a thing. I've been around him for so long; I'd have sensed it.* Then, in an agonizing drawl, she decided to press the matter.

"Chris, I understand that only the Erudites should know the naked truth, but just look at us." She pointed at the stained clothes. "What's the point of hiding it from me now? I want to know the truth. How did we get here?"

"Drew..." He hesitated for a long while. Daring to look no more than a second into her eyes, he took a deep breath and swallowed. "It couldn't be otherwise. Although it is hard to believe, it all started just 60 years ago..."

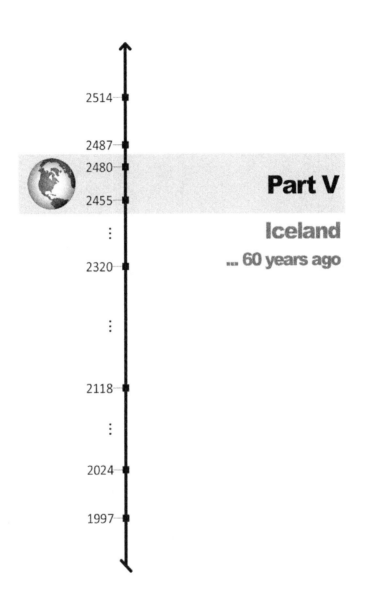

2514—

2487—

2480—

2455—

⋮

2320—

⋮

2118—

⋮

2024—

1997—

Part V

Iceland

... 60 years ago

Chapter 38

"Today we're going to change this corrupt president of ours who's been robbing us blind for years!"

That's what the young man told his grandmother while donning his new T-shirt. It was way too important of a day not to wear it; the day when the whole country was going to vote.

He had been franchised two months ago and now promised to change the fate of the country along with most of his fellow young citizens. A country like none other among the nations all over the world had been purposely held back in a primitive age. They lived in a century where the agricultural production methods were so developed that food was no longer a problem anywhere in the world. However, the young man's family lived from hand to mouth, starving more often than not, their house nothing but a door-less, dusty hut without electricity.

Young people were proud as the polls showed the defeat of the tyrant who spelled misery and indigence, setting up a system to loot the country's resources for the benefit of a few rulers.

Special air vehicles gathered villagers from all across the country to fly them to the polling places. Our young man was among them. Once they arrived at the nearest town, they were left right next to the polling station where people crowded the entrance.

"Any giveaways?" he inquired.

"Warm food and nutrient packs," a dolt, feeble old man answered. "They say that pack alone will last a guy three months."

"They must be doing that to make us vote for that bastard!"

"No, my lad. They ask nothing, tell us nothing! They say it's an organization that works for the people's welfare...and they have come to dish out food."

"Ah, good!" He was pleased.

On the yard by the polling station, there were hundreds of long tables where the future voters waited some minutes before getting in line to cast their ballots. But these were the minutes that would change their decisions; these were the tables on which sat the warm food to keep the country under corruption and tyranny for another five years.

A flowless technological recipe conceived by sick minds hidden within some businessmen's skulls was the spice appropriately added to the dispensed food.

Billions of nanobots and chemicals now ran freely through the bodies of the future voters; the host's brain was the target. The nanobots assessed the intention to vote, altering thousands of connections and spreading key substances to all the right places. Everything was followed by the self-destruction of the nanobots and the removal of all traces that might have indicated they'd been there.

THE SECOND DAY. IN A SMALL ICELANDIC TOWN

...a poll indicating that the current leader would lose the elections even in urban areas was proven yesterday to have

been a complete misrepresentation. Either it had been rigged by the opposition, or simply badly done. What's certain is that yesterday the population of the African nation showed by a majority of 73% that they want their "beloved" leader to remain in power for one more term...

The news was interrupted by Chris's angry voice. "What's that, Nemilo?" The two were sitting in the board room of the small presidential building on the island, from which they ran the daily Tentorian governance activities together with other Tentorian leaders.

"There's a lot of money at stake, my friend—a hell of a lot of money. If you only knew what natural resources lie idle in that country—"

"I don't care about money made by methods well beyond the limits of ethics!" Chris was red with fury and his blood throbbed through his prominent veins. "I went speechless when I heard of the despicable method you resorted to. Who came up with this horrible idea?"

"You have to admit, I'm a genius!"

Chris snorted indignantly.

"Since the client has paid for the most subtle resolution of the situation, we had to come up with something ingenious. The man was clearly losing the election. All international organizations were closely monitoring this event, thousands of observers were there; there was no way for us to go unprofessional."

Nemilo grinned proudly while Chris paced the room rubbing the top of his head. "I'm leaving you, Nemilo!"

The longhaired thug woke up abruptly from his self-glorifying thoughts. He froze, gazing at Chris. "And...where are you going? What are you gonna do?"

"Anything but that."

"That's what it means to be a Tentorian, my friend. That's the way we live: state-of-the-art technology to the fullest! All nations know it."

"We can change all that! Tentorian shall no more mean murders and dirty business."

Nemilo flared his nostrils. "As if we're the only ones playing this dirty game!"

"Huh? We just about have a monopoly over the worst offer in the business."

"That's not enough," Nemilo said. "And we're not alone, remember? Our clients, too, are in it. Companies eager to make money from everything: security solutions against our illegal practices on the one hand, and the illicit development of technologies supporting such practices on the other. Ironic, huh? *They're* the dirty ones." He snorted again, louder. "I bet if we stopped, others would take over."

"Let common people make such bets. Let's give mankind a better chance!"

"Come on, Chris. Quit the talk about mankind! It all began many years before we even existed, as early as the 21st century."

Chris pondered on the highly regarded technological explosion of that time; the progress worked wonders. In the 21st century, everything looked like it would be fine in the long run—the future held promise. Automation was making people's lives more beautiful and easier; it laid everything at their feet.

"But now we're the thirsty ones, the destroyers, Nemilo. Can't you see?"

Nemilo rolled his eyes and said grudgingly, "In the human DNA lies the urge for more, the instinct to advance; to get better, more intelligent, more beautiful, to live longer, to have more. As a matter of fact, they are the thirsty ones. We're just their product—their mirror image."

"With such thinking as yours, more hatred and hunger for power has come into the world. Don't you see that step by step, we overtook every limit in the chase to get more and more?"

Unwillingly, his thoughts turned to the past again. In the 21st century, all the greed had led to increasingly numerous, severe global incidents, creating a melting pot that led to another world war—a war that broke out quickly early in the 22nd century. Media liked to call it a "world war"; they said "If it does not look like the previous world wars, it does not mean it should be seen just as a major conflict." Indeed, it had looked nothing like the wars before. It had been subtler, without clear battlefields, without a lot of physical battles, and without large armies standing face to face. Most battles had been informational, waged by way of computers on the cyber front. Only the manipulated idealists, the poor, the uneducated, and people in underprivileged areas were the real victims. Sadly, they were many...*and many died.*

Chris did not try to mince words. "If you don't stop now, you'll turn into a monster. A soulless mobster. And a whole nation along with you."

Nemilo did not appear hurt by such words—just the opposite. Then he was amused by the thought that he could stop his hearing and let him chatter. Instead, he ignored him and looked out the window at a geyser. A column of hot steam suddenly burst out and it seemed to him that he could see a rainbow appearing. *I could see the same show even if the geyser was artificial... and it would have a bigger rainbow than that.* Then he asked himself whether that geyser was still entirely natural. *How stupid! Just as stupid as this guy's idea to stand against my businesses. I was a genius out there, in Africa!* Nanotechnology joined with artificial intelligence and medical developments were putting massive amounts into the pockets of those willing to play the dirty game; and Nemilo knew he was the ideal player.

"If everything sounds possible in theory," he said, "why not put it into practice?"

Chris did not wait to see a self-satisfied smile on the longhaired man's face. "Because most nations and international organizations have long decided to ban these unethical practices, *'because if further used,'*" he remembered word for word what had been said, "*'mankind would lose its essence; its DNA'*".

He recalled that amid all those interdictions, imposed mainly by the Luxembourg Treaty, the Tentorians managed to thrive on an exponential manner; what was illegal was even more expensive. It was like a new drug, and the wars and conflicts around the world proved to be a fine incentive for this illegal industry.

They had once been only a few thousand World War survivors—bionic people trained and equipped to fight, to influence key people, to influence the masses, to constantly adapt, and to act for just one collective goal: the conquest of new territories through economic and administrative control. But, with time, their appearance had evolved, too; they had long ceased to be easily told apart from the masses. They had also evolved in terms of numbers, multiplying both naturally and artificially in laboratories, trebling every half a century. They aspired to be more numerous and powerful, ready to stand behind over 80% of the illegal practices around the world.

Nemilo gave Chris a taunting look. "And if you leave the leadership, how will you make ends meet—if you don't mind my asking?"

"By enjoying being honest; being human. No one has died of hunger that way."

The arrogant leader burst into a crooked laugh. "Now you've got my undivided attention...so what are you gonna do, pal?" he repeated the question.

"You'll find out when I make up my mind. For the moment, I resign all my leadership duties. Don't rely on me and don't ask me anything!"

Chris walked out, his head down, not looking back, under Nemilo's baffled, loathing gaze. He walked until he found himself alone and halted, sat down beside a wall, put his face in his hands, and asked aloud in a despaired, quivering voice, the question running through his mind: "How did we end up here?"

In the year 2455, many boundaries had been left behind. Technological revolutions took place unbelievably fast. Every field, every industry had been soaring to new heights every year. Everything was increasingly automated, digitized, virtualized; even the imagination of humans and their creative power had been surpassed by machines.

"Are you okay?" the voice of a child awoke him from his ramblings into the past.

Chris looked around. Although he'd been there many times before, the walls of the passageway where he had stopped seemed so strange. Attached to the child's arm, he noticed a sticker-like device. *It's a...toy device*, he thought. The kid didn't wait for an answer; he raised his arms horizontally as if trying to fly and walked away, still engrossed in his incomprehensible game. *Virtual...* Chris mused. *How did these kids end up having access to everything? What's the point?*

He thought of the human body merging evolutions in the medical and technological fields and goose bumps formed on his skin. These facts should have frightened any sensible mind. Knowledge of the human body had reached depths never before seen. Cellular and molecular life, reactions of all kinds happening within the body down to the smallest sizes had become known at length and *everything could be controlled.*

A tear had dried on his gloomy face. Chris stood and started walking back home, reeling. While his steps took him down a road enlivened mostly by virtual images rather than flesh and blood, his face lit up as an idea struck him. He stopped and raised his eyes to an empty blue space in the middle of a cloudy grey sky. He merely whispered, for fear someone might overhear him, "Eureka!"

Chapter 39

...In the businessman's opinion, it looked like a large-scale action, carefully coordinated and painstakingly prepared. It all began when his biometric identification data was stolen from a government database. It went on with the theft of his personal banking information and ended up by using the latest medical and cybernetic technologies to entirely transform a John Doe into an identical clone of Jean-Pierre, who showed up at the bank headquarters to complete the transactions. Nobody suspected a thing. That was how the richest man in the world, businessman Jean-Pierre Albert, got robbed. Until then he thought himself invulnerable on account of his colossal wealth and the security system around him.

The bank director told us that he knew Jean-Pierre personally and before closing the transactions leading to his fortune being halved, he insisted on having a talk face to face. Even now he couldn't believe the person who showed up at the bank was a clone. The bank's position was clear: as long as a procedural error cannot be ascertained, the bank shall be discharged of any liability.

Might have been the Mob involved or the person who showed up was Jean-Pierre indeed? As yet, it's anybody's guess...

Chris' connected brain had just received this news, and the thought of a similar incident happening only several months after the Africa one beclouded his face. He immediately asked the communication device to connect him to Nemilo.

"I want us to meet face to face," Chris spoke his mind.

Nemilo's taunt was not long in coming. "What's the point, with all this technology? I am practically in your room, if you allow me."

"I'm in no mood for jokes. It's a very important matter I need to discuss with you."

In less than one hour, the two were in Nemilo's office.

"A couple of months ago I promised to let you know what I decided," Chris said.

Nemilo stopped him with the air of someone wishing to show who was in charge. "First of all, a drink! What will you have?"

"A...whisky please."

"Fetch me a beer only you know how to brew." Nemilo looked up as if someone had been listening to him the whole time. "When I taste it I wanna feel like I'm in Amsterdam in the year 2000."

The drink bottles flew to them from a bar, seemingly unsupported; they landed plainly on a table. Chris poured his whisky into his glass while Nemilo sipped his beer straight from the bottle. He gave it a pleased once over as he set it on the table.

Chris watched him patiently, but now he seemed to find something wrong even in holding an artificially produced beverage in his hand. The guest took stock of how deeply everything had changed in the last century. Everything well-meant when it started ended up being used in practices beyond the borders of ethics; reality was no longer confined even to the imagination. Not just the drink in his hand, but even the brain, one's thoughts, intelligence and more could be designed, modelled, enhanced, altered, or obliterated. The bank incident had once again proven to Chris that facial or full body transformations going to the point of a complete identity change were relentlessly busting through increasingly fewer ethical barriers. Information technology and nanotechnology had become so advanced as to perform the transformations with precision, making everyone ask 'who is who?', 'what is what?', 'what does somebody or something really look like?'

He looked into the whisky glass and didn't feel like taking another sip. *This glass could just as easily be filled with water...or a virus.*

Nemilo's listless voice brought him down to earth. "You have my attention now!" He took another gulp of beer.

Chris' face lit up. "It's a plan for the future you could be part of if you wish."

Nemilo raised an eyebrow. "I like the plans for the future."

"I want to build a region or...better still, a nation—a country—to go back in time and live by the rules and technology of the late 20th century."

"What do you mean?" Nemilo smiled.

"We destroy everything we touch. Don't you see? I want us to change that; I want to be seen as a *man* making a difference, changing the rules of the game. Now that we have plenty to work with, we can change that."

"We haven't destroyed anyone, pal."

The guest protested calmly, "Look around you. We started from a small town and now we've spread more or less all over Iceland. The people who have lived here for generations are starting to leave."

"No one threw them out."

"They are afraid, Nemilo, of banding with us, sharing the same territory."

"Very well then. Good riddance!"

"We're ruining such a beautiful country. Soon the nations will realize what's going on and will attack us here, where the people once welcomed us with open arms."

"Rubbish!"

"I can't stand any more of this dirty business. I'm afraid to even ask whether you have a hand in the Jean-Pierre Albert incident."

By way of an answer, the smug leader's lips puckered. Chris let out a disgruntled sigh.

"I thought as much."

Nemilo stood as if already bored. "You have any more...brilliant sci-fi ideas? What you want is to basically give up everything defining us, providing us power and wealth, and live like primitives?"

"No, my proposal is to make history and lead a *human* life! Aren't you tired?"

"Absolutely not!" came the resolute reply. "Every nation in this world has been using the technology of the last centuries. Maybe less than us..." Nemilo smiled wickedly, "but, well, that's their problem."

"But we can make a difference; we can set an example. I have this dream and I want to show the world that it can be done!"

"I think you need to get some rest. Everything you say sounds wacky to me and I actually have some work to do. I accepted your resignation when you asked for it. I think you're already going haywire."

Chris straightened his back and his voice grew deeper. "I don't need rest, Nemilo. I will set up this territory without you. All these practices will be prohibited there. This wretched technology that destroys everything in its path, destroys lives...I'll have none of that there."

"Very well," Nemilo cut him short, "let me know when you've done that. Maybe I'll pay you a visit! Now, if you will excuse me, more important things than tear-jerking meetings need my attention."

He turned and left the room, trying to impersonate Chris a few months back when he resigned.

Chris raised his voice to make himself heard. "I'll take my brother with me!"

Nemilo stopped for a second before he went on his way.

Chris's "brother" was not a blood relation. He was in fact a boy with whom he'd grown up. They were born the same day, in the same incubation process. *It's been so long since we both saw the light of day together,* Chris thought. *So many years...*

He remembered that such a long life had once seemed like daydreaming. Now, in the 25th century, it was proven that through constant transformations and redevelopments of the body, everlasting life was within reach. Hence, thousands of conflicting questions about ethics for some, and religion for the few believers left.

Chris and his "brother" had also been the offspring of the latest technology; the outcome of the global war had spawned the world's first generation of Tentorians, they themselves political pundits. Until a few years ago, they had been close-knit, spending their spare time together, with their families, thinking the same way, working together on projects, and both of them in the Tentorian leadership next to Nemilo. Although they still saw themselves as close to each other, they had slowly become estranged in time.

Not with Nemilo! What was I thinking? I'll lay the foundations of this new nation with my brother, Chris mused as he sat in the aircraft taking him home after the meeting with Nemilo. He stared out the window while his eyes brightened like a wonderful spring day. From up here, Iceland looked beautiful. Lakes and thermal springs shone in the sunlight like quicksilver, while beneath his feet was a vast carpet dominated by the blue of lupine flowers interspersed with the green of wild herbs and the dandelions' yellow hues. From up above, he could also see the steam in the Geysers Valley, and the geysers spluttering in white jets like whales. On the horizon, the sun crawled up the highest mountain ridges to wallow into the blue sky. At the foot of the mountains, the black grey of the upland lava desert blended with the golden yellow of the sulfur-covered hills consistently bordered by the birch trees' whitish green tints.

This was the island the Tentorians had picked to settle on. They could by no means be called tasteless; its unsurpassed beauty and the increasingly pleasant climate had reigned in the last centuries. The temperatures, once steeply lower, were now ideal; in the last few hundred years, global climate changes turned Iceland into one of the best places on Earth to live.

We spread like a contagion! Although at first they had only settled in a small town, they had over time scattered across the entire surface of the northern island. From there, they conducted business throughout the world. Some of the Tentorians understood they were treading treacherous grounds, but most of them just became greedier and bared the fangs of the monster lying inside their primordial structure. Human cloning, brain transformation or control, illicit cybernetic or medical activities of any kind, crimes that could not be proven, identity changes, overnight conversions from one religious belief to another... the list could continue indefinitely.

Not with Nemilo! the thought came back.

"Call Arnar Arnason," he said to the aircraft computer.

Arnar's voice came through immediately. *"Speak, brother!"*

"You remember the project we both dreamed of a few years ago?"

Half an hour of conversation later, Chris understood he was thoroughly alone in this project.

"I can't do it now, brother. Everything representing me is right here," Arnar concluded.

"You're sure you don't want some time to think?"

"Admit it, Chris, it'll never work."

"Maybe not, but at least I wish I knew you out of that bunch. They're monsters, Arnar. Monsters!"

"They told me they wanted to make peace with the nations."

"It's a lie; they want to use you because they know you are well connected and have political clout! You can be a renowned Tentorian at another level too; you don't have to stay so high in the leadership forever."

For a few moments, the conversation fell prey to silence.

"Chris, you are happy, so what's your problem? Why do you want to...complicate your life?" Arnar struggled to find the right words.

"Deep inside, I don't feel human. I'm not happy..."

The rest of the conversation came to a quick end. His own brother had stabbed him smack in the belly. He could have sworn they would be together forever, no matter the path he took. He was wrong. Chris now found himself lonelier than ever on an adventure he wanted to begin regardless of the costs.

Other nations had also enforced regulations that restricted in one way or another the use of certain practices or technologies, but no one had done what he was imagining. It was an ambitious project—it was an insane project. *It's hard to become human once more,* he thought sadly.

Chapter 40

"It's been three years today since we began enjoying the air of the 2000s by using none of the following years' technology. We live like humans, we feel the energy of each passing day, real feelings, and tastes. Everything is real, no more a dream or an illusion; we are no longer led by technology."

Thousands of thunderous cheers filled the auditorium. Chris raised a hand.

"Ladies, gentlemen...it's your merit. Congratulations. I hope our dream will continue to be real for the rest of our lives."

Rank and file and important people alike stood up to applaud.

This was the locally broadcasted conference held at the end of each year, where the representatives of the newly founded region presented the track record. Chris succeeded in making his dream come true. He closed his eyes and relished the moment. He was no longer interested in the outside world; he felt truly happy in the midst of the community of one million people who had chosen this path. He enjoyed the fact that all the nations had saluted the project and talked about it as the new and maybe only hope for mankind. The Icelandic authorities had also backed them fully and unconditionally provided the area of the West Fjords to be settled by this community. They also acknowledged its separation by a border, the sole purpose of which was to isolate the region from 25th century technology. No technology above that of the 2000s could cross that border any longer, and no person could step outside. It was the responsibility of each member to comply with the commonly endorsed rules, but it was a community that had freely chosen to live this way, perfectly aware of what lay beyond its border. Outside that territory, however, in the rest of the island, things were taking a turn for the worse. The spread of technology and of the Tentorians themselves grew more and more bothersome. Only the new community in the West Fjords still gave Iceland some hope.

One hand went up from the crowd as soon as silence had fallen again. "Does that mean you won't approve Maya's cure?"

Chris hesitated at first then spoke calmly, "Madam, I am not God, nor do I wish to make any decisions concerning anyone's life by myself. We all ended up here because we wished for one thing and one thing alone: to no more use outside technology. As you might have heard, I'll push forward for all of you to decide on this case by voting."

Worried looks were cast at him from all over the hall. Maya's case had been making headlines. Maya, a 60 year old woman suffering from a rare disease, could have been cured only by way of the outside world's cutting-edge technology. She wanted dearly to be cured but also didn't wish to leave the community forever; she wanted to stay near her family.

Chris took out his handkerchief and wiped the sweat covering his forehead. Then he carried on talking to the woman having asked the question, concealing the struggling of his heart from his voice.

"But let me ask you one thing: are you ready to take responsibility for creating this precedent, when three years ago you swore you would not use any of the new technology again?"

The lady stammered, unable to utter a word.

"No problem, ma'am," Chris came to her aid. "You don't have to answer me! It's just a thing we should all meditate upon. I thank you all; I wish you great success in the New Year and don't forget to lead a humble life and live like real humans!"

Chapter 41

YEAR 2482. VESTFIRDIR (THE WEST
FJORDS), ICELAND

Chris climbed on stage behind the microphone,
looking blankly in the direction of the spotlights. He was in
the same auditorium, and nothing had changed in the seven
years between now and then. He faced almost the same
crowd and the same cameras. Unfortunately, this hall was
one of the few things that still reminded him of the 2000s.
He stared vacantly and felt the pressure of the lie
surrounding him. The words left his lips devoid of any
emotion:

"Only seven years have passed since the first precedent:
the nation's vote to send Maya outside to be healed." The
prattle in the hall was broken off immediately by his voice.
"She came back in less than a week, younger and healthier
than many her age..."

He took a break and tried to look as many people as
possible in the eye.

"Then, within several months, the second case came.
Why should someone die when they could have lived tens or
hundreds of years more? It all seemed natural; a new
precedent had been created."

He cleared his throat and inhaled; he was afraid of his
words sounding strange or offensive.

"Then, there were many cases and we ended up dealing

278   TENTORIA with embarrassing situations of...beauty interventions, which otherwise would have turned into," he cleared his throat, "suicides: the well-known case five years ago, when a gentleman got it into his head his life was worthless without that aesthetic surgery."

Again, his gaze swept over the crowd.

"Ladies, gentlemen, allow me to read you this year's track record—at least in the manner it was presented to me; I am sure the figures are way more disturbing. Out of a population of eleven hundred thousand people, we had more than twenty-five thousand medical interventions outside the West Fjords with state-of-the-art nanotechnology; over fifty thousand beauty interventions, tens of thousands of cutting-edge technological devices reported as existing within the territory, even the use of 25th century industrial practices with people being replaced by machines..."

The bustle in the hall drowned out his voice for a few seconds.

"Maybe it would not sound so awful and some could say it's the evolution which we must take advantage of, but for the following figures, I have also received proof of the same evolution."

He looked at the sheet he held and sighed. After moving closer to the microphone, he read.

"The last year's track record submitted by the police authorities: a 250% increase of crimes and a 180% increase of manslaughters; 36 cases of identity theft, 23 disappearances—have they gone up in smoke? Where are they? Does anyone know?" He raised his eyelids to the crowd before he continued reading from the sheet. "Three cases of cloning! A home disintegrated in one second just because someone got angry with his neighbor and made up his mind to try his new *gadget*; two facial aesthetic surgeries done without the subject's consent—out of jealousy."

Chris raised his voice, speaking loudly and clearly, baring the despair and anxiety in his soul.

"A monster's record: 38 rapes in only one week; that was his age and that's how he thought fit to celebrate. We all wondered how he could prey on so many people in such a short span of time without getting busted. We found out later: by way of the new technology, ladies and gentlemen!" Only a woman's sobs were heard—the mother of one of the victims. "They fell prey, unable to fight back, as you well know," Chris carried on. "A simple device smuggled into the West Fjords made all that possible."

Other seconds of silence descended on those present.

"Fourteen kids kidnapped by another felon, after giving them nanotechnology-laced sweets. From that moment on, it could no longer be called kidnapping—the children came on their own. Fate was direr to them than to the 38 women; we all mourned three days for these innocent angels."

A tear was about to trickle down his cheek; he wiped it away as quickly as possible.

"So I ask you now, where have we gone? Let me answer, too: probably not far from where we've come from."

He almost whispered the last words, folded his sheet, and left the stage without looking at the crowd again.

Chapter 42

THREE MONTHS LATER

The three naked women were completely wrapped around him, undulating and moaning. Nemilo lay in bed smoking a cigarette, feeling them down to the innermost recesses of bodily pleasure and ogling them.

Boss? a voice jarred in his head.

He started as if electrocuted. *What the hell? This'd better be important! Arnar, I told you not to contact me directly unless that was the case!*

It is.

Although the two weren't actually speaking, Arnar was baffled by his reaction. Usually he loved to use this technology. It was one of the very few situations Nemilo was loathed the direct neuronal communication through his implant.

Spit it out! Nemilo rushed him.

The President of Iceland wishes to speak to you.

The boss coughed convulsively. He cleared his throat and the hologram of the three women disappeared. His pleasure had been cut short anyway.

"Put me through!" he spoke out loud.

In merely a second, the voice of the President of Iceland was heard in the background. By the whisperings at the other end, Nemilo counted at least 20 people in the same room with the president.

"You know, I was in the midst of a very important activity," he began the conversation.

"I'm sorry, I wasn't told that," the president excused himself.

"What's all this about?"

"I'll be very brief. I am in an extraordinary presidential meeting with other dignitaries. This call is an ultimatum. All I need you to know is that we endorse the Alliance's plan and that we have joined them. In only two hundred years, you have destroyed one of the few natural heritages still existing on this planet, you have destroyed the land of the nation that I lead, and in the last thirty years you have indirectly driven away almost the entire indigenous population to other parts of the world."

"Yes...you've told me that before. Everyone's free to adapt to change—to evolution."

A sizeable pause made space for the whispers bursting out in the room.

Arnar was listening, too. After trying to make out the voices at the other end, he unwillingly came to contemplate the situation they were in. And his thoughts went to the country of the man with whom Nemilo was talking.

In Iceland, for years on end the incidents had spiked; people increasingly left their homeland because all of their hope had vanished. The native population went down, but Tentorians—once a minority—had spread and multiplied, now making up the vast majority of the population. Iceland had been conquered from the inside. Of the entire island there was but one territory to which the Tentorians had no access, nor did they have any desire to visit: the West Fjords; the region Chris had founded.

As for the rest, each inhabited region of the island turned

into a downright modern ghetto of the Tentorians. Of them only a small fraction disapproved of their leadership's actions, thinking anxiously about the nation's future. However, they were afraid that an uprising would spell doom for them; they had to play the same game, to shut their eyes and obey. The vast Tentorian majority, however, continued to fully endorse everything forbidden by the Nations and implicitly sent just one message to the world: they wished to remain the way they had been designed, soulless machines in a bionic world addicted to technology, in a world devoid of real people.

When the whispers in the room reached a consensus, the President of Iceland coughed shortly and resumed his sententious tone.

"I believe that the message I am sending you now will be very clear: you have exactly three months to leave the island. This is my final offer, not one day more! Otherwise all that's left of the Icelandic authorities as well as the Icelandic people on this island shall join the Nations to wage a war you have never seen. This Alliance has declared zero tolerance of the present state of things."

Nemilo grew smug. "Okay, anything else?"

"I'm afraid not."

Although he should have been irked by the way the Island's President was not mincing his words, the longhaired man smiled arrogantly. He was pondering the outcome of the largest deal in Tentorian history he had just successfully concluded. *Maybe that's what chafed them,* he thought, *but it was worth it; I'd do it again anytime I could.*

He had sent a thousand people into a conflicted area with only one objective: to fan the dissention to the point of generating a large-scale war. The payoff? A multiple-figure sum coming from a corporation producing weapons and security devices. The Tentorians had enforced their trademark methods: human cloning and inroads into people's minds. It was easy to spark a conflict between the followers of two rival religions, a couple of years earlier; with the help of the Tentorians, it was spread across two continents. This was enough to cloud the minds of many and lead them into radicalization. The end result: 30 million victims.

It did not take long for these details to come to light, but the Tentorians had cashed in their money and the epic proportions of damage had been done.

"It's gone too far," the President of Iceland thought out loud after cutting off the conversation. He looked round at the representatives of dozens of nations that had joined forces with his country. This time, having them on his side, he felt he could wipe out the Tentorians. This Alliance had the strength to counteract the Tentorians' actions, and if necessary, fight them directly. They had voted on everything they needed for an impending onslaught in Iceland; they were prepared to use whatever methods required to crush the troublemakers.

Chapter 43

"Ladies, gentlemen, today I declare myself defeated in the face of the fundamental instinct of acquiring as much as one can, of being as beautiful and accomplished as possible. I declare myself defeated by the blind desire of the human race to merge with technology, by the machine which keeps pushing us further. I declare myself defeated in the face of evolutionism, which seems to be moving in only one direction: the man-machine, the Man-God. I feel small and powerless before what mankind has turned itself into!"

His heart was gripped by the claws of the silent, frozen crowd. From the stand in the middle of the stage, Chris swallowed hard.

"Once," he started off in fairytale fashion, "we all said that time, no matter how limited, can seem an eternity if we knew how to spend it. Saving time through the use of robots for any task in order to only spend it later in a virtual reality isn't doing us much good. We all said that the beauty of everything real was lost that way. Today, in the West Fjords, many of you changed their minds. They forgot why we all came here in the first place."

Some whispers cut through the tension-laden atmosphere like sharp blades.

"There was a time when all of us here realized that if

everyone was undergoing aesthetic surgery, correction, changing their appearance and body overnight to become models, then there would be no physical criteria to tell us apart. The beauty thus acquired would practically be pointless. The next step would then be trying to set ourselves apart otherwise...in insane ways: through body part and personality adjustments that had nothing to do with being human, through pointless body marks or blending advanced technologies with human functions—namely bionic mutations."

The speechless crowd gazed at him, mesmerized by the words striking a deep chord.

"We used to tell ourselves that we wanted everything to be natural so nothing could change us. We said that we wanted to be born, live, and die; that we had no desire to live forever because we'd go crazy anyway. We wanted to concentrate all our happiness on the number of years nature provided for us. Eighty, ninety, or one hundred...we wished no more!"

He rubbed his eyes and forehead. Chris had summoned them on short notice to give them this speech, which was also his last. Street riots were intensified by arguments over what must be allowed and what not, and soon people began leaving the area. The West Fjords now faced problems of an equal magnitude as those existing in any other part of the island.

"Today this community is like any other. There's nothing different about us, there's nothing that makes us better, and we can no longer say that we are fully *humans*. I had a dream, and the dream fell apart. I bow to the future, I will forget the past, and I will forget the true values of humankind. I regretfully conclude that there is no turning back."

He ended in a waning voice and left the scene without anyone having the pluck to speak a word. Reality was dire and their project had failed. They had all failed.

Chapter 44

The grey haired man stood before the people at the round table. The prominent bags under his eyes spoke of many sleepless nights and his uncanny drive to try to save his country. There were not enough seats in the room to accommodate all those wishing to be there in flesh and blood. Many white haired people, lots of insignias pinned on chests, and many stiff suits. It was way too important of a decision for the ministers, generals, and presidents from all over the world to miss. Still, the meeting was held behind closed doors with no media, and the public knew nothing about it.

"Gentlemen," the man said, "the Icelandic Ministry of Defense confirmed that the entire population has been evacuated. I confirm the same for all armed units we had in our territory."

Some of the people began whispering over the much-debated decision, while a middle-aged lady kept on anchoring the meeting. "Thank you, Mr. President! Mr. Samuelson, you have the floor!"

A tall, stylish, and sophisticated man rose. "Thank you. As you have seen displayed, the status of the interventions in the places agreed upon looks encouraging. Allow me to read you some figures about the action I managed with you."

His gaze went to the table that had turned into an immense display from which he read.

"The worldwide operation took place simultaneously in 3058 sites in 96 countries; 9250 people were detained, of whom approximately 7500 we believe are Tentorians; 450 businesses that were proven to cover illicit activities were ceased; the body count..." He paused, glancing at the entire audience, "is 1296 people, of whom 130 were ours." He bowed his head for a moment. "It was a blitz operation that took exactly two hours, and now we have to do questionings, checkups, take legal actions, and the like."

The man's speech continued with a review of the current state of facts, aiming to prepare the audience for the true highlight of the meeting. He reminded them of the last half-year of heavy fighting between the Alliance of Nations and the Tentorian Forces. Inside the so-called Tentorian "hive" on the Icelandic territory, they had waged the greatest battles, the latest military technology had been employed, but the blows dealt to the Tentorians failed to stop them. Most of the inhabitants had left Iceland for safer territories long before the last 24 hour's official evacuation. The West Fjords project was over, while the inhabitants of the area had also left the island some time before.

The Alliance was concluding a time of mourning, and the man was not shy in pointing it out. The Nations had already made a great mistake by going to such a war on the island. They thought they could save it, they thought they could defeat the Tentorians on their own turf, they thought they could divide, repel, and scatter them. They had aimed high but were proven wrong. They lost way too many people and equipment in this war—twice as many as the Tentorians. It was obvious who the real war expert was from the economics to the hand to hand conflict. It left no doubt as to the master of the real military technology—in particular inside the "hive". The last battles heartened the Tentorians. More than ever before, they saw themselves undefeatable.

It took a stroke of genius from the part of the Alliance—a stroke that could eventually lead to victory in this war. They had finally put an end to the battles that led nowhere. They decided to create a crisis cell supposed to end it all in the course of a 24-hour operation. The first two phases of the plan had been completed successfully: a rapid evacuation of the island and a blitz attack all over the globe in places where the Tentorians operated. The third and most important phase was now at hand.

When the tall man mentioned that the evacuation message had also been officially transmitted to all Tentorians, who had to agree to live in a community controlled from outside of Iceland, two gentlemen pulled faces.

"May I remind you, gentlemen, that this was the majority vote," he replied promptly. "If you please..."

The man specified some of the Tentorians had understood the impending danger and left the island, agreeing to be registered and follow the program imposed by the Nations. They were guaranteed their freedom, "Provided they leave the island without any of their personal belongings, got checked out, and identified by the International Court of Justice to prove they were not involved in actions the Nations deemed unlawful". However, many remained, refusing to evacuate. Some deemed themselves invincible and wished to waste any Alliance soldier who set foot in their territory, while others felt responsible for too many transgressions against international laws. There were also those unwilling to comply with the official evacuation plan and getting ready to leave the island unofficially, shunning the control and seeking refuge in one of the safe havens they still had on the planet. They planned to later return to what they knew best.

"Ladies and gentlemen," Mr. Samuelson continued, "first I'd like to congratulate you for the success of the first two phases, and especially for accomplishing the second one in a record-breaking interval."

In the council room, silence stressed the unassuming stance of those present. They only bowed their heads in acknowledgement. In the last 24 hours, the Tentorians had been dealt a real masterstroke. Panic had replaced their usual conceit and defiance for the first time. It built up gradually in their minds and exploded. Their lust for power and cruelty were now shrinking. No one knew exactly what was behind this evacuation, but the remaining Tentorians were preparing for the worst. They had geared up with the most advanced fighting technology on the market, ready to face anything on their turf.

The man cleared his throat. "Unfortunately, we have data on a number of Tentorians that have been very active in the last few hours. They fled the island and skirted our check up program. The Tentorian leadership may have understood what's coming by now and could already be on the run. Therefore, I think we need to launch phase three immediately."

After ten minutes of intense arguments, a dignitary wearing many insignias pursed his lips and broke the murmur in the room. "We confirm that the missiles are in launching position."

Mr. Samuelson spoke again, this time looking in the

direction of the President of Iceland. "Dear comrades, Mr. President, everything that moves on the island, everything that has ever been built—and I mean *everything*," he emphasized and paused briefly, thinking of the non-nuclear advanced weapon of mass destruction they had fine-tuned, "will be vaporized within several minutes! Now is the last chance you have to raise any objections to this decision."

He waited calmly for all five seconds of silence while some people looked at each other or to the ground.

"In this case, I consider the decision made and approve its immediate execution. Before that, allow me a brief personal comment. We lost too many people and too many resources in this war, so there's no doubt in my mind this is the right decision." He turned to the man brimming with insignias. "General, please start the launch."

2514

2487
2480

2455

⋮

2320

⋮

2118

⋮

2024

1997

Part VI

The Fate of the Island

Chapter 45

JULY 18, 2514, THE PRESENT TIME. THE ISLAND

The Erudite had long stopped telling his story and only a dense fog floated before his eyes, similar to the one that hovered over the island for several months after the surprise strike of the Alliance.

"Hey, are you in there?" Drew tried to snap him out of it. "I asked you how we got here on the Island—on the island of former Iceland. Me, you, everybody else?"

Chris wasn't speaking anymore; the pain shot hard throughout his body.

"You have to hang on!" she urged him quietly.

The same ground floor staircase next to the main entrance sheltered the two of them. Their clothes were soaked in their own blood. They didn't know what they hoped would happen while sitting there, but they were too weak to face the enemy.

Thoughts throbbed in Drew's head. *This must be the reason the Tentorians want the Island back—it was their home. But how did they infiltrate their allies here? The other Tentorian in the leadership must be the traitor—the one who prepared their arrival, who prepared their base...*

A loud creak came from above where the cement hung heavily overhead as if it was about to fall on them. Her blood curdled in her veins. Nevertheless, she quickly came to her senses, keen to wrap her head around something that made sense. *Is the traitor by any chance...Arnar? How long had he been here on the Island? And Chris, too. He's been here for how long? How is it possible that Iceland recently belonged to Tentorians, but it was also inhabited almost at the same time by us...and then bombed? Are we really in the former Iceland? That's not possible!*

The first Tentorian cargo ship, followed by several fighter-ships, arrived over the Island's shield. They all stood still and waited like ravens ready to swoop down on their prey. Above them, under a withered blue sky, the clouds scuttled away as if they did not wish to witness what was about to occur.

A convoy of military reinforcements rolled down the highway to the Backup Center. Trucks loaded with Island troops and armored combat vehicles were now just three kilometers away. Cole and Claire's motorcycle sped up from a dusty side street. They joined the convoy, one single question slipping through all their minds: what would they find at the Center?

Ahead, the landscape was downright sinister. Only a few had survived the attack launched by the Tentorian allies under Kaligor's lead. Those still alive were also down, too badly injured to fight back.

About twenty Ragons were watching the area in front of the main building. They had taken it, it was theirs, and they wanted to keep it until the shield was deactivated. Some were placed strategically behind sandbags, while others lurked inside armored cars. They all had only one purpose: to kill everything that came through the gate. A high-caliber machinegun was at the ready in a man's hand, eager to feel the hot bullets dashing for bodies. A missile launcher was also at the ready on another man's shoulder, prepared to wreak havoc.

Relaxed, a Ragon sniper lay down on his stomach on the roof of the building, looking through the scope of his rifle deep into the forest and spotting the military truck heading the convoy.

"They are coming close," he communicated through his radio. "Five hundred meters away."

He took a deep breath, ready to fire the first shot; he was aiming for the truck driver. "Three hundred." The orbits of his eyes glittered like his sweat-drenched slimy arches. Then he heard something above his head. *A whirr?* He looked up, puzzled. A weapon floated one meter above his skull.

"What the he—"

The cartridge thud froze all the allies' hearts in their chests. Their teammate's gun with the suppressor should have sounded entirely different. The radio hummed him promptly: *"Li, are you still there?"*

The Ragons were turning around when another gunshot hit their ears. And another one. Bullet rounds started flying indiscriminately and panic set in among them. Although the Island reinforcement troops were not yet in sight, they were losing.

A man with missing teeth who usually hid his dental wasteland opened his mouth wide and desperately pointed his finger in the mini-drone's direction. "Look, over there!"

The high-caliber machinegun sprang into action, and the bullets flew closer and closer to the retreating drone. Its magazine had become empty, but not a single fire was shot without taking down a target. A bullet whizzed a few millimeters by the mini-drone, then another one and the weapon was hit. After another, the drone was left without a camera.

While the still-standing Ragons grinned at their flying target, two missiles hurtled from the forest towards the first sandbag mound. They shattered it into a cloud of particles while countless pieces of lead and hot metal shards shot lethally from both sides.

Claire was there to tip the balance. She behaved as if trained to waste not a single bullet. Concurrently, a thousand thoughts struggled inside her mind; was she gripped by madness or just love? Did she want to save the Island or just get to her father as quickly as possible to save him?

Like someone dashing over the last lap, she went straight to the building entrance, followed closely by Cole. She neither faltered, nor crouched nor zigzagged. She was not afraid; no weapon could be aimed at them without its owner meeting their end. In less than a minute they both made it through the main entrance while all the Ragons were down, breathless. Only one Tentorian was missing: Kaligor.

Some of the troops followed them while the remaining ones geared up to secure the perimeter.

"Avoid destroying the monitoring and control system," an order came through the radio. *"Take out any enemy inside the building."*

But no one seemed to be alive inside; only the remains of a relentless war and a strong burning smell.

A formation of six crack servicemen warily approached the lift door leading to the underground monitoring and control room as Claire and Cole stood by the entrance door to cover them. After glancing at the others for visual confirmation, one of them held out his hand to the tactile screen and punched in the access code.

The screen turned green: *"Access granted"*. The elevator's doors opened. A pile of boxes rose to the ceiling. One soldier scrambled out to the base. Two wires were sticking out of a small electronic device. That was not supposed to be there.

"Bomb!"

A split second was all they had. Some made it behind the walls, which were too brittle to provide much protection.

Cole and Claire plunged outside the building just in time. The charge proved devastating—well beyond the amount needed to completely destroy the building. A cloud of fire billowed upwards, then smoke and dust.

"Wow!" Kaligor shouted, shocked by the tremble. A hoarse, inane laughter came with his raving satisfaction while a grey cloud rushed out of the elevator.

Within a few seconds, the smoke and dust flooded the monitoring room.

Stifling coughing fits overtook him until the dense dust curtains settled in a thick layer on the floor.

"*Kaligor,*" the voice came through the radio, "*good news: we entered the system!*"

"Bingo!" he exclaimed between coughs. The heavy tension suddenly waned away.

"*We're trying to switch it on manual command,*" Tentoria transmitted again.

"I'm looking forward to it! To command this stinking system," he whooped, "and get the hell out into the light."

The half-cut concrete staircase created a shelter for Chris and Drew. Scores of bricks and large amounts of debris were also crammed within those two cubic meters. Several rays of light creeping through the ruins brought their wounds into plain sight. Chris's feet had no room inside that small space; they were crushed and almost severed from his body under one of the concrete slabs. Drew was also injured in too many places to know exactly which one was driving her mad with pain, yet her condition was better than Chris's.

"Why? Why did it have to be this way?" the Erudite raised a moot question.

"Calm down. It does not matter anymore," Drew soothed him and wiped his forehead. "While it lasted, it was just right; we were humans." The Erudite gnashed his teeth. "I'm sorry, Chris. I'm sorry for the moment I doubted you. As a Tentorian you are better than most common people. You and the other Erudites did your best to make sure this Island accommodated the most handsome people and the most beautiful thoughts this planet has known this century."

Chris tried to smile and hardly cracked his lips. "Don't flatter me too much. I'll die anyway...soon.

Beneath the layer of tile dust that had settled after the explosion, the main monitor displayed the outcome of the cyber-attack:

Manual command mode enabled.

A confirmation came from the Tentorian city: "*Kaligor, you have total control.*"

The corners of the bald man's mouth rose to his ears.

"Good! Well then..." He directed his attention to the control panel. "System, deactivate the protection shield!"

„Shield deactivation. Switching to stand-by mode. Please confirm," the computer demanded.

"Let me think," Kaligor cracked a stupid joke, "Dammit, I CONFIRM!"

He uttered the last word clearly and emphatically while his demented laughter went hand in hand with the message displayed on the screen:

`Shield deactivated.`

Kaligor observed the airships rolling in on the monitor in no time at all, advancing to the area where the invisible wall had stood shortly before. The path was cleared. The Island was theirs.

Excited, he plopped into one of the chairs, gazing contentedly at the grimy screen. A black square descended slowly, followed by many small dots—the Tentorian airships.

"Welcome, cavalry!" he howled as if out of his mind.

Drew leaned her head back against the brick. She felt it rather soft. Anything was more pleasant than the pain shooting through her entire body. With one hand, she rubbed her forehead while the other held Chris's head like a mother would hold her dying child.

"You could've saved yourself," she whispered. "You could have had access to all the technology in the world...and yet you chose this."

"Everything was faked out there, distorted...counterfeited. My brother and I made up our minds to flee all of it once and for all. The whole Island decided to keep none of the new technology—*nothing* save the monitoring system and the shield."

"Who decided? What brother are you talking about? What are you saying?"

Chris coughed, and blood trickled from the corner of his mouth.

"Who's the other Tentorian?" she kept asking.

"Arnar...he was like my brother...he is, but he knows no more. He did not want to know."

So it's Arnar. The suspicion in Drew's mind blew up. *It's obvious he made everything happen...the Tentorian base, their allies, everything. He played dirty, the phony bastard.* She could no more rein in her outrage and said out loud, "What brother? Why are you so gullible? He was a mole!"

"No...you're wrong! He's my brother, but he doesn't know anything anymore."

"How's that?" she whispered, worn out.

The Erudite closed his eyes. His life was ticking away.

Drew shook him. "You can't die now; you must hang on! Tell me, is this truly Iceland?" She pointed at the ground. "Chris, what's the truth about all this? I need to know!"

"The Island..." he found the strength to say and took a deep breath of air, "has a history of just 27 years. Iceland had been completely razed before that."

Drew clasped her hands in bewilderment. Her wounds seemed easier to bear than the raw truth. Although she didn't yet completely understand, she felt Chris was too weak to answer now. Still, she dared ask him two more questions nagging her.

"Me, my parents...how come we don't know all that?" She counted in her frenzied mind. "27...years is like nothing! We couldn't land here without knowing. We have an entire history. I have clear memories from 28 years ago and yet...in them I was also here. Who built the Island then?"

"You did, Drew. You, us, your parents, Arnar...we all built our dream with our own hands."

How? The question appeared plainly on the deputy general's lips. Rays of light were now shining right onto her face.

The Erudite went on feebly. "We couldn't afford another West Fjords-like failure. This time it all relied on a secret, a vow taken by all of us. That is what made everything possible. A ray...I see a ray of light..." But there was not light on his face. "Memento mori. I said that for the first time 27 years ago. I'm going. Now I can be sure I am...human," he murmured and smiled one last time, at peace as his eyes finally closed.

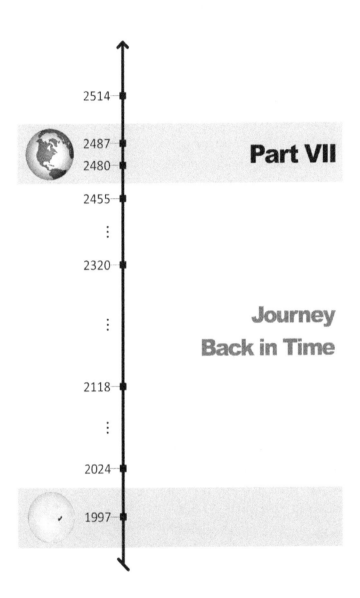

2514

2487
2480

Part VII

2455

⋮

2320

Journey
Back in Time

⋮

2118

⋮

2024

1997

Chapter 46

Arnar watched as the last white-grey metal cubes were built under the searing rays of the sun. From where he was, it seemed they formed out of nowhere; walls growing all by themselves, centimeter by centimeter, each time he blinked. *You can only love progress!* he thought. He was also pleased that he was allowed to choose the architecture himself. The pyramids of cubes standing several hundred feet tall were not supposed to accommodate too many Tentorians; there were only a few tens of thousands still alive.

They had signed a truce with the Alliance to cease all unlawful activities against any state recognized by the United Nations. In exchange, they were allowed to live in peace in this new town built on a few dozen square kilometers, henceforward named Tentoria.

The entire Tentorian community was reeling after the defeat. Most of their kind had perished, and the recollection of that day was saddening to Arnar. The worldwide Alliance operation to hunt them down had succeeded. The last of them, lost in various corners of the Earth, were now finding a home in Tentoria. The illegal actions of the past were now almost absent—or at least kept to a minimum the Nations tolerated. The press said the victory over them had been so devastating that the Alliance could afford to turn a blind eye to those remaining. They were a seemingly insignificant mass and, more importantly, deprived of influence or financial clout.

Arnar was one of the few in the Tentorian leadership that had passed the verification process demanded by the Alliance. It had been grueling, involving many compromises on both sides. The Nations were aware they had to leave behind some well-known Tentorians from the former leadership—especially those with tolerable dossiers. A radical action would have made them face a totally new situation without known discussion partners and influential Tentorians to negotiate terms and conditions. What the Nations did not understand—or rather tolerated without concern—was that some of the former leadership were still alive, unchecked by Justice and hiding behind Tentoria's walls. Nemilo was one of them.

Still, the war dragged on too long for the Nations, the accumulated losses proved too high, and every day of conflict exacted a heavy toll on the global economy. They wanted to cease all actions against the "soulless people" since they had defeated and significantly weakened them. Any action could have been possibly seen as a conflict, and conflict meant instability, unfavorable economic speculations, high security measures, restrained human rights, and embargoes. Nobody wanted any more of that.

The armistice had been clear on one point: Tentorians had to have a new leader. And so, a new image was spread along with the building of the new Tentoria: Xilo. Compared to Nemilo, Arnar had pictured him as far less hungry for power, a Tentorian holding on to principles despite that fact that he was like all the others. For the Alliance, what mattered was his promise to try to lead his people down a better path. As a result, they accepted him, striving not to show total hostility to a race of "humans" when a glimmer of hope could still be seen in some of them. Although Arnar was aware there were indeed better Tentorians, the thought made him smile. He knew the Nations, in fact, had stopped believing in the Tentorians' decent human qualities, instead hiding under a convenient mask that their utter extinction was unachievable. International humanitarian organizations would never have condoned such "genocide", stating that "among them are humans that have a soul, that have ethics!"

From where he stood, Arnar also saw the cube he was going to live in and for one brief moment he hoped for a better Tentoria, for a less bleak future. He saw his family having to spend only a short while there before the Nations allowed them once again to integrate into the world at large. He loved technology but hoped things could be different by refraining more and proving to the Nations that some of them were good to have around. For an instant, he daydreamed.

Arnar also no longer had to serve Nemilo directly. That thought brightened his face similarly to the sky above. Nemilo had been removed, yet he remained close to the leadership as the unofficial general of the army, pulling strings behind the scenes. Even to Arnar that looked like a good plan. It was the insurance policy the Tentorians had secretly built within their internal organization; one of the conditions forced on Xilo when he'd been elected their leader. Tentorians feared the Alliance might try to wipe them all off the face of the earth, and Nemilo was the right general to keep an army ready to defend them.

Chapter 47

The blond Tentorian girl fell to her knees. She stared for a moment at her own blue eyes in the puddle left behind by a shower that had passed over the Tentorian town at midday. They were plainly visible for just a second, until a tear dropped and spoiled the angelic image. Just an hour earlier she could have sworn it was the most beautiful day in her life; she had won the Miss Freshman title. For the last ten minutes, however, she had been swearing to herself just the opposite; she had recognized the face of the most notorious serial killer. The bastard liked to show his true face before attacking his victims to make sure he was recognized.

The young lady rose and shouted one more time for help as hard as she could. Someone heard and started running to her. *Too late*, she told herself; she had already felt the sting to her shoulder. This was the method of the "blonde brain stinger"—a stupid nickname, but one the killer enjoyed. That was how he liked to call himself. After pricking her with the needle, she saw him moving away, hardly having time to shed a tear before the last second of true consciousness.

"Are you fine, Miss?" the man who had run to her asked with bated breath.

The blond woman wiped the tears from her cheek. "Yes, I'm fine. I was just upset for falling out with my boyfriend. Thanks for asking."

"Are you sure? You've cried for help."

"Yes. I realize I shouldn't have done that. I'm fine, thank

you!" And off she went, under the man's astonished gaze.

Five minutes later, the girl was in the bastard's car, perfuming herself and smiling at him. He smiled back in an animal-like growl and headed for the outskirts.

The young woman happily entered the sinister-looking room. "I would like to spend a night with you."

Those were to be her last words. The nanobots that had passed from the tip of the needle through her blood proved deadly. The mix of technological nanoparticles meant to modify the part of her brain responsible for logic was enough to make her end up where she was: In the bastard's lair.

The man sporting a bushy moustache that grazed his chin yawned once and rubbed his eyes. Water poured itself into a glass floating through the air supported by dozens of minuscule, nearly invisible drones. He grabbed the glass and gulped it down. It was too early to wake up, but a loud voice had jolted him out of sleep. *Who is she talking to at this hour? Who would be calling her?* He went to the hallway on the west side of the cube apartment and looked into the girl's room. It was empty. *Why isn't our child home yet?*

"*Yes, I beg you, just tell me now!*" he heard his wife again, this time yelling.

He rushed downstairs to the living room. "What happened, honey?"

"No, no, no...how's that possible?" Her voice was strangled with pain before she burst into sobs.

Arnar watched her, shocked and writhing with fear. His wife's angelic blue eyes, which matched her daughter's, were lost along with their child's life. She grew more and more pale, unable to speak. Finally, she fainted in his arms.

Chapter 48

Arnar slumped before Chris and cried in his blood-covered palms. Though he'd scraped away with his own nails the skin where the Tentorian symbol had been tattooed, it was not the wound he was crying about. He wept with the pain invading his soul and relentlessly gnawing at his heart, making it bleed more horribly than ever before as he wept for the loss of his beloved child.

"I want to die! I was wrong, brother...I was wrong!" he wheezed between his fingers.

Chris stroked his head like the good brother he was, squinting to prevent tears running down his cheeks.

They had not seen each other for a long time, but felt they'd always been together. Chris shivered and hugged him.

"It will be okay, brother. It'll be fine."

He did not believe that himself. Now more than ever he wanted to leave this cursed city and disown his nation. He had failed once in the West Fjords, and since coming back he felt everything was gloomier than ever before.

They faced each other, speechless for a quarter of an hour when Arnar removed his hands from his face. "Brother, I want us to rebuild a nation full of real people, like the one you dreamed about. We can do that together!"

Chris looked through him and answered rather instinctively, "What are you saying? I don't know what you've heard, but the project did not succeed...it couldn't. There I understood one thing: humans are meant to evolve, to merge with technology; they are meant to become...inhuman."

"No, I don't believe that! I was so very wrong about what we must be, have, or know. I should have listened to you..."

"What are you saying?" Chris insisted. "It did not work out, brother. It did not work out and never will! Now it makes no sense to think of anything of that sort—"

"I have an idea!" Arnar cut in as if he hadn't been paying attention. He wiped his face, but his eyes remained vacant. The streaks of blood smeared from one cheek to the other did nothing to make him more convincing. "I know how this might work!"

"Arnar, you're tired. We'll talk some other time."

"Listen to me," he said calmly. "As I was coming to you I had only one thing in mind: I want to forget everything! I want to shake off losing the dearest person in my life...and that I have served a robotic, soulless nation—tyrants and criminals! Chris examined him. "Just think of this technology we possess," Arnar went on. "It brought us where we are, but it can also help us return to what we truly want. What it can do for me is alter my memory, so I would remember nothing at all about this suffering, about who I was, about being a Tentorian. Others, however..." his voice quivered while he lifted a finger in the air like a madman, "get to forget that this very technology ever existed and live for real in the age you considered for your project: the 2000s."

I'm not dealing with a raving screwball, Chris thought. His face lit up and he got on his feet.

"What went wrong..." he started thinking aloud, "was the people knowing what was out there, the advancement of the 25th century! You are right, brother; we must totally isolate ourselves, forget everything quite literally. Nothing must transpire—absolutely nothing..." He was astounded by his fresh take on things, while Arnar watched. "We just have to find a place to isolate ourselves completely from this world; to reset all the minds so they won't know what's out there; to create a system that will keep everyone in—a system that would cut off all ties with the outside world."

Chris ended in a whisper, reflecting to himself. *That way no one will know. We'll be able to live happily until we die; we'll be able to be human beings.* It felt like a recurring dream.

"The island of former Iceland...the war razed it to the ground," Arnar said. "It was abandoned. We can try it over there. I'm sure we'll be backed; it's a good opportunity to rebuild it."

"With the current technology we can rebuild it the way we want in a matter of months," Chris supported him ardently, almost speaking over him. "We can recreate any environment no matter the year in just a few months," he repeated in a whisper.

"We will recreate forests, rivers, wildlife—everything," Arnar followed his lead like a child. "We will give the island a life to define it forever, away from the very technology meant to resurrect it."

"The former Tentorian home can become the home of a radically different nation," Chris added, seemingly startled by his own words. *Such irony! So strange, and yet so possible.*

Chapter 49

"I've just seen your message. What happened?"

"I need to talk with you at once about yesterday's vote on the Island project." Arnar's voice had a strange bitterness about it, and that worried Chris.

"Okay. I'll come to your place. I wanted to go out for a walk anyway."

Six months earlier, a plain-titled message had circled the world: "Do you want to become truly human?"

Chris and Arnar had obtained the preliminary agreement of the President of Iceland and the Nations to implement their project on the island of former Iceland. However, there was one string attached: to have at least one million followers—the future inhabitants of the island.

Only one month later, the project caught the eye of the entire globe and was backed by dozens of organizations ready to chip in funds. Chris and Arnar got ideas from thousands of enthusiasts and a community starting to minutely outline the project already took shape. A new nation to be simply called by its citizens: *The Island* – a name meant to stress to its future inhabitants the thought that it was a unique piece of land and not just a country among many others.

While waiting for Chris, Arnar carefully studied his face in the mirror. He could not remember seeing his face any differently than it was today; it was as if he'd never been younger or older. With the help of advanced cosmetic interventions, he remained the same for decades...*maybe even more than that?* he wondered. *What's the point?* He had "aged" young and unhappy. *Each can have the body he wishes just by snapping his fingers. What a crazy world!*

When Chris entered his cube-shaped apartment, Arnar started as if waking from a bad dream.

"I'm sorry, I should have announced myself," Chris said. "It seems I'm cleared to enter your place straight away."

"And you'll always be. No matter; I'm not bothered. I was waiting for you."

"Tell me, brother, what can I do for you?"

Arnar hesitated before speaking. "I...saw you voted for me to be an Erudite like you."

Chris said nothing, but he moved closer. A chair materialized from the wall and slid next to him. He seated himself, looked down, and listened.

"I understand you don't want to lose me, Chris; you don't want me to lose my memories of you, my only real brother. My heart bleeds, but understand me, I beg you: I need to stick to my initial intention! My past is causing me too much suffering; it's too heavy a burden. The twelve Erudites will be like before. They will know the naked truth. I want to know nothing, not even once being a Tentorian."

"Then...after the moment zero you'll stop being my brother...can you understand that?"

"I want to be like everybody else," Arnar agreed. "I want to go back in time by way of a memory alteration, as they all willingly and unanimously agreed."

After "moment zero", all inhabitants would be genuinely convinced that they were all living in the year 2000. They had all understood the system that needed to be set in place. What to other people seemed plain madness was a heavenly dream for the new nation's backers. The future inhabitants of the Island had been victims of the time in which they were living for far too long; of being dependent on technology or forgetting what being human truly meant.

"Don't you want to think more?" Chris asked doubtfully.

Arnar pressed his hands to his chest and added simply, "Chris, there are few moments when Helen and I don't cry, and then we can't stay indoors. I went around this wretched wall too many times. Our longing for our daughter is killing us, Chris. If I accept this position as an Erudite, I will always remember. I don't want that...unfortunately this means I won't remember you were my brother either." Tears welled in his eyes. "That's my wish though. I want to lead me and my wife into a life of oblivion until we die a natural death."

Chris grabbed his head with one hand, took a breath, and exhaled slowly. "I'll...learn to live with that, brother, because I know what you've been through. But then I want you at least to join me in a governmental position, whatever that may be. My heart would hurt if I didn't see you at all. If you'll be among the 55, you will know nothing of what you don't want to know. I want you to think this through. Do it for me, please!"

Shortly before the new community had completed outlining the Island's control and protection system, they agreed the Erudites were necessary in order to control the system, make sure nothing would take a wrong turn, that the project went the way it was meant to, and that the truth they all wanted to forget would never be learned. The twelve Erudites were going to be mortal themselves, unable to use technology either for furthering their own interests or for living longer. They also were going to vote the future generation of Erudites. They were the only ones to whom the entire truth would be passed down.

While musing over Chris's proposal, Arnar knew that the 55 had been voted in as main backers of the Erudites—a handful of people with clearly defined functions and positions, including the Governor. They had to lead and protect the Island alongside the 12. They were going to know about the existence of continents and other civilizations outside the Island, but their memory would undergo some alterations like everyone else's so they didn't know a number of details that would lead them to suspect where they came from—or to possibly leave the Island. Therefore, they were to also have a clear history in their minds, to really believe themselves they had been born on the Island. They would also pass their version of truth to the next generations of Leaders or Governors once the previous ones died, retired, or withdrew from office. Other people chosen to support the system in addition to the 55, such as the servicemen in the House of Defense, would know they had to protect the interests of the Island, but this would be introduced to them as a special program. They would be ordered to defend the Island if faced with outside threats without being provided with any real details. To them and to everyone else, the Erudites would be regular House of Defense officials— nothing more; nothing that would raise suspicions.

Arnar seated himself on a soft, curvy, S-shaped lounger. It had materialized from the same wall as Chris' chair, taking shape the very moment the host mentally asked to have it. First its bulging parts had appeared from the wall, then it had come fully in sight, shiny like molten mercury, while in the end the texture became creamy and soft. He felt relaxed now, after speaking his mind.

"Look outside," he said, and the outer wall became

transparent. "I can't wait to forget about all this!" In front of them loomed other large cubed pyramids while the military base sprawled beneath it all, covered in countless lights like a dog swarming with glimmering fleas. That night, the moon was hanging majestically above their world, and the wall at the edge of their city shone in its light.

Arnar ran his eyes over it again. "It's so bizarre to have to move from one isolated world into another."

Judging by the tone of his voice, he seemed to be enjoying the idea. In the corner of his bushy moustache, Chris thought he could even make out a trace of a smile, and that delighted him. He found Arnar much too sad lately.

"Another isolated world," the host added, "but this one we can physically leave, unlike the one that we want to build. And even so, I can barely wait."

Chris smiled too, and from the idea of isolation sprang the thought of solutions that had been voted on to prevent future adventuresome Islanders exploring the ocean beyond the borders, where they could find the truth again. The community had agreed on governmental prohibitions and had devised customs and motives to keep as many people as possible on dry land. No matter how the Island was going to develop, no one wanted to have the slightest contact with the people outside.

"I can't wait either," Chris agreed. "Both of us and eight million others."

"Eight, indeed. Phew! Can you imagine? I didn't dare to think of so many when we put the idea forth some months ago. That's pure madness!"

"And just look at them. They work so hard side by side...from all over the world."

"It's the project of their lives. I must admit I'm taken with it as well."

Chris and Arnar had set up a system whereby each individual could help build the dream of the new nation, forward ideas, and vote. The results were not long in coming. They had voted for a religious, dogmatic, and communistic leadership system, which would make it easier to curb technological growth. The history of the Island was to be created in such a way as to make its residents believe it was the only piece of land in an ocean of water. All the memories imprinted in the minds of the future citizens as well as the ones in books or in electronic databases were going to be devised in such a way as to make perfect sense. All the information passed from the true year 2000 on Earth to the Island would be filtered. From music, films, important historical characters, industries, cars, and every subject down to the smallest detail, everything was set in place by eight million minds with the help of cutting-edge data-analysis and data-processing technologies. There was no room for even the tiniest mistake.

In the guest room, moonlight was brighter than the blue lighting artistically shaped in lines on the walls.

"I don't want to be here any longer," Arnar repeated to himself, eyes lingering on the city skyline. With a mere thought, he changed the walls and the ceiling of the room into screens with images so real that the guest felt himself being teleported into the heart of the mountains. "I want to be here."

In the dead of the night, a wave-less sea caressed by a gentle breeze lay far and wide ahead of them. Below, a handful of boulders jutted out from the water to relish the wind. He's transformed the room to appear as though it was near the sea. Halfway through the wall and extending to the ceiling, an aurora borealis spread across the sky in fluorescent waves. Between water and the heavens, a rocky mountain thrust its ridge upwards to the green hues floating over the horizon like a morning mist. Farther up, the green blended with violet in scattered whirls amid thousands of stars enlivened by erratic glimmers. At the base of the mountain, boats sat on the water to witness the magnificent show of nature.

When he opened his eyes wider, Chris felt breathless despite knowing he was in the same Tentorian cube.

"How could I not recognize Iceland?"

"A 21st century reproduction," Arnar confirmed. "That's what I dream of: the true northern lights as seen there, from the Island." He took a breath. He wished he relished the air there too, but he couldn't feel the shoreline breeze, only a light spring wind coming in after a bad winter. "How I miss that island. Before moment zero, I hope we can reconstruct the wildlife and flora just as they were before the island fell prey to our abjectness."

"Nothing is impossible with our technology. We can recreate a natural paradise there, from windswept glaciers and stately fir trees down to the arctic fox."

When the images faded, the same transparent wall let the moonlight roll into the room again. Chris noticed the old-style clothes Arnar was wearing: a white cotton shirt with brown plastic buttons, blue woolen pants, and a brown leather belt matching his shoes and wristwatch. "Nice timepiece."

"I am seriously getting ready for going back in time. Helen says it makes me look sexier," the host joked. "Soon we intend to get rid of this technology, too." He flung open his arms to indicate. "We'll build our house in the style of those years, at least on the inside. As I understand, they have voted for a type of architecture that was common in 1990 in Europe. So that's what we'll build."

"Yes, and this decision is not likely to change. I noticed in the beginning two groups wishing more for the style of their regions, but now everyone looks pleased."

"I think they realized it wouldn't matter anymore since their memories are going to be altered."

At first, Chris believed the change Arnar and his wife were planning was a desperate refusal to live in present-day Tentoria. Then he saw in it a hopeful passion. *Why not?* If Arnar was not going to be an Erudite, no matter how strange he and Helen now looked, their minds would be better adapted to the lifestyle they'd already embraced. *Maybe it's better for them to forget already,* he thought.

"I liked the proposal to restrict Internet use," he said after a while.

"Yes. I'll send everyone a study we discovered in the archives about the true satisfaction the Internet gave humans around the middle of the 21st century."

Chris squinted. "And what did it say?"

"It seems excessive Internet use was a hotly debated issue at the time. First, they all admitted it was a discovery humankind couldn't do without, but once overused it turned into the main trigger of an evolution to unsuspected levels of insecurity, social withdrawal, and reality rejection, and then a rush into the virtual world. For instance, the study confirmed that, although the people using such an interconnection in a restricted manner had fewer friends, they were closer to them; face to face communication formed true friendships. On the other hand, the use of the Internet also allowed access to any information led to the progress we know and deeply regret today."

"That means it will be a very good thing for our little Island."

"Right. We'd better restrict the network to a controlled, mediocre level by way of the communist-dogmatic system. We'll better enjoy the time spent away from those interconnected, all-knowing computers."

Chris went to the window to take in the skyline. "What tragic irony! This precise technology and the way we are interconnected furthers the construction of the Island. With it, we can process a large enough amount of information to build our history before moment zero, but when we're entirely back in time we'll forbid its existence. To us, anything newer than the year 1997 will be gone, bar none. And why not?" He laughed.

"Our Tentorian God will disappear." Arnar laughed as well.

"Speaking of God, what do you think about the discussion on religious matters?"

"I don't know. I think I'm going to take your advice. We, the few Tentorians who are future Island residents, should stay away from this vote. As far as I'm concerned, there shouldn't be any religion."

Chris furrowed his forehead and analyzed a few stars. "What's strange is that religion also gives them that spark of life we cannot feel...but I agree. Let the others decide on that. It seems we are not very good at determining what humans really want."

"From what I see, even to them this is a difficult discussion. Almost everyone wants his religion to exist on the Island."

"That way there's the risk of a religion based conflict

breaking out. It happened countless times in history."

"And too many times it proved deadly," his host backed him up. "We can't leave any room for such a flaw."

"Although I don't know what belonging to a religion truly feels like, I think the direction the voting is leaning to right now is the best compromise. It's also tightly connected to the control system."

"We'll see. Within a week we'll have the final vote."

The vote aimed at the invention of a unique Island religion all were supposed to more or less believe and feel it as if it had been there from times immemorial. The new religion, said those forwarding it, would have appropriate shrines, symbols, and customs and would be tightly connected to the state apparatus to keep them as secluded as possible from the outside world.

Arnar broke the silence. "Do you know what I did today?" Chris studied him. "I drove a 20th century car for the first time in the simulator. I ran a route in southeast Iceland in the former Höfn."

"And how was it? It's a fairytale land out there."

"That may be," he snorted, "but I could enjoy nothing. It was very strange to find my route confined to a long strip of asphalt."

Chris's laughter filled the room. "They call it highway."

"I could only move on that highway and had to input commands into the car...on and on. It hardly does anything by itself. Luckily, it has a motor and spares you pushing it." He, too, laughed.

"Now you understand what I meant when I said this was what got the best of me in the West Fjords. Soon I'll have to remember how to drive."

"Huh! I thought about you, you know. Especially since

you'll know it can be otherwise. Another vote against the position of Erudite."

The guest seemed disinclined to dispute this and replied jokingly instead. "I'll live with this, but you know what will truly kill me?" Arnar raised his eyebrows. "The limited number of models. Take a look yourself!"

Arnar searched mentally for the information. He accessed the chat platform and pursed his lips. "Yeah, they only roll out a few makes, not to mention the limitations set on technology and on the automotive industry competition."

"What can I say? For such a small territory and population, we cannot have several car manufacturers. I think we can't help that."

"Instead, look at the vote on the future common language."

"Here I don't think they'll reach a compromise any time soon."

"Me neither. Two groups of crazy people who must have their own language no matter what—besides English. They will not yield."

"They will not. Allegedly the simulation proved that their neuronal structure would change too much if they had their native language completely erased. Their personalities would be somewhat altered."

"Whatever! As long as they come up with a credible history explaining the existence of three languages on the Island, I don't think it should bother us."

Their conversation continued far into the night, both delighted to have a good time together after so long. Before parting with Chris, Arnar placed a hand on his shoulder. "One more thing."

"Tell me, brother."

"If I choose a position in the leadership, promise me you'll never tell me the truth. I don't ever want to know it."

"I promise, brother. I promise." Chris hugged him. It was one of the last times he was able to do so.

The young Asian man reached the office that had been pointed out to him. The system had automatically announced the purpose of his visit, as well as when he reached the door so he didn't bother to knock, instead waiting quietly. The scar he wore on his left cheek from the age of five could have been removed long ago, but it was his father's decision to keep it as a reminder that the payment for any mistake could be dire. His father ordered this after he'd carved his cheek with his heavy, sharp metal hand. The kid had paid back this lesson to his father, more hurtfully and for good, at the age of eleven. Now he enjoyed wearing the scar to remember the catchword that had made him a criminal at an early age. *Payment for any mistake can be dire,* the words echoed in his mind.

The door opened automatically, vanishing into the wall.

"Come in," came Nemilo's invitation.

He was alone in a room that was almost empty save for a table in the middle, and he didn't seem to have that fierce expression the young man expected.

"Greetings."

"Ohhh...what a pleasure. Hoshito, the golden boy of the future Island!"

"Sounds good," the young man answered from the doorway, "but I don't really get what you mean."

"Take a seat, please!"

He sat down in a chair that materialized in a couple of seconds in the middle of the room.

"I'm surprised someone like you is interested in someone like me wishing to shake off all the past and live on the new Island."

Nemilo laughed. "Believe me, you do not want to give up everything!" A smile flickered in the corner of Hoshito's mouth, and the longhaired man knew the boy would be easily talked round. "I'll cut to the chase. We need someone to just sit quietly on the Island when the connections are cut and the territory is isolated."

"You know they are going to set up a well-controlled system and a state-of-the-art shield to physically separate the Island and cut off any communication and so on. I don't know what you can do about that."

"Yeah, I heard." *They are completely mad!* He did not speak his mind, somehow Hoshito being part of the same community, but tried a slightly easier tack. "But don't you think it's overkill?"

"I guess." The Asian faltered. "It's still under discussion; we don't know how isolated it will really be."

"Believe me, I know. It'll be as isolated as possible. Otherwise the idea can't work. Everything put forward," he hesitated, "makes sense. The two worlds must be perfectly separated and probably no uncontrolled object will be able to pass through, no telecommunication wave; sounds, images...everything will be screened. Only a handful of inside people will be able to control all these, and only by having physical access to the system."

"That's possible. How do you think I can be of any use to you?"

"We don't know whether the Island will ever be of any interest for us, but in case it is..."

"In case it becomes of interest, I will be your golden boy."

"I already like you. You are catching up fast!"

Hoshito chuckled. "That's what everyone tells me."

Nemilo poured himself a glass of rum, took a thick notebook off the table, and handed it to him. "All you have to do is to put this notebook in your future house on the Island, in a place where you are sure you are going to find it and read it after moment zero."

Hoshito took it and flipped through, stunned. "I haven't seen information written on paper except in the history museum."

"You're going to be in one large museum on the Island, believe me! You can read it, but don't try to memorize it, because you're going to forget all about it anyway once your memory is reset."

"What's it all about?" He turned the pages awkwardly.

"I won't spoil the surprise for you, but in a nutshell, it's a plan—a plan full of ideas and information helping you develop a small business on the Island. A business which cannot fail to make you rich in just a few years."

Hoshito buried his face in the notebook. "Hmm."

"Your group will be called the Ragons," he began reading a paragraph. *"You will be in the shadows as much as possible and will act discreetly, without attracting too much attention." The Shadow Ragons,* the guest thought and grinned.

"You'll soon be able to control the black market of the 2000s: all sorts of small, primitive things," Nemilo enticed his mind. "Then, in time, you'll develop, you'll have power, you'll have your men, you'll have women, you'll have everything you want."

"Doesn't sound so bad."

"Once you have read it there, on the Island, you'll also learn how to avoid getting caught. We've learned a thing or two from history." The host's cheeks went up again and he showed off by closing an eye. "This'll make you happy."

"Wonderful! So now all I have to do is think hard and find a proper place to put it in my future house on the Island? It would need to be somewhere I can get to it easily after the moment zero."

"That's right. I did not expect you to be so quick on the uptake!"

The young man curled his lips and puffed. "And what's in it for you?"

"You also have a head for business. What's in it for us? Support. Support in case we ever need something on that Island. You'll find that explained in the notebook."

Hoshito grinned joyfully and squinted at the bottle of rum. "You really wanna drink alone?"

Chapter 50

11 million people had finally subscribed to be part of the new nation. It was a day of excitement. They were already settled on the island and with bated breath, they huddled in front of their television sets and watched Chris' speech.

"My dear fellow citizens, everyone in this room and all those in front of your TVs, already in your future houses on the island, you all look around and see things as strange and old. Many of you may still ask how you will get along without the technology you've had for so many years. If everything now looks bizarre and pointless around you, tomorrow it will all have a clear meaning soundly imprinted on your memory. Your life will go on as if you had lived the whole of it up to that moment on the Island."

He scanned the hall, trying to see through all the stage lights. "Tomorrow I would love to tell you: you did it. Unfortunately, I won't. I do not have this right. You will never know you have succeeded. You will just do it; you will be in 1997, leading that life you chose in your last year of preparation."

He pursed his lips thoughtfully. "I looked in the mirror

yesterday and I noticed I looked just as young as ten years ago. Why? Because I've used this wretched technology to go unchanged. I'm not proud of myself. I understood, like you did, all these things came at a steep cost." He bowed his head and doubted for a second he is the right person to speak to them. *A Tentorian rising to the ranks of a human being.* The audience fell into a deep silence.

He raised his head resolutely. "After the West Fjords project failed," he spoke into the microphone as if yarning a story, "I met a young man who'd lived there all those eleven years. Barring the way things evolved from good to bad and the project failure, the young man wanted to share with me what he truly felt, now after having experienced both ways of life. He told me he'd drawn some conclusions considering the time he'd spent in both worlds. In the West Fjords he went to work for nine hours every day as a public servant for the local town hall. He spent another hour on the road. At home, he cooked maybe for one hour a day, preparing the courses himself, one by one and, he said, it took him rather a lot of time. Then he had to clear the table and do all kinds of chores which now would seem strange not to be done automatically by robots. On the weekend he wasted about three hours cleaning up or fixing things around the house."

Chris cleared his throat. Millions of eyes stared at him. The spotlights stressed his gentle appearance and the sparkle in his eye.

"Then, he confessed, after having been all forced to leave the Fjords, his time was divided completely different: only five hours of work, the rest of the time free. Cooking, cleaning, and the house chores were all done for him by robots. All he had to do was eat and go to the toilet, but he could do even those smoothly to save on time. I then asked him why he came to tell me all those things if he regretted having lived in the West Fjords." He took a longer break to explore the still faces in the room.

"'The fact is that my life's totally meaningless right now,' he told me. 'The work I do is virtual and only requires me to maintain the technology in the areas it cannot do it on its own. I don't have to lift a finger and I don't have to meet any of my co-workers. We have robots doing everything, even 'meeting' with one another for us. I spend my spare time struggling to keep myself fit...and a lot of struggle it takes, too! I run alone on a treadmill in a virtual space or artificially grown park instead of going to work somewhere and burning that extra energy with other people in a social environment. As a hobby, I took up gardening. After all, that's also something I could do with a robot's help. It would do a better job than me anyway. Any of the jobs I did back in the Fjords could have been a hobby for me here, but there they...made sense. An entire social universe was created around me while I was busy doing my work, which I had to do because that way of life was primitive, or inefficient, as the new humankind now likes to call it. Now I'm having fun in a virtual world and I communicate virtually,' the young man said to me. 'And these are turning more addictive, hooking me in. I ended up lonely and blue, not knowing how to tell the difference between virtual and real, or which senses are true or false. Everything that seemed difficult there actually had a meaning, which jazzed up my life. Here everything grows more and more blurry, unreal, pointless...soulless..."

Chris paused a moment to pull himself together. He saw Arnar in the second row beside Helen, dressed in a cream-colored suit with brown pinstripes and a white wide-collared shirt. He wore his watch proudly on the same arm that held his wife. The blond hair outlined her angelic face exquisitely, and her suit, of the same blue as Arnar's tie, was befitting the blue of her eyes. Chris was so proud of them. Perhaps because they were Tentorians, or because they were his friends. It did not matter any longer. Helen smiled at him and Arnar leaned forward.

"Dear future Islanders, we only have years ahead to live. Once we get there we'll live by a totally different set of rules and lead a life that will someday come to an end." He glanced from one side of the room to the other. "*Memento mori*, remember that you will die. This was an old Latin saying which people forgot in recent times. I'd like to point out its beautiful side: we will make every day count, we will live our lives fully and give them the respect they deserve!" A thrill warmed his heart.

Christine and George Williams wiped their tears, smiled and hugged each other. They were in their future home, glued to the cathode-ray tube television set, taking in each word spoken by Chris. Although the matte beech wood cubic box framing the color screen grew increasingly familiar lately since they'd started working through the new house, they still thought it strange to get the news that way, aired by the main TV station on the Island. For them, like many others, television was a long outdated media they had not experienced at all before.

Life had been tedious in recent years; progress pinned them down in a world they never wanted. Now, however, George was holding their two month old boy in his arms and saying to himself he would have a better future. This Island was all they wanted for their little Cole.

Chris started talking again in the same frank tone. "I

want to confess it was your enthusiasm which drove me into this mad project. A project for the future…to go back in time. I bow to your courage of using this technology for the last time in such a radical way—adjusting memory to start a completely different life."

Applauses were not long in coming. Chris applauded too. A similar picture came to his mind from day one of the West Fjords project, 15 years ago. But now he knew it was all different.

"This land of Iceland…has seen many things. Together you've managed to build everything that exists today in less than a year. I was walking the streets yesterday and couldn't believe my eyes. Everything looks so authentic, so…1990s. All the rules, laws, structures, symbols, history…every detail we decided on now exists on the island. From tomorrow onward we will be away from this world that cannot lift a finger without resorting to technological advancements—"

A round of applause interrupted him again and, while it lasted, he had time to notice the refined fabrics behind the loges and the nature-inspired ornaments engraved into the delicate birch panels on the walls. He also took in the six bearing columns draped in white flags guarding the hall on both sides. The future insignia of the Island, a flower framed by a five-pointed star, had been embroidered in silk onto every flag.

"Today the Island shield and the Command Centers, the ones that are going to keep us away from the world of the future, were successfully switched on. Children less than three months old and the 12 elected Erudites will be exempt from being administered the memory adjusting formula. As I will be one of the Erudites, you will not know anything about me starting tomorrow; you have to enjoy this!" Chris' joke managed to wind down most of them. "Hence, from this desk, more often than not the Governor of the Island and the Leaders you voted for will speak to you. By and large, your families and your names will remain the same, as well as the conscious and unconscious characteristics that make up your personality. You chose where to live, your neighbors, the job you'll have, the house to live in. Any remaining contemporary technology will self-destruct tonight. The entire island will go back in time 490 years, on the same spring day. Basically everything you see now outside will follow its course: the weather, the clouds, the insects, the flowers...tomorrow morning all these will not *know* that they belong to another world. At 3:25 a.m. the formula will begin to take effect and last five minutes. Each of you has clear instructions on where to be at that time." He paused before he spoke his last sentences. "Let me congratulate you once again for making our dream possible! I watch you in respect, 11 million people ready to forget the future. Let's meet again safely on our Island in the year 1997!"

FEBRUARY 20, 1997, SUNDAY, 03H31 AM, MOMENT ZERO. THE ISLAND

The sound of a baby crying echoed in Christine's ear. She woke and let one hand fall on the alarm button of the mechanical clock. For a moment she thought she had heard it ringing and it was time to go to work, but it sat quietly on the wooden bedside table. She remembered quickly: *It's Sunday...I can sleep my fill!*

Through her barely open eyelashes she saw George, who had stood up and gone to the baby's crib.

"Hey, how's lil' Cole? Bad dreams, huh?"

He took him in his arms and returned to bed. They snuggled Cole between them, wrapped him up with the goose down duvet gifted on his birthday, caressed him, and went back to sleep.

27 YEARS LATER, JUNE 9, 2024/2514. THE ISLAND

The African-looking man, aged with wrinkles and white hair, stood in front of the 55 attendees in the meeting room. Among them was the Head of the House of Defense, Arnar.

"I'll conclude this meeting by saying: we succeeded in sustaining the welfare of the Island through this year as well. Thank you for that!"

After applauding himself along with all those present, he left the room, closely followed by Arnar.

"Mr. McCain, just a moment please!"

"Yes, Arnar...but I say to you again, call me Chris."

"Okay, understood. I wanted to tell you...Chris, that our recon airship made it back at last."

"Interesting."

"Unfortunately, we couldn't retrieve it. It stopped responding to our commands and entered the self-destruction procedure according to protocol. It fell into the ocean close to the beach in the western area of the Island."

Chris stared blankly as he thought, moving. "Any

witnesses?"

"As far as I've been told, none."

The Erudite nodded, closing his eyes. "Thank you, Arnar." He tapped him on the shoulder.

The general thought for a moment. "There was something else that made us doubt what really happened there. Twenty minutes ago, a clerk at a local post office was reported missing...on the very same beach." He tightened his lips. "His dog returned home alone. At the alleged moment of disappearance, the man was walking the dog on the beach. No such incidents have been recorded before in that area."

Pensively, Chris ran his fingers over his wrinkled face. "We can only hope the two events are not connected. I hope the man will return home. Even so, until tomorrow when I go to the Center, I'd like you to keep me informed about this case."

"I will," the general assured him.

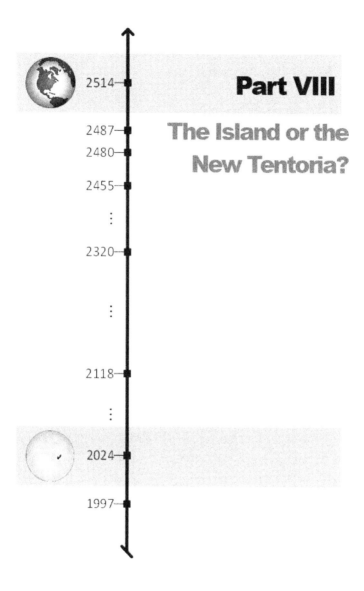

Part VIII

The Island or the New Tentoria?

2514

2487
2480

2455

⋮

2320

⋮

2118

⋮

2024

1997

Chapter 51

The only sounds heard inside the military unit allotted deforested square were the strangled, painful moans of some servicemen from beneath the ruins and the desperate yells of those looking for them.

"Hang on there, we're digging for you!"

A wound in the right arm and a severe laceration by the belly were still healing on Claire's body.

"Son of a bitch!" She gnashed her teeth, exhausted.

Claire waited no more for the last slivers of her skin to heal; she pulled herself up and went straight to the mini-drone. The little imp was hovering in the air several feet away, waiting for her like a faithful follower without complaining about the bullet it had sustained. The camera was struck but it could still fly. She pulled the weapon off it and let the pasty material take the shape of her right arm. The dull black wrapped itself around her wrist and twisted about the fingers to become part of her own hand as a function smoothly attached to it.

There was no time to lose. She had to find out what was going on in the Control Room, so she sprinted to the hole she was about to jump into. What had been the main building of the Backup Center only minutes before the explosion in the elevator was now a heap of ruins and rubble. Amid it loomed an enormous crater, while the remains of the building had been blown right and left as if a volcano had erupted over a radius of about one hundred meters. The elevator shaft could be made out several meters below the surface.

She ran through the crater and jumped right into the dark hole leading underground. After going down one meter, she raised her right hand to be supported by the drone. Although the drone started to pull up with all its power, Claire knew the little imp could not support her entire weight. Thus, she sought desperately to slow herself down by dragging her left hand over the wall. Her fingernails scratched the walls and soon parallel blood lines smeared the concrete. Then the fall turned erratic with brief blows against the walls, and she ceased minding the pain. Only the buzz of the revving drone rang in her ears.

When she felt the elevator's cement shaft with her foot, she flexed her knees and braced herself to lessen the fall. She landed half crouched, fingers splayed against the ground like an athlete ready to run a hundred-meter race. A small cloud of dust formed around her.

Pain throbbing all over her body as her nails rebuilt themselves and her wounds healed. Her tense eyebrows rose, allowing her sight to shoot ahead down the corridor. From behind a mass of red hair, her eyes were nothing but target-seeking arrows.

"Welcome, cavalry!"

The hoarse, Russian accented shout of satisfaction came from the other side of the corridor, from inside the Monitoring Room. The vibrations of the muffled voice pushed their way through fallen blocks of cement and cables dangling from the ceiling.

Claire pulled out her gun cautiously and trudged ahead.

Even though she'd picked the best path, the rubble still squeaked slightly under her feet. She wished she could float like her drone to avoid any noise. A few steps later, she stopped. A silhouette on the other side of the aisle, just outside the Monitoring Room, took shape on her retina. She immediately recognized Arnar. He was leaning against a wall while the machinegun he gripped looked like his only friend left in the world. Dazed, he was holding it and aiming at Claire, who calmly raised her hands in the air. The general examined her tensely a few long moments before lowering his weapon. He then glanced around the corner to the Monitoring Room, and, under the Tentorian woman's desperate gaze, started crawling towards Kaligor.

A burst of bullets startled Claire immediately after she lost sight of Arnar.

"Who do you think you're trying to kill, stupid man?" The voice rumbled out and one of the Erudites' chairs turned around slowly.

The bullet-riddled back of the chair spun round and Kaligor's obnoxious grin came into view. He put his hand to his chest, extracted a blood-drenched bullet from his flesh, and threw it to the floor like a cigarette butt.

"You were one of the topmost Tentorians and now you're shooting at your brethren!" he continued.

Arnar's mouth contorted. "What nonsense are you babbling there? I was born here on the Island, you bastard!" he snapped and pulled the trigger again.

A bullet pierced his heart at the flick of Kaligor's wrist.

"You really know nothing anymore," the Tentorian exclaimed in astonishment. "I wish I could tell you more, but I've no time to spare on you, sorry." Another bullet shot through the general's heart. "Before you die," Kaligor said,

"I'd like you to know I've personally met the guy who ended your precious daughter's life. He is a good lad."

"What?" Arnar managed to moan and collapsed, lifeless.

"Bastard!" Claire's shout resounded through the corridor.

She pulled the two weapons from her waist and started running. When she entered the Monitoring Room, Kaligor was nowhere in sight; only the general lying on the floor, next to other Islanders.

Two monitors displayed the still image of the deactivated shield and red-lettered information flashed on all screens. On one of them a radar terminal indicated a black spot heading towards the Island's airspace, almost past the now imaginary line of the shield. It was the Tentorian cargo airship.

"Damn," Claire exclaimed, eyes frozen on that screen. She then looked to the partition wall of a technical area. "Show yourself, you coward, and let's get it over with!"

A click at the back of her neck made the words on her tongue fail: a pistol being cocked. She also made out the distinctive buzz of a mini-drone carrying it. She closed her eyes.

"You're too late, traitor." The voice flowed from behind the partition wall. "Good bye."

The gun at her nape was suddenly discharged and the bullet hissed past her ear. Although this had become a familiar sound, she felt it as terrifying as any that had come before it. In a last-minute inspiration, she had cast her own drone against the pistol levitating at the back of her neck, hitting it right before it went off.

She could take no other chances. Claire ran her hand under her armpit and shot directly into the hammer of the pistol mounted on Kaligor's drone. She also fired a bullet straight into the drone itself. Then she turned to the wall the hoarse voice was coming from behind and made a dash for it, firing shot after shot. Kaligor jumped out, leaping at her feet, and they both ended up on the ground with no weapons. His hands gripped Claire's frail body harder and harder. She searched from the corner of her eye for her weapon. It was too far.

When the Tentorian's fingers curled to grab her mane of red hair, the rank sweat on his face dripped onto her cheek. Now he felt in control, pulling himself over her body to better subdue her. He mumbled into her ear, "When I get back to Tentoria, I'll look for every one of your family members, down to the remotest cousin, and I'll kill them one by one with my bare hands. It'll be my pleasure. Don't you get that even the slightest amount of your genes have to disappear? Don't you get that such primitives have no place in the 26th century? Don't you get that we want this island back?"

His face shook, flinging sweat in every direction. He reached down to his boot to remove his knife.

"This isn't just an island," she said sternly, "it's the best part of our planet!"

The drone hit the hand thrust into her hair and an elbow struck Kaligor's hairless skull, throwing him sideways. *The weapon!* Claire thought and stretched her hand at it while kicking her boot into his slimy cheek.

A frontal shot; two, three...smack into his shiny skull.

A loud groan escaped his mouth and, although unconscious, his wounds began to heal. Claire frantically scanned the room. She saw the metal leg of a broken chair, grabbed it, and straining wildly, landed it into the back of his head, straight into the capsule. She pulled it out and pushed it in once more...and once again. Only the metallic clang of the capsule, muffled by the dust layer, stopped her. It popped out of Kaligor's nape and rolled on the marble floor into a ball of dust.

The Tentorian tyrant's open eyes remained glued to the technological metal as if it were a lost treasure. The luminous T mark of the capsule went dead, tyrant along with it like a robot running out of energy.

Almost worn out herself, Claire let the makeshift weapon fall and stumbled over to the laptop connected to the system. As soon as she disconnected the cable, the text displayed on the central screen went blue:

```
Restart...
Restarted
Access denied to all users
All interfaces to the system are blocked
Activating shield...
```

In the air, far above the Island, the Tentorian airship was sailing through the area where the shield was present a few minutes before. Fighter airships followed her closely.

Two more lines appeared:

```
Shield activated
Self-control mode active
```

And Claire could only imagine what was going on up there. An invisible force like an electric wall sliced the cargo ship in two. The metallic behemoth was split open much the same a smoothly sharpened blade makes a perfect cut through an apple. A barely visible incandescent line now marked out the forbidden territory along the ship. At first it seemed harmless, only to prove deadly with each second ticking away along with the space growing larger and larger where the core of the flying behemoth had once been. Piece by piece, the side of the ship above the incandescent surface crumbled into the shield and kept on exploding, gulping down the entire heap of metal. The side that had gotten beneath the shield free fell and turned into huge balls of fire which came apart in the sky.

The first fighter ship in the escort understood too late what was going on and failed to avoid the shield impact. It went to pieces in no time at all, outlining a part of the forbidden wall in a ball of fire. The others hardly maneuvered their way out of harm's way.

Dazed, people huddled on the sidewalks, pointing the sky. They paid no attention to the deafening screech of a car's wheels. The driver eventually released the floored brake and felt like screaming at the piles of cars jamming the crossroads. His words stuck in his throat when he opened the door and saw the sky. He went still too, staring agape.

The sky turned purplish while somewhere far away a glowing cloud threw bolts of lightning. *There's a storm up there...a peculiar storm,* a thought whisked him to the confines of his knowledge. Not far below the cloud, a meteorite-like rain fell from the heavens. The ever smaller flaming pieces ended up colliding against the Earth's surface somewhere over the sea.

Thousands of miles away, the neural connections in Nemilo's brain received information on the disaster in the sky. His cheek vibrated while he blinked spasmodically at every fragment of the airship falling faster apart into smaller and smaller pieces. He sensed each explosion occurring above as if the metallic behemoth had been part of his own body and pierced each of his nerves. The 2000 vintage beer bottle slipped from his hand and smashed onto the floor. He, too, slumped into his chair, looking frenzied up to the skies.

In the Backup Center, the smoke failed to dispel, the smothering dust was long in settling, and painful moans accompanied the promise of death. The Tentorians had been so close to the prey, and yet they had failed. The heart of the Island was soundly beating again.

A dirty hand surfaced followed by another. A red mane of hair climbed towards the light. Claire looked above at the shield that had performed its duty. The streaks left in the sky by the fire balls brought a glimmer to her eyes—a glimmer so bright it shone through the black mud on her face.

She wandered among the soldiers who were searching for survivors and noticed Drew on a stretcher, receiving care. The deputy general had the strength to raise a hand. She waved back, smiling faintly, glad to see her out of harm's way. However, there was only one person on Claire's mind;

all her senses cried for just one human being. A few dozen yards away, she saw a shape tucked into a plastic sheet. *No, it's not Cole. It can't be him! The height and the edge of the cuff coming out from under the sheet are wrong.*

She ran where the elevator blast threw her and took to searching thoroughly. Her cybernetically-enhanced organism was doing nothing but computing and looking for signs. No other body function had precedence now. She seemed to have forgotten even how to walk, or maybe it was the rubble.

The shape of a boot appeared on her lens through a thick layer of sand. *It has to be him!*

"Cole...Cole!" she shouted, full of hope. Desperately digging barehanded through the jagged rocks, she called him again. "Cole!"

She pushed aside one half of a metal door and a web of tears came into her eyes. A mask of dirt shaped Cole's head.

"Hey." His voice came out as a whisper.

She stroked his face, gently removing lumps of dirt. His face was covered in brown gunk made of blood and grime. His tousled hair scattered white dust into the air. His ragged clothes revealed blood drenched punctured flesh, while the fringes of what were once his pants could no more be made out against the red background of his grazed feet.

She grasped his hand in a desperate attempt to feel his pulse. It was weak. *Far too weak.* After a rapid scan, she understood that his internal organs were also severely affected.

"Please hold on. You are the one that I love on this planet!"

The brown-eyed Islander squeezed her hand and swallowed hard. "I love you too," he hardly whispered, "but my journey on this Earth will end here. Who would have thought I was going to die this way?"

"No, no..." Claire murmured.

"Run and rescue your father." A last urge could be read on his lifeless lips.

"I'll run to him soon enough, but you...you are not allowed to die! Understood?"

She put her hand at the back of her head and waited for the wonder barrel to pop into her hand. It pushed its way out of her body, and the hole it came out of healed itself. *Come on!* The last roots receded from the flesh and the capsule landed in her palm, the blood stained pivots still moving back into it.

Hastily, she pressed against the edge of her wrist device, which immediately opened its protective screen. Her hands were trembling, deprived now of that sense of security she had implanted moments before. From now on she could only use her own focused strength. After inserting the barrel into the empty chamber, she clumsily unfastened her wrist strap. "You must hang on." She could hear her heart beating in her ears as the young man in front of her no longer moved. "You're the reason I want to live!"

In two movements, she positioned the device on his wrist and pressed its screen several times. She halted. She had done her best. Claire stared into his eyes, unable to hold her breath more than a few milliseconds. Her lungs forced out air as soon as she inhaled with a rhythm to which she wanted Cole to breathe.

She checked the rectangular screen again and begged it, "Please!" But the device failed to understand that command. She thrust her finger into the screen again, but it wouldn't listen to her. Then she stood still, staring at him hopefully.

Cole's body was invaded by millions of nanobots, soulless creatures having been assigned a mission brimming with uncertainties. The screen now read 16%. Unfortunately, that meant his vital signs. The streaks of nanobots had entered his veins, arteries, capillaries, and deeper into tissues and organs, covering every inch of his body. Large cuts were slowly starting to join together. Hard to hear muffled sounds, like those of bones popping, came from inside his body.

The Islander twitched once again and closed his eyes.

Chapter 52

The warmth of the blanket caressed his body. Several rays made their way through the curtains and stroked his face. He felt as if he'd just woken up from a bad dream. His eyes moved quickly behind closed eyelids as he sensed sunlight on the other side. He moved a hand, ran it over his cheeks and the eyes he still didn't dare to open. He was waking up and yet his head wasn't aching. Something was wrong. He raised his other hand to his head, running it through his hair and trying to get a good feel of his head. *Have I dreamed it? The strangest nightmare; people from outside the Island?*

Finally, he opened his eyes. The same ceiling he knew, his teenage room with the same dog-eared posters with vintage cars and motorcycles pinned up side by side on the wall; nothing had changed. *And my head still doesn't hurt!*

A beep came from the bedside table. It was his cell phone. His mind still wandering, lying in bed, Cole grabbed it and brought it close to his face. He read the SMS twice, closed his eyes, and smiled—a smile he relished with his entire body. Now he knew. He opened his eyes and read it again:

"I had to go back, but I miss us already. I need you here in Tentoria. Claire."

Contents

A note from the author

Thank you for reading this book.

It's no secret book reviews are critical for independent authors. They encourage more people to discover the story and the authors to write more.

If you enjoyed "Tentoria" I would be very grateful if you could spend a few minutes leaving an honest review on Amazon; it can be as short as a sentence or two. Thank you.

Printed in Great Britain
by Amazon

60908335R00200